A NOVEL

NEW YORK TIMES BESTSELLING AUTHOR
DEBORAH BLADON

FIRST ORIGINAL EDITION, NOVEMBER 2016

Copyright © 2016 by Deborah Bladon

All rights reserved. No parts of this book may be reproduced in any form or by any means without written consent from the author.

This is a work of fiction. Names, characters, places and incidents either are the product of the author's imagination or are used factiously. Any resemblance to actual person's, living or dead, events, or locales are entirely coincidental.

ISBN-13: 978-1540448644
ISBN-10: 1540448649
eBook ISBN: 978-1-926440-41-5

Book & cover design by Wolf & Eagle Media

www.deborahbladon.com

Also by Deborah Bladon

THE OBSESSED SERIES
THE EXPOSED SERIES
THE PULSE SERIES
THE VAIN SERIES
THE RUIN SERIES
IMPULSE
SOLO
THE GONE SERIES
FUSE
THE TRACE SERIES
CHANCE
THE EMBER SERIES
THE RISE SERIES
HAZE
SHIVER
TORN
THE HEAT SERIES

Chapter 1

Ellie

"Ginger, you need to get your ass out of my boyfriend's lap."

Ginger? Seriously?

What she lacks in originality she makes up for in appearance. Statuesque with long dark hair and a crimson dress that looks like it came straight off a Paris runway. She's just as striking close-up as she was when I first spotted her across the restaurant. The difference now is that I know her ugly little secret.

"My name isn't Ginger." I extend my hand toward her. "It's Ellie. Ellie Madden."

"I don't give a shit what your name is." She dismisses my words with a nod of her chin, her hands tightening their grip on her silver crystal clutch purse. "Why are you still here? The excitement is over."

I consider arguing that point with her. Since I lost my balance and fell into her boyfriend's lap, his excitement has grown. It's grown impressively. I'm not the jealous type, but it's hard not to be envious of the fact that this is her lover. I'm getting a thrill just from feeling his erection rubbing against my ass through the tailored gray slacks he's wearing.

I don't even know what the man looks like. My eyes haven't left her since she exited the ladies' room to set her meticulously orchestrated plan in motion. Once I saw all I needed to, I was on my feet so I could call her out on her bullshit. I kept her in my sight as I weaved around tables and dozens of people all captivated by the award-winning food they came here for.

She managed a distraction when she bumped into a male server who was carrying a tray filled with appetizers. Silverware and small plates with delicious creations crashed to the floor around her feet. She feigned shock, and I ended up in the direct path of four staff members racing to the rescue. That's when I felt two strong hands grab hold of my waist to catch my fall when I stumbled.

"I work here." I look past her to where my best friend, Adley, is sitting. She's ignoring the salad in front of her. Instead, she's focused intently on the phone in her hands. "Today is my day off, but I work at this resort."

"Who cares?" The brunette shrugs her shoulders. "So your name is Ellie Maddox, and you work at Echo Resort and Casino. Are you going to tell me your astrological sign next?"

"It's Madden, and I'm a Leo."

I hear a low chuckle behind me as her boyfriend adjusts my weight so I'm leaning back into him. This man is hard as a rock everywhere. I'm not about to complain. There's no skin on skin contact, and this is a hell of a lot better than listening to Adley talking about the man she recently broke up with back home in New York.

"If you want to be useful, help them clean up the mess they made." She points her finger at the servers who are still on their hands and knees retrieving forks, knives, and wasted food all while avoiding the shards of glass that litter the floor. "I came here to have a quiet dinner with my man, and now I've lost my appetite. I want to leave."

"You can't go," I protest. "Did you order the duck? If you did, you have to try at least one bite. I'm not a foodie, but I think it's the best dish on the menu."

She lowers herself into the chair across from me, her brown eyes narrowing beneath the false eyelashes that frame them. "You're getting off on this, aren't you? You know girls like you can never get a man like him, so you're taking some perverse pleasure in having his hands on your hips."

"Girls like me?" I turn slightly so I can lean forward to rest my forearms on the small square table. "Explain what that means."

"You're nothing special." She pauses for a few seconds, her gaze smoothly moving from my face to the front of my black dress before she levels her eyes on my mine. "You're a redhead with freckles and average size tits."

I arch my back, sliding my ass along her boyfriend's lap. "You're a pretty brunette with long legs and a stolen wallet in your purse."

She glances over my shoulder as she bursts out in laughter. "That's absurd. Look at me. These earrings are each a full carat. I spent more on this dress than most people make in a month. Why would I steal anything?"

I feel her boyfriend's thighs tighten beneath me as I look at her. "I can't answer that. You're the only one who knows why you took it."

"I didn't take anything," she seethes before she shifts her attention to her boyfriend. "Why aren't you stopping this? Tell her she's wrong, Nolan. I want you to take me out of here now."

"Open your purse, Shelby."

His voice is deep and smooth. There's a rasp beneath the subdued anger of his tone. It's so disarming that I turn, without thinking, to finally look at the face of the man whose lap I'm sitting in.

Blue eyes, a shade darker than my own, stare back at me. He studies my face as I study his, the physical closeness only adding to the intensity of our exchange. He's undeniably gorgeous. His nose as strong as his clean-shaven jaw is rugged. His hair, a rich chocolate brown, is styled to perfection. I shiver when his eyes move to my mouth and his lips curve into a small smile.

"I've never been so offended by anyone," Shelby snaps, jerking his gaze back to her. "We're leaving, Nolan. I can't believe you're letting her accuse me of these things."

I stand and adjust the front of my dress. Nolan's touch lingers, his fingers finally drifting away from my hips when I step to the side to face Shelby. "On your way to the bathroom, you stopped to talk to the older couple seated three tables to your left. You picked them because the man's wallet was sitting on the table."

"I spoke to them because they remind me of my grandparents." Her hand drifts to her neck, her long index finger moving in a slow circle on her skin. "You're making a fool of yourself."

I ignore her blatant attempt to deflect. "As you approached them you dropped your bracelet on the floor and kicked it under their table. It was a subtle move. You've obviously done it before."

She glances at her bare wrist before she looks at Nolan. "The bracelet my aunt gave me. Someone took it. I had it on when I met you here."

"Save it, Shelby." I roll my eyes.

"Shut the hell up," she scolds me. "I love that bracelet. If you saw it on the floor, I need to go pick it up."

She starts to slide her chair back from the table, but I place my hand on her shoulder. "You probably buy those bracelets in bulk. You dropped it there so on your way back from the bathroom, you could pretend to spot it on the floor. You asked the woman if it was her bracelet knowing that both she and her husband would look down. That's when you slipped his wallet into your open purse. You counted on the fact that they'd be busy trying to find the bracelet's rightful owner so they wouldn't notice immediately that the wallet is missing. By the time they did, you'd be out the door."

"You're insane." She tries to rise against my touch, but I don't relent. "You're harassing me. I have a headache. I want to go."

I drop my hand to my side. "I gave my phone to my friend and told her to call my supervisor. Resort security will be here any second. You'll need to stay to speak to them about the wallet."

"I don't need to do anything." She shakily gets to her feet. "You're wrong about what you think you saw. The only wallet inside my purse is my own."

"Prove it." Nolan empties the tumbler in front of him with a single swallow before he stands.

His tall frame is imposing. The stern expression on his face only adds to how intimidating he is. He leisurely buttons his gray suit jacket, his eyes capturing mine for a brief second before he looks at her.

"You're not funny, Nolan." She chuckles nervously, her hands cradling her clutch to her chest. "You can't seriously think I would do this. You have to be joking."

"Do I look like I'm fucking joking?"

I wait for Shelby to answer but the only sound she makes is a faint wheezing noise. I've seen this happen to other people caught with their hand where it shouldn't be. She's on the verge of a panic attack.

"You don't look like you're fucking joking," I say, peering up at him.

I see the corner of his mouth dart up quickly before his lips firm into a straight line. "Open your purse now, Shelby. If you have nothing to hide, there's no harm in it."

"I have personal things in here," she whines.

"Such as?" he asks with an arch of his brow.

"I was hoping you'd invite me back to your suite." She exhales slowly. "I have condoms, Nolan. I bought condoms for later. I have them in my purse."

"You wasted your money," he says flatly.

"What?" she snaps back. "What are you talking about?"

"We went on two dates last month, Shelby." He crosses his arms. "They were fine. You were fun."

"They were the best two dates I've ever had," she confesses quietly. "We have something special."

It's impossible not to feel as though I'm eavesdropping, yet I don't move a muscle. I stand in place, riveted to the conversation happening in front of me.

"You repeatedly called me your boyfriend just now." He sighs, shaking his head. "I'm many things, but your boyfriend isn't one of them."

"You are my boyfriend," she insists with a lift of her chin. "This is our third date. You made love to me twice. Technically, that makes you my boyfriend. Any woman would tell me I'm right about that."

No. Any woman would tell her that she's lucky, not right, but damn lucky.

He glares at her. "We had lunch and then we fucked. Two weeks later, we had dinner and then we fucked again. Technically, that doesn't make me anything to you."

"It makes you my boyfriend," she argues. "You asked me to join you here in Vegas. Why would you do that if you weren't my boyfriend?"

He adjusts the knot of his navy blue tie. "You're here for a modeling job. I'm here for business. You're the one who suggested we meet here at Meadow Grill for dinner."

"Yes." She nods eagerly. "That's what couples do when they're in the same place, Nolan. They have dinner, and then they spend the night together."

"We are not a couple," he growls.

She dismisses his words with a wave of her hand in the air. "Yes, we are. This is just an argument. We'll kiss and make up later."

I'm tempted to step in and explain to her that she's delusional. I've heard enough to know that she's fallen in love with him, or maybe just his cock. I can relate. I'm infatuated with it after the brief time I spent perched on it. I can't blame her for wanting to hold onto him. On the surface, he appears practically perfect. The only thing I can see wrong with him is his taste in women.

"We're way past an argument." His jaw clenches. "You're about to be arrested."

"Arrested?" Her eyes pop open as realization washes over her. "You're not going to defend me? You know I wouldn't steal a thing, Nolan."

"You told me your ex was lying when he went on record saying you stole all that shit from him." He scowls. His long fingers circle the silver cuff link attached to the arm of his blue dress shirt. "What was it? Cufflinks, a bracelet, a fucking video game. There was more. The list was long."

"Philip is a liar." Her voice cracks as she straightens her stance. "He went on that stupid talk show to boost his career. He hasn't had a hit movie in more than two years. He used our divorce to put his name back in the spotlight."

"You took it all." He rakes both his hands through his hair. "I watched the interview. You said he was acting. He was fucking serious. You slipped all those things into your greedy palm too, didn't you? You're a goddamn thief."

"I'm not." She inches back on her heels. "You're making accusations you can't prove, Nolan. You can't talk to me this way. You'll regret it."

"I have few regrets in life, Shelby. I assure you that walking away from you and never looking back will not be one of them."

He turns toward me, leaning down until I can feel his breath on my cheek. His blue eyes are fierce, guarded and tamed by something impossible to place. "I'm Nolan Black, Ellie Madden. It's been a pleasure meeting you."

Before I can say anything, he pivots on his heel, brushes past a stunned Shelby and walks out of the restaurant just as security arrives.

Chapter 2

Ellie

"We can skip the magic show, Ellie." Adley scans the floor of the casino. "You put on a kick ass show of your own back there in Meadow."

I watch as she tightens the elastic that is securing her high ponytail in place. I've always admired Adley York's effortless beauty. Not one blonde hair on her head is out of place. Her makeup has held up through early evening drinks, our drawn out dinner at Meadow and a quick stop to play the slots. Lady Luck may not be shining her bright light on us tonight, but spending time with my best friend feels like winning the jackpot to me.

"You told me you've always wanted to see that magician. That's why I bought tickets." I wave to Jersey, a gray-haired man who arrives like clockwork at the same time each night to play a twenty on his favorite penny slot machine. I've been assigned the late shift virtually every day I've worked here. I tell myself it's because they want the brightest and best on the floor during the casino's prime hours. The truth is that the senior security guards pull rank and take the early shifts so they can be home when the clock strikes midnight.

"I know I did," she concedes with a nod of her head. "I get that you spent your hard earned money on those tickets, but we haven't celebrated our birthdays yet. You haven't forgotten that we weren't together on my birthday last month, have you? It was my twenty-fourth. I only get one of those."

"We weren't together on my twenty-fourth birthday last week either," I point out with a wink. "I thought the whole purpose of this trip was so that we could have dinner at Meadow to celebrate my big day."

"Our big days," she corrects. "I'm only here until tomorrow, Bean. We've spent most of my visit playing catch-up. Tonight we need to party."

"Don't call me Bean." I push the *Cash Out* button on the slot machine I've been playing. "I've been asking you to drop that nickname since we were in middle school."

"You're my jelly bean, Ellie Bean," she sing-songs. "I'm never dropping it."

I know she won't. I'm secretly grateful even if I'll never admit it to her. "So you want to ditch the magic show and party instead? Where is this party taking place?"

"You, my very best friend in the entire world, are going to get us into Shade Nightclub."

I hold up the printed slip from the slot machine and wave it in her face. "With the way my luck is going tonight, we won't get anywhere near the inside of Shade."

Her eyes zero in on the paper. "Twenty-seven cents? That blows."

"I lost ten dollars in the blink of an eye," I say on a heavy exhale. "I worked hard for that money and now, poof, it's gone."

She takes the slip of paper from my hand. "Your boss should give you a bonus for catching that woman who stole the wallet in Meadow."

"It's part of my job." I look over at where Jersey is sitting. His left brow is raised. That's a sure sign that he's on a winning streak. "I don't get bonuses for nabbing petty thieves."

Adley frowns. "That's a crime in itself. That poor man would have spent the rest of his vacation trying to replace his credit cards and crying over the lost money in his wallet. You saved him from that headache. You should at least get your picture on a plaque on the wall for the employee of the month."

I smile. When two of the senior security staff arrived at Meadow, I briefed them on what I'd witnessed. They approached Shelby and the owner of the wallet. She was taken to the central security office on the third floor once she realized that she couldn't talk her way out of the fact that the man's wallet was in her purse along with a credit card belonging to another female hotel guest.

I graciously accepted the praise my supervisor gave me along with a hug from the couple who Shelby had duped. Once I'd filled out my incident report, I was free to go.

The wallet is back where it belongs, and Shelby is at a local police precinct, waiting to be booked.

"It's my job, Ad." I pluck the printed slip from the slot machine out of her hand. "I'm going to give this and the tickets to the magic show to my friend Jersey."

RISK   *Deborah Bladon*

"You're talking about Wally Hampton, aren't you?" She wiggles a thumb in Jersey's direction.

"Wally Hampton?" I pause and look at Jersey. He's still winning. The toothy grin on his face is a dead giveaway. "That's Jersey. Does he look like someone you know?"

"He looks like Wally Hampton because he is Wally Hampton. He just so happens to be the greatest quarterback ever to play the game." She shakes her head. "You're going to give him your measly twenty-seven cent voucher and two tickets to a magic show? The man is worth a fortune, Ellie."

"That can't be right," I whisper even though Jersey is out of earshot. "He's never mentioned football to me. He's a big baseball fan. He's always wearing that Yankees ball cap."

"He's retired." She shoots me a look. "Do you know how much his autograph goes for? If you ask him to sign one of his jerseys, you could sell it online and spend your days living the high life in Vegas instead of busting your ass catching purse snatchers and chasing minors out of the casino."

"I happen to like my job." I open my purse and pull out the folded piece of paper I printed our tickets on. "I'm giving him these so he can take his wife to the show."

"He's a huge deal, Ellie. If he wanted to see that magician, he'd just have to show up at the door and they'd seat him in the front row."

"To do that he'd have to be Wally Hampton," I say quietly. "Tonight he can sit in the tenth row and he can just be Jersey. A man on a date with the woman he loves."

13

***

"I thought that you'd be able to leapfrog the line since this club is technically inside the resort you work at." Adley scrunches her nose. "There are at least a hundred people in front of us."

My gaze wanders down the line of people all waiting to get in Shade. The club opened two months ago in the new wing of the resort along with several high-end boutiques including Belese designer handbags, Whispers of Grace jewelry and the soon-to-be-opened new location for Matiz Cosmetics. Celebrities and their entourages have been descending on the property in droves.

The only impact it's had on my job as a casino security guard is that I have to hover if I'm assigned the task of watching over someone recognizable when they have the urge to gamble.

When a gorgeous actor and his pop star girlfriend indulged in a night of poker last week, I spent my entire shift on a comfortable chair inside Ollie's Room, the high-stakes playground. I lucked out that night, but the actor didn't. He lost more money than I'll make in two years. It didn't seem to faze him. He was all smiles when he walked out of the room with his arm around the woman who has the number one song in the country right now.

"I might know the guy working the door tonight." I half-shrug. "If I do, it'll be an easy in."

"I'll do whatever it takes to get us inside." Adley traces her fingertip along her bottom lip. "If you know what I mean."

I rub at my forehead. "You didn't just tell me that you're willing to blow some random to get inside Shade, did you?"

She nods. "It's the hottest club in Vegas. I want in."

"You told me you hated going down on Leo." I grin at her. "Weren't you the one who said blowjobs are overrated?"

She chews on her lip. "Leo's penis was not appetizing. It scared me."

"You were together for two years, Ad. You were getting it on with his scary dick that entire time."

"We did it in the dark." She glances at two women who join the line behind us. "I saw it on our second date, and after that, we only did it with the lights off."

"I didn't need to know that." I tuck a lock of my hair behind my ear. "I'm going to go see if I can get us in. Promise me you'll stay in line."

She stomps both her heels on the black marble tile. "I'll hold our spot, but I'm counting on you to pull some strings. If you fail, I'll have no choice but to resort to plan B."

"Plan B?"

"A blow for the bouncer," she says it with a straight face. The only indication that she's joking is the faint lift of her right eyebrow.

"Keep your lips together, Ad." I tap her chin. "I'll be right back."

"Roger that, Bean." She offers me a mock salute.

I turn toward the club. All that stands between my best friend and I having an unforgettable last night together in Vegas is the long line of people in front of us all wanting the same thing we do. The temptation of the buzz from a stiff drink and the allure of getting lost in the rhythmic beat of the music are irresistible. I have a feeling this will be a night to remember.

Chapter 3

Nolan

"Ellie Madden," I say it without the slightest hint of a variance in my tone. That, in itself, is a fucking miracle. Before I'd said it aloud, I'd whispered her name to myself. Not once, but twice since I left the restaurant an hour ago and went straight to my suite to pour myself a stiff drink. The name is unfamiliar. The exquisite redhead claiming it as her own isn't. "It's my understanding that she works at the resort."

The woman behind the counter laughs. It's not lighthearted and filled with the promise of an entertaining story about Ellie. It's sinister, bordering on that edge of evil most of us have skated on at some point. I'm there now; teetering on the brink of something I instinctively know isn't good for me. "There are strict guidelines in place regarding the privacy of our employees, Mr. Black. You don't expect me to break any rules for you, do you?"

I know she'll cave. The way she's twisting the plain gold band on her ring finger tells me she sees something in me her husband doesn't own. Maybe it's virility or charm. For all I know it's a full head of hair. Whatever it is, this woman wants me to pay to get her to play my game. I want details about the woman who fell into my lap, so I'll up the stakes.

"You remind me of my first girlfriend," I lie. The woman I'm negotiating with is at least fifteen years older than me. My first girlfriend was born three days before I was, which means she's due to celebrate her twenty-ninth birthday a mere six months from now. "Have you ever lived in Manhattan?"

"Manhattan?" Her face lights up like Times Square on New Year's Eve. "I've lived in Nevada all my life. I've always thought about taking a trip to New York."

"Stop thinking and do it," I cajole. "You haven't lived until you've seen the city. A woman like you will fit right in there."

I have no idea where this bullshit I'm saying is coming from. All I know is that her beaming smile just got brighter. I'm gaining ground and I'm not about to lose traction now.

"Would you show me around, Mr. Black?" She licks her red lipstick stained lips. She's wearing that cheap all day lip tint that never wears off. She would have gotten better results with a red permanent marker and a magnifying mirror. Coloring within the lines isn't her strong suit. Apparently, being coy isn't either.

"Show you around?" I volley back. "As in, take you to see the tourist hot spots?"

"That's not what I meant." She pauses to bite the corner of her lip, imprinting an uneven red line on her two front teeth. "As in, show me around your place."

"You don't beat around the bush, do you?" I ask with an entirely straight face. Encouraging this woman to visit me in New York will only complicate this exchange. All I'm searching for is something trivial that will lead me to Ellie Madden. I want to

18

RISK   *Deborah Bladon*

know when her next shift is. I'll settle for the name of her boss.

I view this awkward conversation as a shortcut to my end goal. I need details about the woman I've never forgotten, even if she acted like she doesn't remember me.

"We're both adults." She adjusts the name tag pinned to the lapel of her resort-issued black blazer. "There's no need to waste time. I'm not big on foreplay. I'd rather get to the meat of the matter."

There's no fucking way I'm acknowledging any of that.

I scan her name tag, realizing her name doesn't suit her at all. "Lacy? I can call you that, right?"

"Oh yes." She squirms on the stool she's perched on. "Your voice is so deep. I've never heard my name said that way before."

I resist the overwhelming urge to roll my eyes. "I was supposed to meet a friend at Shade ten minutes ago. If you tell me where in the resort Ms. Madden works, I'll be on my way."

"I can do one better than that, Mr. Black." She stands and quickly rounds the counter. "My shift just ended. You can buy me a drink at Shade and I'll tell you everything you want to know about Ellie."

***

Her offer was too enticing to resist. I waited while she reapplied her lipstick, again missing the natural contours of her mouth. In addition, she went for a layer of eyeshadow. The color isn't on any

19

palette I've ever seen. This woman is a living, heavily breathing example of the *before* picture in a cosmetics ad.

"Well, damn." Lacy stops in place when we near the entrance to Shade. "Look at that line to get in. We may have to go to my place for a drink."

I never say never to a threesome unless the second is this woman and the third her husband. I'd bring up the fact that she's still sporting a wedding ring, but I'm not crossing any lines with her. Visiting Lacy's place is penciled in my never-going-to-fucking-happen calendar.

"I'm on the VIP list," I say in a low voice. "I'll buy you one drink. I'm not promising more than that."

"You say that now, but wait until we slow dance."

"I don't dance," I quip. "I have two left feet."

She looks down at my shoes. "Those cost a mint. You're loaded, aren't you?"

"I can spare enough to buy you one drink," I say gruffly. "One drink, Lacy. That was our agreement."

"You're kind of bossy." Her legs twitch. "It does things to me."

There's no way in hell uncovering the truth about Ellie Madden is worth this much bullshit. I need to cut this woman loose now before my buddy Crew sees me with her. I'll never live this down. This will trump the time I asked Marilyn Finnegan to prom in high school. Crew still brings that up and it's been ten years.

Dinner without me may not be what Lacy's after, but it's the only consolation prize I'm offering. I want this woman far away from me. Now.

"What's the name of your favorite restaurant in Vegas?" I shove both my hands in the front pockets of my pants. "If you could eat anything tonight, what would it be?"

Her eyes fall to my belt and then drop lower. There's no subtlety at all. "You're setting me up, aren't you? Do I have to come out and say that I want to …"

"Get your hands off of her, you jerk! Do it now!"

That voice. The voice yelling those words is the same throaty voice I heard earlier in Meadow Grill.

I turn away from Lacy as she lists the things she wants to do to me and I turn toward the voice of the woman I can't stop thinking about.

Dressed exactly as she was earlier, Ellie's long red hair is flying over her shoulder as she single-handily drops a man double her weight to the floor.

Chapter 4

Ellie

"You're going down for this, Jerry." I squat on the floor next to him; my hands wrapped tightly around his wrists. I squeeze as I press them both into the small of his back. "You crossed a line this time. I can't believe how fucked up you are."

"How fucked up I am?" He squirms beneath me, his chest pressed against the cool marble. "You're the one who tackled me. You broke my nose. I think you broke my fucking nose."

I glance down at the blood that's pooling near his face. "You make me sick. I hope the judge throws you in jail and buries the key."

"What judge?" He turns his head so he can look right at me. "I'll leave, Ellie. I'll walk out and never step foot in here again."

I arch my neck back, an exasperated sigh escaping me. "You're not getting a warning this time. This is way more serious than jerking off in the staff room."

He closes his eyes for a minute. The resistance in his body fades as I shuffle my feet.

"The police will be here soon," I say hoping that someone who works at the club will step into this fray. I don't know how long I can pin down a man Jerry's size. If he pushes back, I'm going to end up with my ass on the floor, and my lace panties on display. Damn this short dress.

I don't look up even though I know that a circle of people has gathered around us. I heard the gasps when I yelled at Jerry. I saw the movement of bodies when I jerked him to the ground as he was trying to bolt. I was so close to the club's entrance, but I couldn't just walk past Jerry when I saw what he was doing.

My duty as a security officer of this resort wouldn't allow me to and my conscience wouldn't either.

"When a woman tells you to stop touching her, you damn well stop," I spit the words out through clenched teeth. "What gives you the right to ignore that?"

"She didn't want me to stop. That '*no*' meant nothing."

"What?" I twist his left wrist. "You didn't just say that."

"You didn't see the way she was grinding on me earlier, Ellie. That chick wants me." He sucks in a deep breath as a drop of blood trails out of his nostril. "She was just playing hard to get in the line."

"You had your hand up her skirt," I say, shaking with anger. "She was pushing you away. I heard her tell you to stop."

"That wasn't real." He laughs. He fucking laughs as blood flows out of his nose and onto his upper lip. "I guarantee her panties were wet. She wanted me. Her body was screaming yes. I don't give a fuck if her mouth was saying '*no*.' "

I look up at the face of the woman who I saw pushing Jerry away. I heard the desperation in her voice. I saw the panic that flashed over her expression when she told him to stop. Her words may have been quiet, but the emotion behind them was loud enough to wake the dead. The tears in her eyes and the stuttering breaths that escape between her sobs, tells me everything I need to know.

"I don't think your nose is broken, Jerry." I stare down at his nausea-inducing face. He's the boy-next-door type. When he worked security with me, women would constantly stop him to ask for directions, or assistance, or his number. That ended the day I caught him in the staff room with his pants shoved to his thighs, his cock in his hand as he jerked off, oblivious to the fact that motion sensitive cameras anchored to the ceiling were capturing his every stroke.

"I fell hard," he whines, the distinct scent of beer on his breath. "I've never had a broken nose, but this feels like one."

I know two wrongs don't make a right. I'm acutely aware that I'm violating protocol by even considering what I'm about to do, but sometimes rules have to be broken and lessons have to be learned the hard way.

I reach forward, grab a handful of blonde hair on the back of Jerry's head and just as I'm about to smash his smug face onto the hard tile to guarantee his nose is indeed broken, I feel something brush against my shoulder.

I turn at the touch, my gaze sweeping over the handsome face of the man whose lap I landed in earlier. Broad shoulders, messy hair and evening stubble greet my eyes. "Hey, Nolan Black. How's your night been?"

RISK   *Deborah Bladon*

***

"You're inviting her for a drink too?" Lacy, one of the resort's deputy night managers, asks. "I thought it was just going to be me and you. You know, just us two."

Really? You'd think after everything that's happened tonight, the fact that Nolan Black is hot for Lacy wouldn't shock me. It does. I get that some men are into older women. I didn't peg Nolan as one of them, but then again what do I know about the man other than he smells fantastic and his ex-non-girlfriend pockets everything in sight.

"Three's a crowd," I announce, loudly, way too loudly. Both security guards leading Jerry away, turn back to look at me. "You two go have fun. I don't want to get in the middle."

I couldn't get in the middle if I tried. Lacy has wrapped her arm around Nolan's waist and with every step he takes to the side, she mirrors it with one of her own. They look like a pair destined for the finish line of a three-legged race.

"Lacy and I are not having a drink." Nolan tries another side step, but Lacy doesn't miss a beat. "We're past that point. There's no need for it now."

"So you're good with skipping the drink and just going back to my place?" she asks in a rush. "I told you foreplay isn't necessary. You're a fast learner."

"Foreplay is always necessary." A man's voice to the left catches me off-guard. "It's often the best part."

25

I'm not going to argue with the handsome stranger. He's almost as good looking as Nolan. His black hair is long enough to skim the collar of the white dress shirt he's wearing. His green eyes are as mesmerizing as his smile. He pulls one hand out of the front pocket of his gray pants as he approaches.

"I'm Crew Benton and you are?"

I reach for his hand giving it a squeeze. He's not my type, but he definitely checks all the boxes on Adley's list of what constitutes the perfect man. If I can make a connection for her maybe Leo will finally cease to exist in her mind and heart.

"I'm Ellie Madden, and I'm pleased…"

I'm interrupted mid-introduction by a woman who taps me on the shoulder. "She's Ellie Madden, and she's officially fired."

Chapter 5

Ellie

"Fired?" I furrow my brow, confused by the word. The head of security at Echo Resort just fired me in front of a bunch of total strangers. "Ms. Griffin, I don't understand what you mean."

"What is there to understand, Ellie?" She peers down her nose at me. "You're no longer employed here. You can collect all of your things from your locker tonight."

"Tonight?" I bark back. "I'm fired as of this minute? Now?"

"Exactly." She taps the toe of her expensive shoe on the floor. The woman is dressed to impress tonight. The pink cocktail dress she's wearing shows off curves I never knew existed beneath her typical outfit of choice. I've never seen her in anything that wasn't navy blue or white. Sometimes it's a skirt with a blazer. On the breezier days, she changes the skirt out for a pair of slacks. A white blouse is always part of her ensemble. If it has ruffles down the front, she's feeling adventurous.

Tonight must be an all-out circus based on the fact that she's wearing makeup and her hair isn't tucked into the tight braid it's usually in. It's a wild, blown-out mess.

"You're firing me because of what I did to Jerry?"

"Jack-off Jerry?" she volleys backs. "What did you do to him?"

Wait. What? Who calls him that other than himself?

I point at the pool of Jerry's blood that is now surrounded by four yellow caution signs that were placed by one of my co-workers. The resort is committed to cleanliness, so I have no doubt that someone with a bucket and a wet mop is on their way. "That."

She looks down at the floor, shaking her head. "Jerry deserves worse. He's the scum of the earth, that one. "

My forehead scrunches as I try to piece together exactly what's happening. I see Adley standing behind Ms. Griffin. She's listening intently to our conversation. She's not alone. Crew Benton, the man who just introduced himself to me before I was promptly kicked to the curb, is also within earshot, as are Nolan Black and Lacy. If my humiliation wasn't off the charts before, it's launched into the stratosphere now.

"Why am I being fired?" I ask calmly, smoothly. If I'm going to have any chance to salvage my job, I need to appear rational, even though I'm in full panic mode inside. "I haven't done anything to warrant termination of my employment. My last review was stellar."

"I didn't say you weren't great at your job, Ellie." Her eyes drift from my face to where Nolan and Crew are standing. "There is security camera footage of you taking a picture in the casino of two guests. You're well aware that's not permitted on the

RISK   *Deborah Bladon*

casino floor, yet you took the male guest's phone from him and happily took the picture while they posed. It's a clear violation."

I rest my palm on my cheek. I know that rule. It's one of the obscure rules that virtually every guard breaks in some way. Most of us look the other way when a guest visiting Las Vegas from out of town takes a selfie or poses next to the screen of a slot machine they've won on.

I've only requested once that someone stop taking pictures when I noticed he had a high-end camera in his hands and an agenda that seemed to be outside the norm for a regular casino patron. I escorted him to the central security office and they took it from there.

"You're talking about the elderly couple from two nights ago, aren't you?" I question. "It was their first time in Vegas and it was her eightieth birthday. I was careful to position them away from any tables or slot machines. I made an exception because they asked politely if I could take the picture instead of just taking it themselves."

"An exception?" She shakes her head. "You're not authorized to grant exceptions, Ellie."

The finality in her tone is unmistakable. I'm not going to win this battle. I'm not sure I want to. This job pays shit. I live in a bachelor suite with no air conditioning, intermittent hot water and a neighbor who plays a medley of classical music early every morning. I love Mozart. I'm a big fan of Beethoven. I just don't want to hear it as soon as I come home from my shift when all I'm seeking is a few hours of sleep.

29

"Why fire me tonight?" I ask because Ms. Griffin doesn't strike me as the type to publicly shame people if it can be avoided. "Couldn't you have done this tomorrow? In private?"

"That was my original intention," she says with a half-grin. "I was going to have my assistant call you in the morning so we could handle this then, but I noticed you on my way into the club. I thought why not get it over with now?"

I sigh, heavily. Instead of enjoying Adley's last night in Vegas, I now have an unemployment cloud hanging over my head.

Way to rain on my party parade, Ms. Griffin.

"It looks like I'm heading to New York with you, Adley." I look right at my best friend. "If you know where I can score a job, I'm there."

"I have a job for you." Crew Benton steps closer, his open hand reaching for me. "It's nice to meet you, Ellie Madden. You're officially hired."

***

I shake his hand again, not sure if this time it's a simple *hello, nice to meet you*, or if I'm making a deal with the devil. The man looks like sin. I can't even imagine what the job he's offering entails.

I draw the line at pet sitting an iguana or wearing a sandwich board while walking around Times Square. I've done both of those things and I know when repeating history is a mistake.

"It looks like you're all set, Ellie," Ms. Griffin says, obvious relief in her tone. "I can offer a

RISK   *Deborah Bladon*

recommendation if need be. Ellie is an exemplary employee when she isn't writing her own rule book."

I smile at her. I sense she's done me a favor. The only reason I'm still in this city is because there's a very slim chance that I might land a job with the Las Vegas Police Department. It's looking increasingly less likely that will ever happen. I have no ties left here. My life is back in New York City. It's where I belong.

She nervously murmurs an awkward goodbye before she darts toward the entrance of the club.

"When can you start?" Crew watches Ms. Griffin walk away before he turns to me with a smile. "We'll cover the cost of your flight back to Manhattan and we'll supply a moving allowance."

Generous, maybe too generous considering I have no idea what I'll be doing once I land in New York.

"What kind of job is it?" I rub my chin. "I appreciate the offer, sir, but I need to know what you'll want me to do for you."

"My name is Crew. You'll call me Crew. No sir bullshit."

I nod. "No sir bullshit. Got it."

"We need a head of security at our flagship store. You'll be setting new protocol in place for our loss prevention team. You're perfect for the job."

"What store?" I raise a brow.

He bites back a smile. "I'm Crew Benton, Ellie. I'm the Chief Operating Officer of Matiz Cosmetics. Nolan is the CEO. We want you to work in our store on Fifth Avenue."

Chapter 6

Nolan

What the fuck just happened?

Crew just offered the sexy redhead a job. Not just any job. The job we've been trying to fill for the past four months. He gave the almost six-figure-a-year job of head loss prevention officer to a casino security guard who just got her ass fired.

"Hold up." I raise my hand in the air. "Wait."

I own the goddamn company. Crew has a small percentage of Matiz Cosmetics shares in his pocket. He handles the front-end of the business, putting himself out there for the press when they want an exposé on what our new product line entails. I'm running the entire show behind the scenes.

I don't handle new hires. Crew doesn't either, but he witnessed the same thing I did. He saw Ellie take control of a man who towered above her. She wasn't taking any shit from that asshole. There was no way in hell she was going to let him mistreat another woman. It took balls to do what she did. The fact that she did it while wearing a skin tight black dress, only makes it that much more impressive.

I scrub my hands over my face, desperate for the clarity I possessed a mere three hours ago. Since Ellie plopped her firm round ass in my lap at the restaurant, my brain has ceased to function in any manner that's the least bit helpful to me. That has to stop now. Matiz is my company. This is where I take back control of this fucked up night.

"We need to discuss this, Crew." I step toward where he's standing with Ellie. "Let's not offer anything before we find out if Ellie is qualified."

Ellie's back stiffens at my words. The more I stare at her profile, the more I doubt she's the girl I've been looking for.

"Are you fucking serious?" Crew asks with a smirk. "You saw what I saw, Nolan. She took that guy to the floor. You're the one who called me when you left the restaurant because she caught Shelby red-handed with a stolen wallet."

I called him because I wanted him to get his ass to Meadow so he could catch a glimpse of Ellie before she left. I needed him to confirm the same thing he does every time I see a gorgeous redhead with beautiful blue eyes. He tells me it's not the girl I've been searching a third of my life for and I tell him I'll let it go. I never do. I can't. The scenario plays out the same way every goddamn time. It never ends with Crew handing a high paying job to an underqualified applicant.

"I admit it's all impressive." I focus on Ellie, but she's looking right at Crew. "We need to be prudent about who we hire, Ellie. We'll need to know your background."

She nods, but doesn't turn from Crew to look my way. "I have a bachelor's degree in Criminal Justice from Mercy College. I attended on a full scholarship. Before I moved to Las Vegas, I worked in Manhattan as a security consultant for Foster Enterprises in their Fashion Division. During my contract, I was able to help lower loss due to theft in their stores to less than one percent across the board. I did that without using security tags on any of their products."

Jesus Christ. A fucking full scholarship?

I limped through college on a ticket paid for by my father.

We're consistently losing three percent in annual sales to theft by customers and our goddamn greedy employees. Lowering it to one percent would mean more than twenty million dollars saved a year.

Ellie takes a deep breath before she continues. "I should also mention that I'm a recipient of the Jane Bishop Medal from the Mayor of New York for civilian bravery. It took getting a bullet in my thigh but it was worth it and yes, it hurt like hell. "

"Good enough for you?" Crew crosses his arms over his chest as he shoots me a look that says wake the hell up, idiot, this woman is our savior.

I don't say anything because fuck me, there are no words. *A bullet? A medal for bravery?* I'm scared of spiders, and this woman is getting awards for her courage.

"I get that you need to check out my credentials." Again, she stares at Crew while she talks. A smile brightens her face. "If you need me to fill out an application or submit my resume when I get back to the city, I'll be happy to come in and do that."

"Give me your number." He tugs his phone out of the back pocket of his pants. "I'll need a few other details too."

34

She steps away with him; her phone clutched in her delicate hands. They're the same hands that most likely could snap a man's neck in two with one quick twist.

"Are you coming home with me or not?" Lacy bumps her hip against my thigh.

Shit. I forgot about her. Her voice, her irritatingly high-pitched, tinny voice had trailed off when I walked over to speak with Ellie and Crew. I assumed Lacy had wandered away after someone else, but that didn't happen. She's still here.

I look down at her, expressionless. There seriously are no words.

"In case you can't take a hint, you're not Ellie Madden's type. The looker with the black hair is." She smirks. "It's fate. The two of us are destined to happen."

I circle my index finger in the narrow space between us. "The two of us? You think this is fate?"

"You haven't been able to take your eyes off of me since we met." She flutters her now chalky eyelids causing flecks of bluish, lime green shimmer to rain down on her cheeks. "We're wasting time standing here when we could be back at my place."

Destroying this woman's ego is tempting, but the fuel of my frustration would be wasted on her. She may be right. I may not be Ellie's usual type, but that unspoken exchange between us, when she was in my lap, was undeniable. I know she felt it too even if she acted like I didn't fucking exist when she was talking to Crew.

"Are you ready to go?" Lacy snaps. "Time is wasting."

"Time has run out." I gesture at my watch with an exaggerated sigh. "It looks like fate has other plans for us. I have an early flight in the morning."

"We'll just pull an all-nighter." Her eyes drop to my wrist. "Jesus. Is that a Rolex? How much are you worth?"

"This? A Rolex?" I tap the face of my watch, one of the *three* Rolex watches I own. "I wish. I got this from a guy working a street fair in Toledo. It keeps time, but the rash it gives me rivals the one on my dick."

"What?" she asks tightly. "You have a rash on your dick?"

I nod. "That's what my doc says it is. He doesn't think it's contagious. My ex-wife disagrees."

"She has the rash too?"

If I actually had an ex-wife, she'd be rash free, just as I am. I'm clean as a whistle and have the monthly test results to prove it. "She's got the rash, the open sores and the non-stop itching. At least, that's what she claims in her lawsuit."

She takes a step back. "She's suing you over the rash?"

I reach down and scratch my dick through my pants, shifting from one foot to the other. "She has to prove I gave it to her. Since my doc says my rash isn't contagious, she can't win."

Her attention is laser focused on the movement of my right hand. "I forgot that I need to give my dog a bath. He needs a good scrub. I'll go home now and do that."

I stop scratching and raise my hand to her shoulder. "I'll help."

Tension tightens her body. She looks at my hand, panic chasing away anything else in her expression. "No. You can't help."

"Why not?"

"He'll bite you?"

"Is that a question?" I quirk a brow. "Dogs love me. What kind of dog is it?"

She retreats so quickly she bumps into a woman walking behind her. "He's a really big dog. You know the kind with the floppy ears and the long nose."

I force back a smile. "What's the name of your big dog, Lacy?"

Her eyes search mine as she scrambles to think of a name, any name that will give her the out she needs to get away from me and what she thinks is my rash covered cock. "Lacy."

"Your male dog is named Lacy?" I ask as she slowly backs away from me.

"That's right. Yes," she calls with a brisk wave of her hand. "He's named after me."

With that, she turns and sprints to a run, racing to the nearest exit. I adjust my suit jacket, smooth my hand over my hair and walk over to where Ellie is still talking to Crew.

RISK   *Deborah Bladon*

Chapter 7

Ellie

What the hell crawled up Nolan Black's ass?

The man was doing everything in his power to dissuade his business partner from hiring me. You'd think after what I did in Meadow Grill that he'd want me on his team.

He was there when I took Jerry to the floor for touching that woman, yet Nolan seems completely unfazed by my drive to do what's right.

After hearing Crew tell me about the job at Matiz, I know I'm a perfect fit. I would do the job well and make the company proud. They're one of the most recognized makeup brands in the United States and also one of the most expensive. It's not my ultimate dream job, but I'll happily take it.

While Nolan was talking to Lacy, Crew explained that the biggest challenge they currently face is theft, by customers and employees. I have the skills and knowledge they need to halt that in its tracks. I conveyed some of that to Crew, but I know he's already on board with hiring me. It's Nolan that I need to convince and I sense that he's the one with the final word.

"Where's your date?" Crew chuckles as Nolan approaches us alone. Lacy is nowhere in sight. "Are you two kids calling it a night? Don't be too loud. My room is next to yours, remember?"

I dip my chin to veil the smile on my mouth.

"Fuck you, Crew," Nolan barks back with a chuckle. "Lacy had to go. She needs to wash her dog."

"She's allergic," I point out. "Pet dander, strawberries, shellfish and soy, I think."

"Either Lacy overshares, or you have too much time on your hands if you're gathering useless intel like that." Crew smirks. "I'm all for having some shit to hang over your co-workers' heads for leverage, but that's information no one needs or wants."

I laugh. "No. Lacy told me. She told everyone when she ate a piece of birthday cake in the staff room and broke out in hives."

"Forget about Lacy and her allergies," Crew says dryly. "Let's get back to business, Ellie."

"Business," I repeat, my gaze darting to where Adley is leaning against a pillar. She's been waiting patiently for me, and I'm eager to get back to her.

I'm moving back to New York whether this job at Matiz works out or not. If there was ever a reason for the two of us to celebrate, this is it. The difference between now and an hour ago is that we're going to pick up a bottle of cheap champagne and toast to our reunion in my apartment while I pack instead of ordering expensive cocktails in Shade.

Nolan clears his throat. "You should get back to your friend. Crew and I will discuss the job and let you know."

I'm pissed. I know Nolan can sense that. I want this job, and right now, I feel like the only thing standing between me and my future as a Matiz employee is him. It's time to revise my approach.

I extend my right hand. Call it an olive branch, if you will. That's how I want Nolan to see it. "Thank you for even considering me for this job, Mr. Black. I appreciate it more than you know."

He looks down before he reaches forward with his hands. He softly wraps my hand in both of his. "I'd prefer if you called me Nolan. Please don't take my hesitation about giving you the job personally."

How could I not? He's essentially discounting me for no good reason.

I smile through that thought as I place my left hand on top of our still joined hands. I slide my gaze up to his face. His eyes search mine, looking for something there. I don't know what it is, but from the urgency in his expression, I don't think he's finding it.

"If I owned a company like Matiz," I begin before I sigh, heavily. "I know that if I was the owner of such a huge organization, that I would be very cautious when it came to hiring anyone. You can't be too careful these days. It's impossible to know who to trust."

He nods slowly, his dark brows pinch together as he looks into my eyes again. "Our ideal candidate will have the experience to spot a potential shoplifter immediately so the security staff can be vigilant about subtly watching their every move. Primarily, we're looking for someone who can think like a thief, so they're always one step ahead. That's a level of insight I'm not sure you possess."

"I understand," I mutter even though I don't understand. I called out the woman he was having dinner with after she stole a wallet just a few feet

RISK *Deborah Bladon*

away from him. No one else in the restaurant, including the wallet's owner, realized what was happening. If that's not insight and experience, what the hell is?

"We'll discuss your qualifications and Crew will let you know either way in a few days."

I pull back. The tug is enough that Nolan releases my hands. I clasp them together in front of me. "I'll look forward to that call."

"We're heading into the club. There's room at our table if you'd like to join us." Crew motions toward the VIP entrance of Shade. Why doesn't that surprise me? When they checked into the hotel, they would have been granted all access to Shade. That's what money buys here in Vegas, among many other things.

"Thank you for the offer, but I can't. I need to give a witness statement to the police regarding Jerry and then I'm going to hang out with my friend at home."

"I'll be in touch." Crew nods as his hands dive into the front pockets of his pants. "Have a good night, Ellie."

"You too," I shoot back quickly.

"We will." Nolan's voice lowers. "Goodbye, Ellie."

I offer a sweet smile that is masking something sinister and then I wait.

They both pivot on their heels and take a step toward the club's entrance.

Then another step.

Crew stops to talk to a brunette with a short bob and an equally short dress.

Nolan continues on.

On Nolan's sixth step I finally unclench my hands. "Hey, Nolan Black. Turn around."

He turns instantly at the sound of my voice.

Nolan's gaze catches mine before it settles on my fingers and the object I'm dangling in the air. His brows arch in surprise. His eyes fall to his now empty wrist before they dart back to the watch in my hand; the exquisite Rolex watch in my hand.

"I believe this belongs to you." I smile, tilting my head as I step toward him.

"How the fuck?" he mutters with a grin and a shake of his head. "You're hired. Can you start next week?"

RISK   *Deborah Bladon*

Chapter 8

Nolan

"It's not her." Crew drops a piece of paper on my desk. "I'm telling you that Ellie is not the little redhead. She's not."

I look down at the paper. It's a copy of Ellie's transcript from Mercy College. Elinor Beth Madden is her full name. She graduated at the top of her class.

It's just another piece of the puzzle I've been trying to put together for the past week.

After she had stolen my watch right under my nose, I gave her the job. She was so excited she almost hugged me. Almost. I wanted her to. I'm all for celebrating in whatever way a stunning woman desires. A hug is a decent place to start.

There were no hugs that night, though. There was nothing other than an hour inside Shade with Crew. I bailed and went up to my suite. I spent the majority of that night, and every night since, researching Ellie Madden. I even had one of my personal security guys run a background check on her.

Everything she told us checked out including the award the Mayor gave her for taking down an armed robber in a pharmacy in Queens. After the madman had fired a shot into the ceiling when his demands for cash and prescription drugs weren't met, he pointed the gun at a woman holding a crying baby. Ellie stepped in the line of fire, and when he pressed

43

the trigger to silence the infant, it was Ellie who got hit.

Thank Christ he was high and a bad shot because she could have lost her life.

Although the bullet grazed her thigh, she didn't step down. She waited until the asshole had what he wanted in his pocket and when he tucked the gun into the waistband at the back of his jeans, she pushed him face first into a display shelf. It gave the police, standing at the ready outside the pharmacy, the slim opportunity they needed to rush in. The man was apprehended without anyone else being hurt.

That wasn't the only time she's risked her life helping others. She stepped in the middle of a purse snatching in Central Park more than a year ago. The mugger was threatening his victim with the jagged edges of a broken wine bottle.

According to an archived article from The Post that I found online, Ellie ran at him full force from the side, taking him to the ground. The impact knocked the bottle from his grasp. She declined to give many details when a reporter who happened to be jogging through the park tried to interview her, only stating her name as Ellie. She was quoted as saying, '*she did what anyone in her position would do*.'

She's wrong. Many people who stumbled on the mugging would have gotten the hell out of there, afraid to get involved.

In the grainy picture published with the article, Ellie is standing next to a gray-haired woman who has her face buried in her hands. Ellie's arm is draped around her shoulder in comfort, concern blanketing her expression.

The woman is a real life crime fighting crusader who somehow ended up working in a casino in Vegas for minimum wage. It makes no fucking sense.

"You looked in her eyes, Crew." I toss the paper aside. "You can't tell me that you don't see what I do. The same sadness is there."

"We've all got some sadness inside of us." He takes a seat in one of the two chairs that face my desk. "There's no way in hell that Ellie is the girl we used to know. Kip was quiet as a mouse. She didn't say more than a few words to us in total the entire time we knew her. Ellie is a force of nature. They're polar opposites."

He's right. Kip, a girl we knew for a sum total of two months when we were teenagers, rarely said anything. She wore a patterned scarf around her neck to ward off the winter winds. She'd pull it up and over her lips, holding it there whenever she spoke, muffling the sound of her voice. She was so shy that she kept her eyes cast to the ground most of the time. It's hard to imagine anyone climbing out of a shell that contained to transform into someone like Ellie.

"They look alike." I sigh, rubbing the back of my neck. "I know I say that every fucking time I see a gorgeous woman with red hair and blue eyes, but I see Kip in Ellie."

"You want to see Kip in Ellie," he corrects me with a rap of his fingers on the edge of my desk. "I've had your back on this fascination you've had with Kip for years, pal. I know you said that some crazy shit went down the last time you saw her, but it would make life so much easier if you would just ask Ellie if she's Kip. It's a simple question. She'll answer and we can put this to bed."

Crazy shit doesn't even begin to describe what transpired that night. Crew may be like a brother to me, but he'll never know what happened between Kip and I the last time I saw her. That's a secret I'll take to my grave.

"It's not that simple." I rake both my hands through my hair. "I can't just walk up and ask her. You can't either. You gave me your word that you'd never ask a woman if she's Kip. I don't think Kip could handle seeing me again. It would flood her with memories of that night."

"Look, Nolan." His voice takes on an even tone. "The way I see it is that whatever happened between you two is in the past. If it's so fucked up that you can't even tell me, you need to drop it. Kip's living her life somewhere and you're living your life here. It's all good in the end, right?"

I hope so. I fucking hope that Kip's living the life she always wanted and that the last night we ever saw each other is just a distant memory to her now.

***

"You have a two o'clock with Brenda in merchandising and then a four o'clock with Old McDonald at his farm."

I chuckle before I look up at my assistant. "Eda, you're a sweetheart. I've told you that today, haven't I?"

RISK   *Deborah Bladon*

"Not yet today, Mr. Black." She shakes her head. The motion causes her glasses to slip down her nose. With one nudge from her index finger, they're back where they belong. "The only compliment you gave me today was this morning when you said I have the legs of a woman half my age."

I straighten my back so I can peer over my desk at her legs. Despite the scorching temperature outside, she's wearing a pair of sheer black hose. "Some women might not take that as a compliment, but you know your legs put every one of the Rockettes to shame."

She giggles. "If a man tells you that your sixty-year-old legs look like they're thirty, you take it as a compliment. Plain and simple."

That's how I'd describe Eda. Plain and simple. The only caveat is that it's those qualities that make her a timeless beauty. She doesn't spend half her day rushing to the ladies' room to check her makeup. Her wardrobe is modest and comfortable, right down to the black loafers she wears.

The woman is more valuable to me than my right hand which is the main reason she's still working for me. She's tried to retire, twice, but I derailed that with a hefty pay raise each time along with a shorter workday. I'll take as much of Eda as I can get.

"Is my date for my four o'clock meeting me here or do I need to swing by her place and pick her up?"

She smiles, her brown eyes widening. "I knew you'd be pressed for time, sir, so I arranged for her to meet you here. I do so love any chance I get to see her. You know that."

"I'll be back here by three thirty." I glance down at my watch. It's the same one Ellie silently stole from my wrist. I've worn it every day since. Her masterful light touch combined with the way she looked at me was enough to put me under her spell. She'd effortlessly robbed me of one of my prized possessions and it only made me crave her more.

Since I left Las Vegas and returned to New York, I've tried to convince myself that my interest in Ellie is solely based on her resemblance to Kip, but my cock, that traitorous bastard knows the truth. I've jacked off twice in the shower to the images stored in my memory of Ellie.

I've come thinking about the fullness of her breasts and the feeling of her ass as she sat on my lap. The dress she was wearing that night fit her like a goddamn second skin. She's petite, yet strong. The nip of her waist leads down to curvy hips. All that softness and strength coiled into one body is the perfect combination for the kind of mind-blowing sex that makes a man forget his own name.

Eda clears her throat. "Mr. Black? Are you still with me?"

I shake my head to chase away thoughts of Ellie Madden and her sweet ass.

When the hell did I revert to a teenager with a perpetual hard-on?

"Yes," I say as I try to will my dick to calm the fuck down. "I have a two o'clock with Belinda and I'm meeting Ronald McDonald for dinner."

"Close enough," she says with a half-shrug. "Whatever you're thinking about, keep it up, sir. You have a sparkle in your eye I've never seen before."

Chapter 9

Ellie

"Hay," I say peering up at him.

"Hey, Ellie." A slow grin slides over his lips.

I resist the urge to reach up and touch him. I want to, for the one obvious reason and all the other reasons that are tied to the fact that he's so good-looking. Nolan Black is at least six foot two, and he has to be near two hundred pounds. He's muscular, solid and right now, with the hint of a late day shadow over his jaw and his hair a mess, he looks ready for bed in a way that has nothing to do with sleep.

"I meant hay as in hay," I correct him with a nod to his shoulder. He's dressed in a black suit with a blue shirt, open at the collar. I doubt there's anything he could wear that wouldn't look ridiculously good on him.

"Hey as in hey, how are you, Nolan?"

I tap my index finger over my bottom lip. "No. Hay as in you have a piece of hay on your shoulder."

He glances at his right shoulder where a single piece of golden hay is clinging to his suit jacket. Instead of reaching up to remove it, he turns back to me. "Tell me about your first day on the job."

I stare at the piece of hay, intent on finding out how it got there. This is Manhattan. The man works in an office in the tower above this store. There isn't a bale of hay for miles. "How did that hay get on your jacket?"

"I suspect it was the goat."

"The goat?" I make a frustrated sound. "What goat?"

"We didn't exchange names when we met. It might have been Billy. That's a fairly common name among goats, is it not?"

I furrow my brow. "I've never met a goat."

"Consider yourself lucky." He glances at the hay again before he turns his attention back to me. "Your shift ended an hour ago. I didn't expect to find you here."

My mind is spinning, but I lurch it to a stop with a deep breath. "The store closes in less than two hours. I stayed to observe the procedure you have in place for that."

"I'm impressed." He scans the area behind me. It's as busy as it was when I first arrived this morning. All day there has been a steady stream of customers, both women and men, filling the large space.

Some people come to Matiz with a determined mission in mind. They know which products they want, so they immediately approach one of the four sales associates who are on the floor at any given time.

Others wander in from the street. The bait that lures them is either the large sign in the front window that promises a free makeover or one of the many ads they've seen online that offers an initial discount of anywhere from five to ten percent.

Some leave with nothing in their hands, but most walk away with a Matiz shopping bag and every intention of returning.

Every staff member in the store including the professional makeup artist, who arranges and personally handles the makeovers, is cordial, kind and incredibly generous with their time.

"Did your uniforms not arrive at your apartment?" His gaze rakes me from my head down.

"They did." I feel my cheeks flush. I chose a simple white sheath dress and nude heels for my first day. The dress is fitted enough that it draws just the right amount of male attention without sending the wrong message.

"Is there a reason you're not dressed in the outfit you're contractually required to wear?"

"When someone enters a retail store with the intent to steal, the first thing they do is identify the security staff and where all the cameras are located." I move to stand beside him so I can survey the store from the same viewpoint he is. "Your security guards are all dressed in black. They wear identical black button up shirts and slacks. When you add an earpiece, it makes it very obvious that if you want to steal something, they are the people to avoid."

"Go on."

I feel his eyes on me. I continue, not wanting to get derailed when I'm trying to convey a message that could potentially save his company millions of dollars in lost revenue. "The surveillance cameras installed in here aren't state of the art. It's a common misconception that if you have cameras in full view that thieves will think twice before pocketing something. That's not necessarily true."

"The security consultant we hired before we opened this location would disagree with you." His breath brushes over my cheek.

I swallow hard. "I'd argue the point with them and I'd win."

I look up at him. He's completely in control. His eyes are focused intently on my face. The man is so breathtakingly gorgeous that he must stop traffic. The more I look at him, the more I understand Shelby's desperation at the restaurant in Vegas when he made it clear they were over.

She had him inside her. She knows the sounds he makes when he nears his release and the smell of the sweat on his skin when he's satiated and his eyes are closing in search of his next breath. It's that one breath that will fill his lungs again after he's used his chiseled body to bring me the most decadent pleasure I've ever felt.

Shelby. I meant Shelby. For fuck's sake. I meant me. I totally meant me. I want it to be me.

"I'll have my assistant set up a time for you to come to my office to further discuss your concerns." He contemplates me. "Are you free tonight?"

"To come to your office?" I question with a quirk of my brow. I'm already working late. I'm not sure I want to dedicate even more time to this job on my very first day.

"No." His gaze follows the curve of my shoulder, up my neck and to my lips. "To meet me for a drink."

"A drink?"

"Alcoholic, preferably." His eyes meet mine. "Consider it celebratory. Let's toast to your new position."

The only new position I can focus on is the one where my back is against the wall; my legs wrapped around him and he's pumping his enormous cock into me, splitting me in two in the most delicious way imaginable. I've sat on it. I know he's got something sizable to work with.

I study his face. There's victory already dancing in his eyes as his lips curve into a smug smile. He's absolutely certain I'll say *yes* because I doubt any woman has ever said *no* to him.

"I have plans tonight." My words are quiet and surprise even me. I'm supposed to share a bottle of wine with Adley at the bar by our apartment once I leave here. We're going to celebrate the fact that I'm her new roommate. "I'm already meeting someone for a drink."

He takes a step back. The assumption that it's a man is written all over his face. There's a sudden dark intensity in his eyes. His smile has disappeared, replaced by a strict set of his jaw.

"Understood," he says quickly before backing away. His fingers finally brush the lone piece of hay from his shoulder. It falls to the polished wood floor as he turns abruptly. A few heavy steps of his feet close the distance between me and the glass door and with a push of his hand, he's out of the store and immersed in the pedestrian traffic of Fifth Avenue.

He's wrong. He doesn't understand. I don't completely either. I just know that the last time I saw that level of triumph in a man's eyes when he asked me out, saying *yes* to him was one of the biggest mistakes of my life.

Chapter 10

Nolan

"Take it as a sign that you need to keep your hands off of her." Crew takes a large bite of pizza, washing it down with a pull from his second bottle of beer. "If you fuck Ellie, we'll lose her, and Matiz needs her."

"Why would we lose her?" I push my empty paper plate aside. "I can fuck whoever I want. This has nothing to do with Matiz."

His throat works on another large swallow. He's shoveling the pizza in at a pace I can't keep up with. I had eaten half a cheese pie before I tapped out. "Every time you bed one of our employees, she quits. You don't give them the time of day after you've had a taste."

"That's bullshit." I swipe a paper napkin across my lips. "You're full of it."

"Name one woman who is currently employed at Matiz that you've fucked."

"Donna," I say smugly.

"She split four days after you drilled her in her office."

I roll my eyes. "Gwendolyn. The blonde from accounting."

"Gwen?" He rubs his stomach through the dark green polo he's wearing. "She left a week after you took her to the Met Gala. That was supposed to be a platonic date, Nolan. She was the best accountant we've ever had and you literally fucked her over. She couldn't leave fast enough."

"Both of those were years ago," I point out. "I haven't screwed anyone out of a job in a long time."

"That's because now you chase women who aren't employed by us." He tips his beer bottle toward me. "Cheers, pal, for keeping it locked up at work."

"It would be different with Ellie," I argue. I mean that in every way. I sense it. Fucking her wouldn't be like the others. I feel it when I'm near her. I know it. I saw it in the way she had looked at me before she told me she was meeting someone else tonight.

I don't understand how she already has a date when she's only been in New York less than a week. Actually, I do understand. What man in his right mind wouldn't ask her out?

"It would be exactly the same with Ellie." He finally rests his napkin on the empty paper plate in front of him. "You're still an asshole to women after you've screwed them. You know that, right? You haven't changed that much."

"I appreciate the insight but you can fuck off anytime, Crew." I laugh. "You should be meeting someone by now, shouldn't you?"

His eyes drop to his watch as if he's checking to make certain he's not late for his appointment to charm a woman, he hasn't met yet, into bed tonight. I've watched Crew in action for years. His method never changes.

He approaches a brunette, talks to her for what amounts to less than five minutes and he's saying his final farewell to her a couple of hours later. He's the quintessential rich single guy in New York City.

I used to be the one sitting next to him, seducing a different woman every night. I'd lose track of who I had fucked on Monday by the time Friday rolled in. It was the life.

Work, wealth and women.

I would have ridden that addictive train forever if I hadn't derailed. That happened one Tuesday night a few years ago. Reality slapped me with her scathing palm right across my face.

"You're telling me you want me to get lost?" He furrows his brow. "Say the word and I'll disappear, Nolan."

"I need to get home." I brush a few crumbs from my pants. "Thanks for coming back to the office. The pizza was good. The company better."

He stands, smoothing his hands over the thighs of his jeans. "If Ellie's into someone else, back off. Let it be."

"I don't see a ring on her finger." I stand too, buttoning my suit jacket. "There's no harm in getting to know her better."

"You're not interested in Ellie because you still think she's Kip, are you?"

I don't fucking know. Kip was pure light. She was everything I wanted to protect a decade ago. She was too young for me to kiss, too innocent for me to dream about touching. She was an angel who ran into the devil's fist one night.

It was the same night I risked losing my future to guarantee she'd have one.

RISK   *Deborah Bladon*

"Ellie is having a drink with some other guy right now." Crew points out as he scoops his key fob off my desk and into his palm. "Leave her alone, Nolan. There are thousands of other women in Manhattan."

That's true, but Ellie Madden is the only one I can't stop thinking about.

***

"I didn't expect you to make a list of recommendations, Ellie." I stare down at the piece of paper. Perfect feminine handwriting details twelve separate items that she'd like changed at the store. At every Matiz store, actually. Considering we have more than a hundred locations across twelve states, this is going to cost me dearly.

"I thought you'd appreciate it." She crosses her legs at the knee.

"When did you have time to compile this?" I go there because I want to know what time her date ended last night. I have no right to know, but that's not stopping me. "You mentioned having plans when I saw you at the store last night and it's now just past ten. I didn't expect you to be this prepared for our meeting."

She gives me a look that I imagine a monkey with two heads would be accustomed to seeing. "Your assistant, Eda, called me at eight this morning and said you wanted to see me at ten with a few suggestions on how you can improve security in the stores."

I no longer have to wonder whether Eda is actually writing down word-for-word what I say when I call her into my office. I thought the pad of paper and the pencil were for show; apparently, she's documenting every word that comes out of my mouth. She must be hiding a third hand behind her back because the pencil never leaves the spot where she tucks it behind her ear.

"I did ask her to convey that message to you."

She fists her hands together in her lap. "Do you want me to go over each point with you, Nolan? I have some suggestions on fixes."

That would make sense, wouldn't it? I'd tell Eda to get us more coffee. We'd roll up our sleeves and get down to business. I'd keep it professional because that's what a man in my position does.

"Did you have fun on your date last night?" I lower my tone, so it's skimming against the dangerous edge of desire. I know I shouldn't do this. It's not just Crew's words that are echoing in my ear. It's my own vow to never again sleep with a woman who relies on me for a paycheck. I'm losing sight of it again as I stare at Ellie's pale skin and her naturally pink lips.

She eyes me cautiously. Her mouth is twitching as she tries to hide a smile. "I never said it was a date."

"You said you were meeting someone for a drink."

"I did say that, yes."

"Did you meet a man last night, Ellie?"

"Several." Her head tilts to the side. "I met Randy. There was Liam and I think I might have met a Drake too."

RISK   *Deborah Bladon*

"I see." I lean back in my chair. "So you're saying you met a friend for a drink? A female friend and the two of you understandably attracted a fair bit of male attention."

"I did meet a friend and we attracted some male attention."

Jealousy, in all its unwelcome glory, slithers through me. Whoever the fuck those three men are they got something I didn't get last night. They got Ellie Madden's attention. I was the one who asked for it, but she offered it up on a silver platter to a trio of strangers instead.

I let out a long breath. Focus is what I need right now. I need to focus on work and not on the mental image of Ellie leaving a bar with another man. I have to concentrate on her security concerns for the stores and not on the way her legs look in the white pants she's wearing, or the sheer black sleeveless blouse that reveals her lace bra underneath.

I hear someone clearing their throat just as I catch sight of Crew in the doorway of my office. The expression on his face is one I'm painfully familiar with. I'm on my feet, my phone in my hand before he says it.

"Mayday." His voice is calm and clear.

I cast my gaze down to my phone's screen. Three missed calls and four text messages, all from the same number. Each attempt to reach me spaced precisely one minute apart.

"I silenced the ringer before my meeting," I tell him. "Where the fuck is Eda? She didn't get a call?"

61

"She takes coffee at ten every day. She's not at her desk. I got a call less than a minute ago. That's why I'm here." His tone is even. "We need to go. Now, Nolan."

I nod to Ellie, round my desk and bolt straight out the door.

Chapter 11

Ellie

"Mayday?" Adley taps her forehead. "Is that some bro code thing? Is it like when you call me when I'm on a bad date pretending you're having an emergency so I can slip away?"

"It wasn't like that. It was definitely something serious." I pick at the fried chicken on my plate. Adley is great at many things. She can tell you at any given moment what the weather forecast in New York City will be for the next ten days. Her ability to sing, without taking one lesson, is inspiring. She can't cook, though, but that's not for lack of trying.

Tonight's main course is overcooked chicken breast and soggy green beans. The appetizer was a spicy chorizo soup that made my eyes water and my throat burn after one spoonful. I'm now filling up on the freshly baked loaf of sea salt focaccia I picked up at the bakery at the corner on my way home from work.

"Mayday is a distress call." She uses the blade of her knife to push all the green beans into a pile near the edge of her plate. "Maybe there was an emergency in one of the stores."

"I hung around until his assistant, Eda, got back from her break." I cut a small piece of chicken in half. "I wanted to see if she knew what was going on."

"Let me guess. She didn't tell you a thing,"

"She told me one thing." I hold up my index finger and wiggle it. "She said that he left the building and might not be back for the rest of the day so if I had anything further to discuss with him, I'd have to schedule another meeting when he's free."

"Are you going to do it?" She takes a bite of chicken and frowns. "This is dry. It's really dry, isn't it, Bean?"

"Am I going to do what?" I ignore the invitation to criticize her cooking. Now that I'm back in Manhattan and I have a job that offers financial stability I can finally do a few things to thank Adley for all she's done for me the last few years. The first thing on my list is cooking lessons for both of us. If I ask her to tag along with me, instead of pushing her to go on her own, she won't be offended, and ultimately I won't have to eat chicken this overcooked again.

"Schedule another meeting with his lap."

I smile, counting the remaining beans on my plate. Seven. I'll eat them all and the chicken too. I always clear my plate. "I didn't sit on Nolan's lap during our meeting today."

"I don't think he would have minded if you had." Adley pushes her plate aside, reaching for a chunk of bread.

I laugh at the mental image of me walking into Nolan's office and settling on his lap. "What happened in Vegas was a one-time thing. I'm back here now and I work for him."

She washes down a bite of bread with a swallow of lemonade. "I saw the way he looked at you in Las Vegas. I'm not just talking about when you were rubbing your ass all over him."

"I wasn't rubbing my ass all over him," I say with an exaggerated scowl. "How was he looking at me?"

"Like you were an answer to a prayer."

"You're such a hopeless romantic, Ad." I flutter my eyelashes. "Unless Nolan Black has been praying for someone to clean up the lax security in Matiz's stores, I'm not an answer to any of his prayers."

"You're wrong, Bean." She slides her chair back from the kitchen table. "He feels something for you and I have no doubt that he'd be okay with you sitting in his lap during every meeting you two have, business or otherwise."

"No more talking about Nolan's lap." I spear a piece of chicken with my fork. "I'm going to finish my dinner. Do you want to go to Cremza when I'm done to split a scoop of cookie dough ice cream?"

She pauses, stopping as she reaches for her plate. "That's a deal as long as I can treat you. It's my turn to pay."

"We haven't gotten ice cream together in more than a year. How do you remember who paid last time?"

"It was the day you left for Vegas." There's a sad note in her voice. "It was one of the worst days of my life. I remember every single second of it."

I push up to my feet, wrapping my arms around her. "I'm back now. This is where I belong. I'm never leaving again."

***

"Randy is meeting me here." Adley glances around the small, very crowded ice cream shop. "I sent him a text on the way over. You don't mind, do you?"

"Randy from last night?" I walk back through my mind trying to pinpoint which of the three men we met last night was named Randy. I didn't care enough to notice. Adley did, though. I could tell when one of the men sat next to her and the top of her cheeks flushed pink.

She nods. "He gave me his number before we left the bar. I was going to wait two days to text him, but life is short."

My fingertips brush over the screen of my phone. I didn't take any numbers last night, although two were offered. My excuse was that I just moved back to the city and still needed time to adjust. The truth was that neither of them seemed all that interesting to me.

"I'll order our ice cream." Adley approaches the counter. "Should we get one or two scoops of cookie dough?"

"One." I smile as she scans the menu hanging on the wall. "We don't want to waste any."

"Ice cream never goes to waste when I'm near it." She pulls a twenty from her wallet. "I'll get one scoop, two spoons."

I step back while she orders, my gaze scanning the people in the store. It's a mix of young professionals on their way home from their offices and parents with kids in tow. The noise level is loud enough to drown out the people ordering but quiet enough to entice me to look for an empty table for us to sit at to enjoy our frozen treat.

I see a man rise from a stool, his order of a pint being pushed across the counter toward him. He turns to leave, but I already know who it is. The back of him is as distinguishable as the front. It's the first time I've seen him in anything other than a suit. Tonight it's gray slacks and a black V-neck T-shirt. He looks elegant in the sea of khaki shorts and tanks tops that are a necessity in August in this city. Even as the calendar marches toward fall, the heat hangs over the city, the humidity heavy.

I look down at the strapless white romper and flat sandals I'm wearing. It's fine for dinner at my apartment and a walk to get ice cream. It's not what I'd ever choose for a chance meeting with Nolan.

"I may be the luckiest man in New York." His voice is deep and delicious as he approaches.

"Why is that?" I ask, my eyes flitting across his face, landing squarely on his ear.

"Out of all the ice cream shops in the city, you walk into mine."

My mouth curves. "Yours? Are you claiming it as your own?"

He steps closer, his fingers grazing my bare shoulder as he shields me from a man pushing his way toward the line. "Am I claiming what as my own, Ellie?"

I shiver, unsure if it's from the intensity of his touch or the air conditioning. "Cremza? Do you own it?"

His eyes settle on the outline of my nipples that have pebbled into stiff points. "I don't. I'm a regular. I live near here."

I cross my arms over my chest wishing I had put on a strapless bra when I decided to venture outside. As much as I try not to, I glance at his ear again. "I don't mean to pry, but is everything all right? You rushed out quickly during our meeting this morning."

He blows a puff of air out from between his lips. "I apologize for that. There was something I had to take care of."

It's a response, intentionally vague. I don't know him well enough to press for more. Not on that subject at least. His ear is an entirely different topic and I'm too curious about that to ignore it.

"I didn't realize you had a pierced ear."

His fingers follow the path of my gaze to his right ear. They flutter over the lobe and the red and black crystal ladybug stud that is there. "It's not pierced. This is a clip-on."

"A clip-on?" I step closer to get a better look.

He leans in until his breath is brushing over my cheek. "You smell incredible. It's Matiz Mist, isn't it? Matiz Mist and you."

"Why are you wearing a ladybug earring?" I tuck my hair behind both of my ears.

"I misplaced the butterfly one."

I stand in silence. I have no idea how to respond to that. Luckily, Adley approaches with a pink cardboard cup filled with my favorite ice cream in one hand and two white plastic spoons in the other.

"Randy's here." Her voice is shaky as she pushes the ice cream toward me. She doesn't look in Nolan's direction at all. "He brought Liam with him. He's totally into you, Bean."

I glance at the entrance to the shop. I see two of the men from last night. I know, just by their appearance, which one is Randy. His eyes are locked on Adley. He's dressed as Nolan was earlier, in a tailored dark suit complete with gray patterned tie.

Liam is the opposite. His shoulder length dirty blonde hair is pulled back into a messy bun on his head. His jaw is covered with a beard. Last night he was wearing a dark, long-sleeved sweater and jeans. Today it's the same jeans, but the tight white T-shirt he has on emphasizes how muscular he is and shows off the black and gray tattoos that cover his arms.

He turns heads, both men and women gawk as he approaches. It's not surprising. The man is a full foot taller than me. He hovers right around the six foot five mark.

"Ellie," he says my name casually. "How's my favorite redhead?"

Annoyed. I didn't take his number last night because I wasn't interested in seeing him again. He's a nice guy, but he's not my type at all. I prefer my men all cleaned up, polished and put together. Liam doesn't press any of my hot buttons.

I feel a brush against my arm as Nolan extends his hand past me. "I'm Nolan Black. I work with Ellie. It's nice to meet you."

"Liam Wolf. My friends call me Wolf." Liam grabs Nolan's hand and gives it a firm shake. "We've met before, haven't we?"

RISK *Deborah Bladon*

"It's possible." Nolan's jaw clenches. The earring is gone, the only hint that it was ever there is the fading red spot on his earlobe. "I have an ice cream delivery to make. It was good to meet you, Liam. Until tomorrow, Ellie."

"Until tomorrow," I repeat as I watch him walk away.

Chapter 12

Nolan

"They're a real life roleplay." Crew dips the tip of a plastic spoon in the ice cream. "He's the big, bad Wolf and she's little red…"

"Jesus Christ," I spit out. "Shut up, Crew. I don't want to hear it."

"You're the one who brought them up." He drops the spoon on the counter. "What flavor is this? It's disgusting."

I place the cover back on the ice cream and shove it in the freezer compartment of the refrigerator. "It's blue bubble gum. Not my first choice obviously, but you know."

"Your lips are blue. How much of this shit did you eat before I got here?"

"A few spoons," I lie, wiping my mouth with the back of my hand. I ate half the fucking pint while I considered adding an Adele song to the playlist on my phone. It shouldn't bother me that Ellie is hanging out with another man tonight, but it does.

Once I reached the doorway of Cremza, I turned to see her looking up at Liam with awe in her eyes and a smile on her lips. That look should be reserved for me. I want to own that look.

"You're going to feel that later, pal." Crew leans against the counter. "We know the guy fucking Ellie."

Anger knots in my gut. The slow and steady burn of frustration takes root around it. I don't need to hear the words aloud. It's all I've thought about since I left Ellie's side. Liam will taste the hint of peppermint that's always on her breath. She'll undress for him, tempting him with each inch of her skin that's exposed. It's his body that she'll cling to when an orgasm rushes through her. That fucker will have everything I want if he hasn't already.

I would have stayed and put a halt to all of it, but I needed to be here. I had to be here.

"I don't know him, Crew. I've never seen him before."

"He's Nick's brother."

"Nick who? Nick Wolf? The guy from high school?"

"The guy who is burning up every bestseller list known to man." He reaches in the fridge for a bottle of water. "One of his books was optioned by a studio in Los Angeles. He's a big deal."

Nicholas Wolf went to high school with us. We didn't hang out often. When we were partying and planning for college, he was submitting short stories to the school's annual anthology.

It paid off in spades for him. His series of detective novels has taken the world by storm. You can't turn a corner without someone talking about his latest book release.

"What about Liam?" I tug my phone from my pocket. "What's his deal?"

Crew's already on it. His fingers are skipping over his phone's screen. "All his social network accounts are locked up tight. They're as private as

RISK   *Deborah Bladon*

Ellie's are. I can hand this off to Kristof. He'll have a full file on your desk in the morning. Just give me the word although, for the record, I'm still one hundred percent against you pursuing Ellie."

Kristof Hellaman used to hold a high ranking position in the FBI before I lured him away. I needed his expertise to solve my own personal whodunit a few years ago. He wasn't successful but he proved his loyalty. Since then, he's been on retainer, never more than a phone call away if I need a background check or an extra set of eyes on me when I travel. He's a valuable part of my team, and he's paid accordingly.

"Between you and me." I pause to circle my finger in the air. "Kristof brought me next to nothing on Ellie."

He chuckles, resting both his hands on the counter behind him. "Kristof brought you all there is on Ellie. You can't accept the fact that the last address he traced her to back then was in Boston."

The street address listed for Ellie Madden's mother more than a decade ago doesn't exist now. The tenement was torn down by a developer itching to build a suite of condos to lure people to Boston's old West End. It worked.

I co-invested with Crew in a pair of office buildings in that area spearheaded by a friend of my father, and the returns have been consistently healthy. Residential dwellings, beyond those in my own portfolio, aren't a magnet for my money. Commercial buildings have always proven to be my golden ticket.

"It's not about Kip." I scrub the back of my neck.

73

"You asked me not to mention Kip to Kristof." His voice takes on a serious tone. "I haven't, though I've never understood your reluctance to get him involved. She wouldn't even know you're looking for her and if he finds her, at least, you'll know she's all right."

I've always used the same excuse when Crew has suggested we get Kristof to trace Kip's tracks. I tell him that it would be a waste of my money. The details we have are so vague that it would be impossible to find her.

I never knew her real name. She didn't offer, and I stopped pressing for it after asking twice and getting only a shrug of her shoulder in response.

I first saw her walking a small, shaggy brown dog on Broadway and Fifty Second Street as the matinee of a musical ended and theater goers flooded the sidewalk around us. She dipped her head and dodged through the crowd, bumping into me and then steadying herself with a torn glove covered hand on my forearm.

I looked down at a petite curly haired girl wearing a worn red varsity jacket with the name Kip sewn onto the shoulder with black thread. Where a circular white snap should have been on the front, a piece of rusted wire pierced the frayed wool. It was woven through the hole left by the missing snap and tied into an uneven, loose knot to keep the mid-section closed. The jacket was at least four sizes too big for her, but it sheltered her from the bitter bite of the cold that winter.

To Kip, I was Rigs. It was the name she heard my grandfather calling out to me when the light turned to cross Broadway. He was in a rush to get home after our lunch in mid-town on that Sunday afternoon in December. I stood in place as she mumbled an apology after touching me. She looked up into my lean adolescent face with the sparse growth of beard dotting my jaw and the rebellious long hair that fell into my eyes. Then she smiled and with a pull of the leash, she sprinted toward Eighth Avenue with the barking dog on her heel. They disappeared into the rush of people heading back to the warmth of their homes or hotels.

It was one of the few times she ever smiled at me.

A week later I was back in the same spot with a brand new pair of red gloves in my hand for her.

"We can kill two birds with one stone, pal." Crew finishes the last of the water in the bottle. "I'll get Kristof to check out Liam Wolf and I'll tell him what we know about Kip. The trail on her is cold, but he's a fucking genius. He'll Sherlock Holmes the shit out of it and you can finally put this to rest."

If Kristof starts poking around in the past he's going to uncover what happened the last time I saw Kip. That will jeopardize my future. As much as I want to know how she is after making it through the hell storm of that night and finding her way out the other side, I can't risk exposing my part in it.

"Don't call Kristof," I say evenly. "We both know that finding Kip is impossible. We know nothing about her. You're right. It's time to drop it."

He shoots me a look that I've seen before. He knows I'll drop it until I see another redhead with blue eyes. Once that happens, the questions will start all

75

over again. It's a never-ending Ferris Wheel of my own misery that I finally need to step off of for good.

She survived that night. That's all that matters. I have to let it go.

"What about Wolf?"

I respond almost immediately. "Don't waste Kristof's time. I'll find out everything I need to know about him from Ellie tomorrow."

Then I'll do everything I can to make her forget him.

Chapter 13

Ellie

"What's the deal with you and Wolf?" Crew asks as he picks up a tube of pale pink lip balm.

I look at him first before I lock eyes with Nolan. "You don't strike me as the type of man who gossips."

He chuckles deeply with a faint shake of his head. "I assure you I'm not. Crew and I went to high school with Liam's brother. I mentioned seeing him last night to Crew."

Embarrassment wages war with disappointment in the pit of my stomach. I feel my cheeks heat. Of course, that would be it. Why would Nolan care if I was hooking up with another man? He had every chance to stay at Cremza to yank my attention his way. It wouldn't have even taken a yank. A faint tug and I would have been focused solely on him.

He walked away, though. He introduced himself to Liam and then he took off.

"From what I remember, he's a good guy." Crew glances at the line of customers waiting to pay for their purchases. "A big guy too. If he needs a job, you have the go-ahead to hire him to join our security team."

"I'm sure Liam has a job," Nolan comments under his breath.

"I can ask him when I have dinner with him tomorrow," I say, leaving out the important detail that Adley, and all her good intentions, invited both Liam and Randy to our apartment for one of her home cooked meals. It's an ill-thought-out effort on her part to impress Randy. He mentioned not having a decent meal in weeks, and she was quick to offer up her spaghetti and what, I think, are meatballs.

It's my chance to get to know them both better since I left Cremza ten minutes after Nolan did. Wolf didn't seem to mind. Two other women had already stopped to talk to him before I finished explaining that I was too tired to hang out.

"You're having dinner with him?" Nolan asks coolly, his eyes buried in his phone.

"That's the plan. He's coming over to my place."

That's enough to not only grab his full attention; it also perks his left brow. "You just met him, Ellie. Do you think it's wise to invite him into your home?"

"I'll frisk him before I let him in."

Crew gets a chuckle out of that. "I've got a meeting across town in thirty. I'm heading out. We'll approve the new cameras, and you can set up an install time, Ellie."

I smile. When they stopped in, unannounced, five minutes ago I knew it was to discuss the cameras. I'd called Nolan's assistant, Eda, this morning asking for a meeting with him and Crew. The new cameras are small and unassuming. The viewing range will cover the entire sales floor. Also, their design will fit in flawlessly with the lights already in place in the

RISK   *Deborah Bladon*

stock room. I know that employee theft is a huge problem and I want to pin the culprit to the wall.

"I appreciate that, Crew."

"I'm considering pocketing this." He looks down at the lip balm. "There's not a lot of color to this, is there?"

"There's a selection of lip balms just for men on the back wall." I point to a display that one of the sales staff spent hours perfecting. "Those don't have any color at all and the packaging is more masculine."

"I had a hand in launching that line," he says with a smile. He rolls the lip balm over in his palm. "I had someone else in mind for this one."

"Who?"

Nolan's question raises Crew's left brow. He stares at him before he finally answers. "My niece."

"She's too young for that," Nolan shoots back quickly. "Besides, she'll appreciate your gifts more if you don't have one in your hand every time you see her."

"Good point." Crew nods, setting the lip balm back.

"Thank you again for trusting in my decisions, Crew." I grin.

"You're the expert." He checks his watch. "I'm confident that you're going to curb theft in this store and then we'll move ahead on implementing your changes in all our stores in the city, and eventually nationwide."

It's a huge testament to his belief in me. He can't know how much I value that.

I turn toward Nolan as Crew exits the store. "Is that all? I should get back to work. One of the other guards is due to take their coffee break."

"That can wait. I need you to come up to my office with me." His hand reaches for my elbow. His grip is firm, yet tender. The whisper of something unrelated to discussions about security cameras and scheduled staff breaks is there.

I breathe in the scent of his cologne. Matiz for Men. I recognize the subtle undertone of white musk and cedar. Beneath it is the fragrance of his skin. He smells as good as he looks. "It will only take fifteen minutes, Nolan. I can meet you up there as soon as I'm done."

"You'll come with me now." His touch is more insistent. "It's important, Ellie, and it's not a request."

Which means it's an order.

An order unrelated to his store or the employees who are now milling about, sudden exuberance in their voices as they greet customers. His presence is feeding their movements. Their drive to impress him is obvious.

The slight change in the tempo of his breathing gives him away. As do his fingers as they press into my bare flesh as a female customer stands near us, spellbound by our unspoken exchange.

I knead my hands together. "I'll come."

The irony of the words isn't lost on me, or on him. That familiar flash of triumph in his gaze is quickly replaced with a hunger I haven't seen there before. It's a bold and unapologetic hunger for me.

***

"I'm not a complicated man," he says with a sigh.

Is he serious?

He runs the largest cosmetics company in the United States with a keen eye on global expansion. His family's fortune has punctuated New York's highest society for decades, yet his personal life is incredibly private. I should know. I searched his name online and the results were bone bare.

I glance over my shoulder to where he's standing near his office door. He sent his assistant to get a folder from marketing. She had to ask twice if he was sure he needed to see the hard copy for a lipstick ad that ran in a national magazine three years ago. He insisted, she questioned again and finally she left. That's when he closed the door to his office before he slid his suit jacket from his shoulders.

"You strike me as a very complicated man," I reply honestly.

"Do I now?"

I watch as he meticulously rolls up one sleeve of his dress shirt and then the other. The result is an unobstructed view of his muscular forearms. My eyes flick across his skin before they settle on his face. "You do, yes."

He tugs on the front of his black pants before he lowers himself in the chair next to me. I anticipated him being in the chair behind his desk where he sits all day as he makes decisions that impact the lives of each and every one of his employees, including me. He's close now. Almost too close given the fact that I still have no idea why I'm here.

"You're wrong, Ellie." His gaze travels over the green skirt and white blouse I'm wearing before it lands directly on my face. "My life is simple. I need very few things."

"What things do you need, Nolan?"

"I need a good bottle of cabernet, a steak cooked to perfection and a beautiful redhead to share them with."

Chapter 14

Ellie

"Just to be clear, Ellie. The redhead I'm referring to is you."

I nod. I didn't respond when he first said he only needs wine, steak and me. As if a man like him could be content with a good meal, a glass of an expensive vintage red and my company. It may satisfy him for a few hours, or an entire night but then he'd be back on the prowl and every day I'd be forced to face a man I once fucked. If he was bad in bed, it might not be a problem. I doubt that Nolan Black has ever fucked a woman and left her unsatisfied.

"That's a flattering invitation." My lips purse. "I can't accept it, though."

He freezes in place, his eyes honed in on my face. "You're not accepting? Why?"

I could use Liam as an excuse, but that would be unfair to both men. Comparing them is impossible. One is friendship material wrapped into a rugged, long-haired beast. The other is refined and cultured. He wears wealth with ease, and his kisses must steal a part of a woman's soul that she'll never get back, even after he's had his fill and left her with an ache between her legs and in her heart.

Nolan Black could destroy me from the inside out. I sense it when he looks at me with his brilliant blue eyes that see into parts of me even I hide from.

"I don't think it's a good idea," I answer evenly. "I found out the hard way that mixing business with pleasure is a mistake."

"I see." He leans back in the chair, his long legs crossing at the knee. His fingers strum a beat on his thigh. "Do you think your job will be impacted if we share a dinner?"

He's smarter than that. He knows exactly what I'm talking about. He wants to hear me tell him that I don't think I can handle a good hard fuck followed by a brief it's not you, it's me speech or a ghosting. That's how Tad Darling dumped me. His name was a poetic parody of the man bearing it.

We met in New York, fucked in Boston and then moved to Las Vegas once I had a massive diamond ring on my finger. It ended as most relationships with affluent, emotionally vacant, pussy chasing men do. With no respect for what once was in the form of an empty goodbye. In Tad's case, the goodbye came two months after he had all my belongings packed up and delivered to my office. His phone number changed, and the locks on our apartment were replaced, just as quickly as I was.

"That's been my experience in the past," I confess. "Dynamics change when that line is crossed."

He studies my face. "Only if the two people involved don't handle it properly."

"Can I ask you a question?"

"Please." He waves his hand in the air before his fingers settle on his chin. "Ask away, Ellie."

"If I have dinner with you, what do you expect from me?"

"I'll pick up the check if that's what you're asking." His voice is smooth. The crisp notes of each word flow together off his lips. I instantly wonder if there's anything he could say that wouldn't sound sexy to me.

"That's not what I was asking," I blurt out in haste, slightly annoyed that he's finding humor in this.

"What are you asking?" He leans forward, resting his elbows on his knees.

I tug on the hem of my skirt. "This isn't really about a good bottle of wine and a steak, is it?"

"What do you think it's about?"

I call him on his bluff because I doubt like hell he's expecting me to. "It's about us sleeping together. That's really what you want."

"Yes, Ellie. I want to fuck you."

***

Breathe, Ellie. Breathe.

Bluff called. Nolan Black answered.

"I don't believe I've misread anything between us." His eyes soften, the intensity gone. "The attraction is strong and it's mutual. If there's a reason, beyond your job, that you'd prefer not to act on it, I'm interested in hearing that."

"Do I need a reason beyond that?"

He takes a deep breath. "You're an asset to Matiz. I'm not going to do anything that jeopardizes that. We don't want to lose you."

It's the beginning of a conversation I never had with Tad. We didn't consider what the end of our relationship would mean to my job at his company. Ultimately, he took that from me too.

"Do you find me attractive, Ellie?"

I scan his face. I can tell him honestly that he's the most attractive man I've ever met, but he's heard that before. He knows it. It's evident in the way he carries himself, in the way he's speaking to me now. "Yes, you know that you're attractive."

"Does your reluctance to have dinner with me have anything to do with your date with Liam tomorrow?"

"Why would it be because of Liam?" I shoot back quickly.

His posture changes, his back stiffening. "I have no idea where you two stand. It's not uncommon for people in this city to devote their attention to one person after a first encounter."

I wade through the verbiage to get to the message he's trying to convey. "You think I hooked up with Liam already and I'm now head-over-heels? I met him two days ago, Nolan. Technically, it was less than two days."

His mouth quirks. "So you haven't slept with him?"

My eyes fall to his hands. His right thumb is tracing tight circles over his left palm. I tilt my head to the side, contemplating not only what I'm seeing but what he just asked. "I don't think that's any of your business. I also don't think it's an appropriate conversation for us to be having during work hours."

"Consider yourself off the clock." His fingers thrum over the face of his watch. "You officially have the rest of the day off."

RISK   *Deborah Bladon*

"No," I say with an exaggerated sigh. "Don't do that. Don't influence my job because of something personal between us."

"You admit that there's something between us?"

I can deny it. I should deny it, but I don't. "I'm attracted to you, Nolan. I'm sure most of the women who work for Matiz are, but that doesn't mean anything has to happen between us."

"You're right." He crosses his arms over his chest. "It doesn't mean anything has to happen, but it will. How long do you think we can resist each other, Ellie? I'm a strong man, but you're the type of woman who can weaken a Herculean resolve."

Words. They're all just words meant to seduce and tempt. They roll off his tongue as leisurely as the comments about the weather he directed toward a man in the elevator with us on the ride up to his office.

I look down at the necklace I'm wearing. It's a cheap piece I picked up at a flea market in Las Vegas. It has no sentimental value. The significance of it is non-existent. Once it breaks, as thin silver chains often do, I'll toss it away without a second thought. It's just like his words, pretty in the moment, but once they've served their purpose, quickly forgotten.

"I'll have dinner with you, Nolan."

"Tonight," he says, not asks, in a tone that reeks of victory. "I'll pick you up at eight. There's a place in Hell's Kitchen that I know you'll enjoy."

I rise to my feet at the quiet rap on his office door. "No, not tonight. Tomorrow."

87

"Tomorrow?" He ignores the tapping as he stands. "You're canceling your date with Liam for me?"

My stomach knots at his blatant arrogance. "No. I want you to come over for dinner tomorrow too. Around seven o'clock would be good."

"With Liam?" He scowls.

"Yes." I glance at his office door. "Are you going to get that?"

"No, I'm not." Confusion etches his brow. "You want me to come to your place tomorrow to have dinner with Liam? With you and Liam?"

"Liam will be there," I begin as I rub my forehead. "My roommate Adley and Randy, Liam's friend, will be there too."

"I'll be the fifth wheel?"

"Or sixth." I shrug. "Depending on how you view her."

"Who?"

"The woman who wrote on your palm. I assume she drew the cute heart too." I turn back as I reach the door. "Bring her with you. I'd love to meet the artist behind that masterpiece."

He mumbles something under his breath, but I don't stop to ask him to repeat it. I swing open the door and almost knock the file folder from his assistant's hand as I breeze past her on my way to the elevator.

Chapter 15

Nolan

"There's no way in hell this is happening." Crew looks right past the woman who opened Ellie's apartment door just as I was about to knock. "Talk about a roleplay. Are you seeing what I'm seeing, Nolan?"

Unfortunately, I am. I see all of it. It's being imprinted on my retinas so every time I close my goddamn eyes from this point forward, I'm going to see this in front of me.

Ellie is wearing a bikini top. The most perfect bikini top ever to grace a female body. Two small triangles of black fabric and some thin black string are all that cover her breasts. The black very short shorts she's wearing sit well below her belly button. Her hair is pulled back and high in a ponytail. She's standing near an open window with her hands on her hips, her skin glowing with a mist of perspiration.

She turns to the side, and I swallow back a moan born from somewhere deep inside me when the profile of her gorgeous ass comes into my view. The thin material of her shorts leaves nothing to the imagination, and suddenly my cock is hard as steel.

The bastard standing next to her is hard too. I'm clear across the room from him but the outline of his dick through the faded jeans he's wearing is obvious to anyone within a mile radius. The tool belt he has on does nothing to hide his arousal.

He flexes then, drawing his arms up over his head. His biceps tense, his abs ripple, and Ellie's eyes are glued to everything but the T-shirt, that I assume is his, bunched in a pile at his bare feet. She's practically naked. He's half-way there and I'm staring at it all with a bottle of wine and a gallon of melting cookie dough ice cream in my hands.

"What the hell is going on here?" I snap.

"The air conditioning stopped working," Ellie's friend says. I remember her from Las Vegas, but apparently not well enough to recall her name. "The building manager told us the repair guy wouldn't be here until tomorrow afternoon, but he showed up fifteen minutes ago."

I glance at her. She's clothed. She's wearing a short yellow dress and a huge smile.

"You're Ellie's bosses, aren't you?" She steps toward us. "I'm Adley York. I'm Ellie's roommate."

Crew pushes past me to grab the woman's hand. "I'm Crew. Nolan didn't tell me where we were headed, but I'm glad I tagged along."

She laughs. "You'll regret saying that. It's like three hundred degrees in here."

"Nolan?" Ellie approaches tentatively, her hands clenched together in front of her. "Crew? What are you two doing here?"

I tuck the bottle of wine next to my elbow before I run my fingers over my brow. I'm burning up, but I can't tell if it's the temperature in here or how Ellie looks. I thought that black dress in Vegas was hot. Now, I can't even remember what it looks like. "You invited me for dinner, Ellie. I brought wine and your favorite ice cream."

RISK   *Deborah Bladon*

"You thought I was serious?" she asks tightly. "I didn't think you'd actually show up."

She doesn't know me very well. I never back down from a challenge. There was a trace of amusement in her eyes yesterday afternoon when she invited me for dinner. I decided by the time she pressed the elevator call button that I'd be at her apartment promptly at seven with a bottle of crisp chardonnay, along with a container of the ice cream I saw her friend give to her at Cremza.

"I'd never turn down an invitation from you." I glance back at the repair guy. His eyes are focused squarely on Ellie's ass. "I would have worn my board shorts if I knew the evening was beach themed."

She looks me over from head to toe. Her gaze lingers appreciatively on the gray dress shirt and black pants I'm wearing. "There isn't a theme. We're not having dinner. We postponed."

"We canceled," Adley interjects. "Bean decided we should cancel after the air conditioner died. I was just on my way out to have dinner with one of the guys who planned on being here."

"Bean?" Crew chuckles. "What's that nickname about, Ellie?"

"I came up with it, "Adley says, pride evident in her smile. "Ellie is my jelly bean. I call her that because she used to sneak jelly beans from a jar in my mom's kitchen. Eventually, my mom just gave her the entire jar."

"You've known each other since you were kids?" I step forward. "Tell me about her back then."

Crew and both women turn to me. It's not my words that draw their attention. It's my tone. Firm and demanding, it's a command for information about a woman who just started working for me. It's obvious to all three of them that I'm not trying to lure playful memories about Ellie's childhood from her best friend. I'm hunting.

"We should take off." Crew shoots me a sharp glance that's spiked with the anger he's barely containing. I was intentionally sparse with the details when I told him we were meeting two beautiful women for dinner.

I accessed Ellie's payroll record to find her address, unsure if Crew had taken note of it when he handed her file to human resources the day she started working for us. He didn't clue in when I asked my driver to drop us a block up from Ellie's building. I told him to call the store in Midtown to check on the shipment of lipstick that arrived earlier today. I did that to keep his focus away from the direction we were headed.

His call ended just as Adley opened the door. The timing couldn't have been more perfect.

"I'm staying," I announce because there's no way in fucking hell I'm leaving Ellie alone with the repairman. If I weren't losing a pound a minute in sweat because of the sweltering heat in this apartment, I would have thought the scene that greeted me when I walked in the door was the beginnings of a poorly lit porn shoot.

The air conditioning unit is definitely not working, and the blond haired guy who is now absentmindedly rubbing his dick through his jeans is focused on only one thing. It's not the screwdriver in his hand. It's Ellie's body which, when covered with a sheen of sweat, looks incredibly fuckable.

"You're not staying." Ellie points to the apartment door. "You and Crew can go."

I brush past her and head directly to the kitchen area that consists of little more than a few worn cabinets, out-of-date appliances and a peninsula that oversees the main living space. I open the freezer door, pushing packages of frozen berries and a bag of cubed ice to the side. I shove the container of ice cream in before I slam the door shut. "I'm going to open this wine, have a drink and then I'll fix that air conditioner myself."

"River is going to fix it." Ellie sighs heavily.

River? Naturally, his goddamn name would be River.

Ellie's eyes target me before she turns to River. "How long before you'll have it working?"

"I need parts, babe," he drawls through a grin. "One of the guys from the supplier will try to bring them over in a couple of hours. We can hang until then. You got any beers?"

I start to unbutton my shirt. "Find someone else to hang with, River. I can handle this."

He shakes his head. "No can do, mister. This unit belongs to the building. I can't just let any Tom, Dick or Harry touch it. The owner will fucking freak at me if he finds out I let you touch the AC."

"It's Nolan," I say dryly. "The owner will not fucking freak if I touch the air conditioner."

He laughs. "Dude, seriously, you don't know him. I talked to the guy on the phone when the boiler blew last winter. He skipped right over the building manager and went straight for my jugular. Shit will get real if you try and fix it."

I crane my neck so I can look at Crew. "You're welcome to step in anytime."

Crew walks across the room and slaps River on the shoulder. "The only shit that's going to get real is the conversation we're going to have tomorrow about that uncontrollable boner you're rocking. Seriously, River. You're on the job. Dial it back."

"What?" River's eyes dart from Crew's face to mine and then back again. "I know your voice. There's no way you're Benton."

"In the flesh." Crew flashes a smile. "I own this place, and unless you're out of here in the next thirty seconds, I'm going to contract out repairs for all my buildings to another company."

Chapter 16

Ellie

"I trust you, pal." Crew claps Nolan on the back. "I don't know if you know what the hell you're doing, but I trust you. Don't fuck this up like you did with the others."

"Did you fuck up someone else's air conditioner?" Adley asks Nolan as she closes the door behind River. It took him less than thirty seconds to scoop up his T-shirt and leave. I was just as surprised as he was when Crew said he owns the building.

"He's fucked up a few," Crew grumbles. "He promised me, this time, it would be different."

"It will be different." Nolan scrubs his hand over the back of his neck. "You have my word."

It's obvious that they're not talking about air conditioners, but Adley hasn't clued in yet. "It doesn't matter to me if you fuck it up because if you do, you have to replace it. That's in my rental agreement. If something breaks and isn't repairable, it has to be replaced within a reasonable amount of time."

"I have doubts that this one is replaceable." Crew's gaze volleys between Nolan and me. "Do what you need to do, Nolan. Bear in mind, that if this goes badly, you owe me."

"Understood," Nolan replies curtly.

"I'm late for my date." Adley leans forward to kiss my cheek. "Do you want me to relay a message to Wolf through Randy?"

"If I want to talk to Wolf I can text him myself," I murmur even though the only reason I took Liam's number when I was leaving Cremza is that he insisted. He thinks he can help me further my career, but I'm not convinced. "Go have fun, Ad."

"You too." A sly grin slides over her lips. "I'll call you later."

"Are you headed uptown?" Crew turns to Adley. "I'm getting an Uber. We can ride together if that works for you."

"It works for me." Adley nods. "What's the name of that nail polish you're wearing? I've been looking for a shade just like that."

All eyes drop to Crew's hands and the bright pink polish messily painted onto his right thumbnail. He wags it in the air. "This is our Pink Twist. It just came in today. It looks like my niece needs to keep her day job. She's not going to cut it as a manicurist."

"I'm buying a bottle." Adley reaches for his hand to bring it in for a closer look. "I think this would look good on me."

"It suits you." Crew cups her hand in his. "Ellie can bring a bottle home from work for you. No charge."

"Seriously?" She holds his hand to her chest. "Thank you."

"No thanks necessary." His smile widens as he stares at her. "You ready to head out?"

"Absolutely." She abruptly lets go of his hand. "I'm going to Axel NY."

"Good choice." Crew gestures toward the door. "I've been. Great food."

RISK   *Deborah Bladon*

Adley launches into a story about the last time she was at Axel. I hear her say something about her ex, Leo, as the door shuts behind them.

"Time for me to get to work." Nolan slides his shirt from his shoulders. "There's a gallon of your favorite ice cream in the freezer if you're hungry."

I smile in spite of my resolve not to. I didn't expect him to show up tonight. I was shocked when I turned to see him and Crew standing in the entryway of my apartment. "Cookie dough?"

"That's what your friend got for you at Cremza. I assumed it was your favorite."

"It is." I draw in a breath. "What flavor were you buying the other night?"

He hesitates briefly before a grin pulls at the corner of his lips. "Blue bubble gum."

I cover my mouth with my hand to shield my broad smile. "I would have pegged you for more of a vanilla or strawberry type."

"Oh really?" A bead of sweat rolls down his muscular chest. My gaze follows.

"Yes, but I was wrong. The secret is out. The owner of Matiz Cosmetics likes blue bubble gum ice cream."

His hands drop to his pants. He loosens the belt and then unfastens his slacks. "The owner of Matiz Cosmetics likes many things. Bubble gum ice cream is right up there with a certain blue-eyed redhead."

"Are you taking your pants off?"

"If that's a request, the answer is yes." He draws in a deep breath. "It's so damn hot in here. I'm just trying to get comfortable so I can fix your air conditioner before I pass the fuck out."

I bite back a giggle. "The only tools we have are in a drawer in the kitchen."

Cocking his head to the side, he looks directly at me. "Show me what you've got, Ellie."

***

"There's an empty furnished apartment on the second floor with a working air conditioner." He pushes his phone back into the front pocket of his pants. "It's a two bedroom. You can stay there tonight and the new unit will be installed here first thing tomorrow."

"So that strange smell that was coming from it was a fried motor?"

"That's the culprit." He looks over at the dismantled air conditioner on the floor near the window. He had the problem diagnosed within minutes, and it took even less time for him to call someone to arrange the delivery and installation of the new unit as well as accommodations for Adley and me for the night. "It's not worth trying to fix it. Someone from the repair crew will have the new one installed in no time."

"Will it be River?" I ask quietly.

His arms cross over his chest. My eyes fall once again to the skin that is exposed right where his pants hang open. I can see the barest hint of his black boxer briefs and the trail of dark hair that disappears beneath them.

"No." He narrows his eyes. "You don't actually like that guy."

"Are you asking me if I do or telling me I don't?"

"I'm stating a fact."

"I might like him."

"But you don't," he says assuredly.

"You don't know that, Nolan."

"I know you like me." He straightens his stance. "River and I are nothing alike, so it stands to reason that you don't like him."

"Am I anything like the woman who wrote on your hand?"

His gaze drops to his left hand. He flips it over to reveal a now bare palm. "Who said it was a woman who wrote on my hand?"

I did. It was an easy assumption to make. An uneven heart was drawn near his thumb. It was a sweet accent to the phrase I LUV U which was scribbled in black ink across the middle of his palm. "A man wrote it?"

"Strike two. You have one last chance before I get to ask you a question."

"You wrote it for someone or maybe to yourself?" I joke.

"If I wrote it I'd take the time to write out each letter. I'm not lazy when it comes to those three words." He studies me, his expression softening. "But no, I limit the self-love to messages written on my bathroom mirror. I try to keep the ego in check in public."

I laugh. "Do you think you're doing a good job with that?"

"Fair." He half-shrugs. "I'd say I'm doing a fair job with it. It's my turn to ask you a question."

My eyes flick over his body. It's now dotted with sweat. I follow the path of his chest, to his neck and finally to his face. His hair has morphed from styled perfection to damp tousled mess. Somehow he looks even more handsome than he did when he first got here. "What's the question?"

"Can I call you Bean too?" His eyes soften as he smiles. "Say yes."

"No." I shake my head quickly. "You can't."

He leans forward until his lips are almost brushing mine. His voice is barely a whisper. The movement of his mouth, so close to my own, drives my pulse to race. "Can I call you my date for tomorrow night?"

I draw in a quiet breath. "I remember something about a good bottle of cabernet and a steak. Is that still on the menu?"

"We can have whatever you want. If you agree to have dinner with me, I'll eat dirt and drink week old coffee. Just tell me it's a go."

"What about my job?" I pause and pull back. "I lost one job because of a man. I don't want to repeat history."

He tips his head. His eyes are pinned to mine. "That man is an idiot. In case you haven't noticed yet, I'm not. "

"I know it's just one date, but I like this job. I want to keep it for now."

"For now?" He studies my face. "You have aspirations beyond Matiz?"

"Of course," I answer confidently. "I'll tighten your security and then I'll chase my dream job."

"What's your dream job, Ellie?"

It feels too personal to share. It's the only job I've wanted since I was a kid. One day I'll be a member of the New York Police Department. I'm determined.

"I might tell you about that on our date if we can come to an agreement about my job security."

He nods. "As of tomorrow morning, you report to Crew. He's your boss. You run everything past him. I have no say in anything related to your position at Matiz."

I bite the corner of my lip. "You'll honor that even if we end up in a place where we're not on speaking terms?"

"That will never happen."

"It could happen, Nolan."

"It won't. I can assure you, that I won't stop speaking to you."

"You can't see into the future," I point out. "You don't know what tomorrow will bring."

"I do know what tomorrow will bring." He reaches forward to push back a piece of hair that has fallen loose of my ponytail. "Tomorrow I'm going to have dinner with you."

I don't move as he glides his fingers from my cheek down to my neck. I'm still dressed in what I hastily put on after having a cool shower when I got home from work.

I meant to throw a T-shirt over my bikini top, but I've been too pre-occupied with everything that's happened since Nolan arrived. For the first time tonight, I feel exposed. Goosebumps crawl up my skin at his touch.

His gaze lingers on my mouth. "So we're in agreement that I'll pick you up here tomorrow at eight for dinner?"

I dart my hand in the air between us. "Yes, we have an agreement. We'll go on a date and Crew is my boss. Let's shake on it."

His tongue slicks his bottom lip as his hand slides to the back of my neck. He cups it, tilting my head slightly. He leans close, his breath rushing over my cheek. "Let's seal it with a kiss."

I breathe in the masculine scent of his skin when I feel his soft lips brush across my forehead.

Chapter 17

Nolan

I should have been all in. Lips, hands, cock. She was right there. Her mouth inches from mine, her breathing as rough as my own.

I wanted the memory of last night just as it was. The lingering kiss on her forehead, her fingers drifting to my bare chest and then my hand tightening its grip on the soft, smooth skin at the back of her neck.

I held back, instead staring into her eyes so she could see something in me that the asshole who fucked her over doesn't possess. I don't know him, but I want to be a better man than him.

When the property manager knocked on the door, Ellie pivoted away from me and the moment was lost. I didn't expect the guy to show up until I'd left, but dropping Crew's name during our phone call was all it took. He was there within minutes with keys in hand, eager to take Ellie to her temporary home on the second floor.

She changed her clothes, thanked me awkwardly while the guy watched our every move and then I left. I exited the building to a warm breeze and air thin enough that I could finally breathe. That's what I did. I stood on the street, looking up at her apartment window and once the light flicked off, I finally turned away. I walked home through the streets of the city I love. This city has taken so much and given me more than I deserve.

It's the same city I'm now surveying from the window of my office. People scatter as they step off a bus. Each of them is in a rush to get to a job that steals hours from their life just to pad their bank account enough that they can barely maintain the cost of living in Manhattan.

Others wander the streets aimlessly in search of anything that will give them the hope they need to make it through another day. Those are the people no one thinks about when they're window shopping on Fifth Avenue. I think about them. I still search their faces looking for Kip.

"You cost me a new air conditioner." Crew chuckles as he walks into my office through the open door.

It's too early for Eda to be at her desk. I was up at dawn, trading breakfast for a call to London to discuss the launch of our first international location. By the time I exited my apartment the sun was flooding the streets with the lazy morning light that lures people from their beds.

I skipped the routine of stopping for a cup of coffee around the corner from my office. The smile of the tall black-haired barista who always wears our Classic Crimson lipstick used to be the perfect complement to my medium cup of dark roast. We never exchanged a word, only a knowing glance after seeing each other at a park on the Upper West Side. I walked right past the café today, my mind consumed with thoughts of Ellie.

"It was worth it," I volley back. "You're here early."

"I'm trying to impress the boss," he jokes. "Why are you here? I thought you'd still be at Ellie's place. That or in intensive care because of heat exhaustion. Jesus, it was hot in her apartment."

He has no fucking idea.

"They needed the new unit." I sit in my office chair. "You should run a check on all the air conditioners in that building if they're as dated as the one in Ellie's place."

"I've already made that call." He settles in one of the chairs in front of my desk. "My dad had those units installed years ago. It's time to update them."

I nod. He opened the door for a conversation about his dad that I'm slamming shut. My relationship with Crew's dad is strained. Our father-pseudo son bond was ripped to shreds when he shoved a corporate knife in my dad's back during his hostile takeover of the small investment firm they launched together.

It's business first, family second for most of the Benton family. It was the same for me at one point. My priorities changed, as have my allegiances.

Crew is the closest thing I have to a brother. I respect his relationship with his dad, but I don't huddle on the sidelines with the two of them anymore.

"The more time I spend with Ellie, the more I realize that she's nothing like Kip."

I'm caught off guard by the words. I glance at him. His face is impassive. There's nothing readable there. To him, Kip was just a girl who lived on the street a decade ago. The first time he tagged along when I took her a sandwich he introduced himself as Jeff. It was just one of the many names he used back then to keep girls from tracking him down after he'd had his fill of them.

He saw her only a handful of times. She was always wearing a black knit cap I'd given her pulled down over her forehead. Their conversations were consistently one-sided with Crew telling her stories about his adventures in Paris the summer before we met her.

He's given me shit repeatedly since then about my inability to forget about her. Even though he continually reminds me that he can't recall the barest details about her, he still weighs in whenever I ask him to.

When we knew Kip, he used to joke that my ongoing interest in her was all about the driving need to be her first. The thought churned my stomach. She was an innocent. Her trust in me wasn't currency I'd use to barter anything from her, especially that part of her soul.

I didn't want her that way. I couldn't imagine her that way. She was too young, and I was too lost in the grief of my grandmother's death that winter to see straight. I saw someone who needed help when I looked at Kip, and I know she saw the same in me.

"They're different," I agree. "Personality wise they are nothing alike. I still think Ellie looks like Kip."

He shakes his head. "I don't see it. I've always said that Kip was close to our age. I know you think she was younger but you're wrong, pal."

RISK *Deborah Bladon*

How do you gauge someone's age when they're thin and frail because they go to bed hungry every night? Skin is deceptive when it's burnt from the bitterly cold winds of a nor'easter. I asked Kip how old she was, but like every other question, an answer never came. It didn't matter to me. It didn't change a thing between us. We were unlikely friends, but for those two months, it worked for us.

"Besides," he continues without any prompt from me, "Ellie would have recognized you by now, pal. If she were Kip she'd know you were Rigs."

Trauma has a way of distorting memories. I should know. I cling to vague images of Kip's face that morph into something different every time I see a woman I think might be her.

"What's on your agenda today?" I easily change the subject. I'm not going to debate the topic of Kip with Crew again. We've done it too often with no resolution. It's always felt like we're digging up the past with two very different shovels.

"I'm doing that marketing meeting at nine," he says, his gaze skimming the screen of his phone. "I'm booked for lunch with my brother, and I'm dedicating my afternoon to chasing down the chemist who is working on that new mascara we want to launch in the spring."

It's a typical day for Crew. Since we graduated from college, he's had a high ranking position waiting for him in a tower across town that bears the Benton name. Still, he took a seat next to me when I inherited Matiz.

I'm not a fool. I know that eventually during one of the weekly lunches he has with his brother,

Kade, he'll make the decision to jump the Matiz ship to work alongside his family. I'm preparing for that eventuality by bringing new people on board at a steady clip. I don't want to miss a beat when he finally takes the plunge.

"You still up for going to Club Aeon tonight?" He glances at me. "We can head out late. Eleven works for me, and it gives you time at home after you break free of this place."

"I'm clocking out at noon today. I'll spend the afternoon at home. I have a date tonight, so you're flying solo to the club."

"With Ellie?"

I run a hand over my tie to straighten it. "We're having dinner together."

"What if it turns into something?" He studies me. "I've seen you around her. You're different. Your dick's not driving this thing. It's more."

It is more. I don't know what it is. I can't tell if I'm infatuated with her or if this is awe. It could be pure lust with a side of admiration. I have no fucking idea what I'm feeling. All I know is that tonight I'll be sitting across a table from Ellie with the intention of going back to her place so I can sink my cock into that beautiful body.

"It's just a dinner, Crew."

He rises to his feet. "Don't let this get ahead of you. If this goes somewhere, you need to sit Ellie down and explain a few things to her."

I know exactly what he's talking about. The reminder is not only unwelcome. It's unnecessary. "I've got it covered."

RISK   *Deborah Bladon*

As I watch him exit my office, I look down at my left hand and the fading message on my palm.

I didn't see it when I showered because I was too busy daydreaming about how Ellie looked last night. I was so engrossed in what I wanted to say during my call to London that I didn't notice it when I was getting dressed.

I see it now. I feel it now.

She was fast asleep when I got home last night so she must have written it early this morning when she crawled into bed with me. The light from the attached bathroom was filtering into my bedroom through the door I'd left ajar to offer her a safe path in case she needed me.

I felt the rustle of the blanket as she settled beneath it and the pull on my hand. I was so exhausted I kept my eyes closed as I listened to her hum a soft melody while she traced her delicate fingertips over my hand. Or what I thought were her fingertips.

I LOVE YOU

Those three words, written with so much care in black ink across my palm, are a symbol of the life I keep hidden from the world. It's a life I protect at all costs.

Chapter 18

Ellie

"You're sure you don't mind, Nolan?" Tilting my head back, I look up at him. "You'd tell me if this wasn't a good idea, wouldn't you?"

"Why would I mind?" His blue eyes sparkle as the headlights from a taxi turning a corner in our direction cast a glow over his face. "I told you I was up for drinking old coffee and eating dirt. I trust that this is better than that."

"They make the best burgers in Manhattan." I gesture toward the street cart. "I missed these so much when I was out in Vegas. I've been craving one since I got back."

"What are we waiting for?" He takes a measured step toward the long line as his gaze darts up to the concise menu printed on a white board near the cart's window. "They've got a few different burgers. What are you in the mood for?"

I smile at the question. Obviously, he's talking about the menu, but ever since Nolan picked me up, I've been in the mood to ditch dinner so I can be alone with him. He's dressed just as he always is, impeccably. Tonight it's charcoal slacks and a light blue button down shirt in the same shade as the sundress I'm wearing. He had a suit jacket on when he knocked on my door, but he slid it off after I asked if I could change our dinner plans.

He tossed the jacket to his waiting driver along with instructions to stay put. He didn't hesitate for a second when he fell into step beside me as we walked the three blocks to this spot.

"We can split a cheeseburger," I suggest. "The fries are amazing. Can you get an order of those too and maybe a bottle of water?"

His eyes flick over my face. "I got paid last Friday. I can spring for two burgers."

I laugh. "I usually only eat half. I save the other half for the next day."

"I'll get one cheeseburger, two fries and two bottles of chilled water." He holds up two fingers in the air. "Fries are my weakness."

"Fries and blue bubble gum ice cream are your weaknesses."

He reaches forward, resting his hands lightly on my bare shoulders as he leans down so his lips are level with mine. "Fries, blue bubble gum ice cream, and a beautiful redhead are all my weaknesses, but not in that order."

"The ice cream trumps the fries?"

"No." He skims his lips over mine in the softest kiss. "Ellie trumps everything. You're proving to be my biggest weakness."

"Me?" I draw in a deep breath, my lips craving another taste of his. "How am I your biggest weakness?"

"I gave up a table at my favorite restaurant and a bottle of the best wine I've ever had to eat half of a burger on a street corner with you."

"You said you didn't mind." I tilt my head to the side. "You won't regret it after your first taste. I promise."

His eyes fall to my lips. "I have no doubt about that."

***

"Adley invited a few people from the clinic she works at over for drinks." I sigh as I rest my phone in my lap. "Unless you want to eat ice cream with an audience, my place won't work for dessert."

He takes a healthy bite of what's left of his half of the burger. By the time I'd finished my meal, he was just digging into his.

After he had picked up the food, we'd sat in two white folding, wooden chairs next to a small table in an area set up to accommodate patrons of the different food carts. While I bit into a fry, he talked about the man who had served the food to him. He's the same man who used to work this cart when Adley and I were fresh out of high school. His smile is infectious, and if you spend just a minute or two talking to him, he'll add a homemade butter cookie wrapped in cellophane and tied with blue ribbon to your tray at no charge. Nolan got two.

When he suggested we go back to my place to eat some of the ice cream he brought over last night, I eagerly agreed. It might have been an easy way to get me to ask him to hang out after dinner, but it was my intention all along. I sent Adley a text telling her to get lost for a few hours. That's when she clued me into the last minute party she's hosting.

RISK *Deborah Bladon*

"I have a place we can go to," he offers just as he brings the water bottle to his lips.

He didn't say it was *his* place. He said it was *a* place.

Tad had a place he took women to. All the women he fucked that weren't engaged to be married to him. I found out about his secret hotel suite two months after he stopped talking to me. It was completely by chance, and if things hadn't worked out the way that they did, I would have dumped him myself after realizing that he wasn't spending his Tuesday and Thursday nights playing basketball with his buddies. He was in a luxury suite in the Lunar Hotel, just off the Vegas strip, with whatever woman caught his eye that day.

His assistant had been on maternity leave when Tad unilaterally decided that our engagement was over. The day she came back to work, she called me, thrilled that Tad had continued the tradition of ordering a dozen red roses each Tuesday and Thursday for me while she'd been away. A quick check of the delivery address and the name of the florist was all the information I needed from her. I spent the next hour fitting together the pieces of Tad's double life.

My fiancé had a standing order in place to have a bouquet delivered to his suite at the hotel at eleven o'clock two nights a week so that the woman that he'd spent the evening screwing would have a memento to take home with her. By the time she got the flowers, he'd be on his way to our condo to get into bed with me.

113

The florist told me that the flower deliveries had started just a month after we moved to Las Vegas. I wouldn't have uncovered that fact if the florist herself hadn't just realized the day before I stopped at her shop that her husband had been unfaithful to her. She was emotional. I was pushy and it ended with her breaking the shop's promise of privacy to tell me all about Tad's deliveries.

My intuition told me never to stop using condoms with Tad even when he insisted. I'm grateful I listened to it.

"Are you one of those millionaires that have a hotel suite that you only use for sex?" I ask because I have a right to know if I'm going to share my body with him.

His mouth twitches. "Is that how you see me?"

I can't tell if the question is serious or not, so I err on the side of caution and put a different spin on it. "You seem like the type of man who would have a neutral and safe place to take women to."

"No." He shakes his head firmly. "I was talking about you thinking I'm a millionaire."

I try to hide my smile behind my hand. "Millionaire. Billionaire. What's the difference?"

"Hard work and a good accountant."

"Are we going to a hotel, Nolan?" I blurt out, wanting this part of the conversation to be over. It doesn't matter where he's taking me. I'll go. I want to go. I just don't want to get there without having the chance to mentally prepare myself for what I'm stepping into.

RISK   *Deborah Bladon*

He reaches for my hand, scooping it into his. He lifts it to his mouth. His lips feather over my palm in a touch that sends shivers down my spine and arousal to my core at the promise of more. "Trust me, Ellie. We're not going anywhere near a hotel tonight."

Chapter 19

Nolan

Ellie threw a wrench in my plans as soon as she brought up fucking. Not only was it a wake-up call to my already semi-hard cock, but it was also a moment of clarity.

After she had told me her roommate decided to throw an impromptu party, I decided we were going to my suite at the Bishop Hotel. It's the only place I've taken a woman to in years. It's fully equipped with everything I need. A box of condoms, a bottle of lubricant, a change of clothing for me and most importantly, an unspoken understanding with the staff that I require and expect discretion, always and completely.

I saw the anxiety marking Ellie's expression when she asked me about a hotel. There wasn't a trace of the playfulness that I always see on the faces of the woman I pick up at clubs or bars. Those women know when I tell them where we're headed that my expectation is clear. I'm not taking them to a luxury suite at one of Manhattan's premier hotels to do anything other than fuck.

Those experiences are empty. They've always been a way to quench the thirst for pleasure. I give, I take, and then I say goodbye. It's fleeting and final. It fits perfectly into the spot I've carved out for it.

I fuck at the Bishop Hotel. I feel in my apartment.

"Is my jaw on the floor?" She runs her fingers over her chin. "Is there a better view in Manhattan than this?"

I take a spot next to her in front of one of the large windows that overlook the city. The views of the city are spectacular, but right now they can't hold my attention. I stare at Ellie. Her hair is loose tonight, a cascade of long red curls down her back. Her dress is simple, but flattering. The straps thin enough to showcase the subtle curves of her shoulders, and the smooth skin of her arms. "I have the best view anywhere right now."

She tilts her head up at me. Suspicion wrapped in doubt is there in her eyes, but a faint smile tugs at the corners of her mouth. "Have you always been this charming?"

"It's not charm, Ellie. I'm telling it like it is."

Her gaze drifts across the room. She kneads her hands together, her top teeth pulling at the corner of her bottom lip. I want to feel that. I want those teeth on my lips, on my skin and after I've felt her come on my mouth, I need to feel the scrape of those teeth on my cock.

"Do you always tell it like it is?"

"I try to," I admit with a nod of my chin.

"I guess that means I should tell it like it is too."

There's a subtle challenge woven into her silken words. She narrows her eyes as if she's studying me with the intent of finding the most vulnerable part of me. Right now, it's my cock, hard as nails, aching from tip to root.

"Tell it like it is, Ellie," I volley back because I like the game. I like that she's not in a rush to fuck. She's biding her time, setting the pace. It's an experience I'm not accustomed to.

"I know your secret," she whispers with a lift of her brow.

I try to retain my composure, but it's a battle I can't win. I stare at her, in silence, dumbfounded by her words.

She knows my secret. One of my secrets. I have many, too many.

"There are clues all over your apartment." Her mouth quirks.

"Clues?" I scratch the back of my head. This game of cat and mouse would be infinitely more enjoyable if I were the cat and she played the role of the mouse, but that doesn't suit her. She's the one tugging on the string waiting for me to take the irresistible bait. "What clues?"

She leans closer so the seductive scent of her hits me. My body's response is feral. A fierce desire burns inside me to push her against the window. I want to fuck her until her secrets are mine. I want to punish her for playing with me. I need her as bare and exposed as I feel.

"There's a picture on top of your piano of Crew holding a small baby in a pink blanket. It looks like it was taken in a hospital room. It must be his niece in his arms." She flashes a smile at me. "Crew looks younger in it. I'd say it was taken a few years ago."

A few years ago, indeed. Five years, three months, twelve days.

"I saw a black marker on the table in the foyer." Her eyes drift past me to the hallway that leads back to the door she followed me through. "It's permanent, but not really. The ink fades once water hits it."

The dots she's connecting make perfect sense to her. The scattered unframed pictures on the piano I never learned how to play, the black permanent marker left near the door by a delivery man with a tight schedule and an absent mind. He handed me the pen. I signed for the package and by the time I was pulling a ten dollar bill from my pocket to offer him, he was back on the elevator.

"You said that the person who wrote on your hand wasn't a woman or a man. That only leaves the possibility of a child."

My chest expands. The air in my lungs stalls as I wait for her next words.

"Crew's niece wrote it when she came to visit you." She smiles. It's obvious she can't help it. I see the relief on her face. I hear it in her voice. The uncertainty about the message on my palm was her last thread of resistance. "That ladybug earring you had on belonged to her, didn't it? Little girls love pretty things."

Seconds pass and I don't say a word. I've never discussed this with a woman. Not even with Shelby and the two other women I saw more than once. I kept everything neutral, only giving meager details about my life as I dressed after rolling off the sheets and away from them.

This is why I only take women to the hotel. I need that barrier between my world and them. I don't want them stumbling into my real life. I'm not looking for impromptu deliveries of home baked goods from a woman I fucked and forgot. I don't want the complications that come when a woman shows up at my place in lingerie expecting a repeat.

There was a time when that worked for me, but no more. Not now.

I'm giving Ellie more of a glimpse into who I am than I have with anyone else, yet it still feels trivial. I should explain everything before I have her. Tell her who she's really sharing her body with.

"Can I tell you one of my secrets?"

"Yes," I say hoarsely, as eager to hear her confession as I am desperate to move the conversation away from me. "Tell me."

She looks up at me, her mouth curving into a small smile. "I'm relieved that a woman didn't write those words on your hand."

If she thinks that's a secret, I need to explain the meaning of the word to her. The relief that she felt was written all over her face. It was there in her body language.

She shakes her head. "I'm not saying that I think this is an exclusive thing. I don't. I know that we're probably going to have sex tonight and that doesn't mean you won't be having sex with other women tomorrow or that I won't be having sex with other men this week or whenever."

"What men?" I cock my head to the side, the bitter unfamiliar taste of jealousy coating my tongue, forcing the question out.

"It doesn't matter," she answers quickly on a sigh. "I was trying to say that I won't sleep with a

RISK   *Deborah Bladon*

man if he's in a serious relationship with someone else. If a woman loved you enough to brand your hand, even temporarily, you might love her back. I'm glad that it wasn't a woman who wrote it."

"What men, Ellie?"

"I don't know." She shrugs. "I wasn't talking about a particular man, Nolan. I was talking in general terms about having sex with other men."

I swear to God my vision is blurring from frustration. Why can't she give me a straight answer, and more importantly, why the hell do I care?

I've been in bed with women I know for a fact were fucking other men the night before I got my turn and I never gave them another thought. One of my friends from college married a woman he screwed an hour after I did at a frat party. I didn't think twice about it. I went to their wedding with a gift from their registry in my hands. I've never given two shits about what guy a woman fucked before or after she's been with me. Right now, the only thing I want is Ellie to tell me who the hell else she wants.

"Are you planning on fucking River?" I ask in an even tone. This is an adult conversation and I can act like a goddamn grown-up when I have it.

"Why are you bringing him up?" Her hands jump to her hips.

"I'm bringing him up because that son of a bitch couldn't keep his eyes off your ass last night."

"He was looking at my ass?"

How the hell is this conversation even happening? My face should be firmly planted between her thighs by now, my hands all over that

121

ass. Instead, we're discussing another man's fascination with her body.

I rub at my forehead. "Are you going to sleep with River or not?"

"I haven't even said yes to his dinner invitation yet."

Fucking hell.

"He asked you out?" My voice sounds strangled. It's a reflection of how my cock feels.

She tucks her hair behind her left ear. "He sent me flowers today and on the card there was a cute poem. He made up a rhyme about taking me to dinner in the form of a poem."

"A poem?" I repeat back, trying to absorb the idea that he wrote her poetry. I bought her half a burger and some fries. "So you're going out for dinner with River after you've had dinner with me?"

"Are you talking about actual dinner?" She purses her lips. "Or are you using dinner as a euphemism for sex?"

I lost my virginity when I was a teenager. Since then, I've never once met a woman I craved this much who I spent this much time talking to before I fucked her. Ever.

"I don't use anything as a euphemism for sex." I cross my arms over my chest. "When I talk about fucking, you'll know it. There will be no doubt."

"In that case, I haven't decided if I'll have dinner with River or not," she pauses. "The poem he wrote was very sweet."

"I'll write you something too."

"You'll write me a poem?" She laughs. "I can't wait to read it."

RISK   *Deborah Bladon*

I've never written a woman a poem. I wouldn't know where to fucking start.

"I told you that I'm nothing like River. It's not poetry, but it's something." I turn on my heel and head to the foyer. I pick up the black marker, unsure if it will even work after all this time. As I approach Ellie, I catch sight of her against the backdrop of the view of Manhattan.

My city, the very first love of my life, is there paling in comparison to the beauty of this woman. This woman who fell into my lap and my life and who I can't stop thinking about even though I've never really kissed her.

I reach for her hand and she gives it easily. I turn it over, pulling the cap off the marker with my teeth. I let it drop to the floor. I write on her skin while she watches my every move.

When I'm done, I toss the pen onto the piano.

Ellie looks down at her palm. She swallows hard and then, without a word, she grabs the front of my shirt, rises to her tiptoes and brushes her lips over mine.

Chapter 20

Ellie

His kiss is demanding. His lips are soft, their touch gentle at first, but then they part and his tongue greedily finds mine.

His moans are raw as his large hands cup my neck, controlling the tilt of my head and the pressure of his mouth on mine. He whispers something against my lips as he pulls back to catch a breath. I don't hear it. I can't make it out, but I sense it.

The desire is there in his kiss, and in his touch.

I reach up to wind my fingers through his hair. That pulls another sound from within him, but this time it's a groan. It's deep and gruff, the sound reverberating through him and into me.

"I'll give you anything you want," he whispers against my cheek as he breaks the kiss. "Tell me what you want, Ellie."

Everything. All of it. I want to feel and taste. I want to touch the skin that's hidden under his clothes. I want to hear the sound of his breathing and then when it hitches I want to savor that, knowing that he came just for me.

"I want you inside of me," I manage to say before his hand drops to my thigh.

His fingers race up my skin stopping when they reach that spot. It's the spot where the bullet hit me. I hated the scar for years. I was wary each time I took off my clothes in front of a man, worried that he wouldn't see anything but the jagged edge of the circular imperfection on my skin.

The men I've been with have never asked me about it, or even acknowledged it. They've all been too busy chasing their own needs. Even the man I promised to marry couldn't be bothered to understand the hidden pain that the scar represents. He knew I'd been shot. He never said the words, but I could sense that it was merely a flaw to him that wasn't worth a touch.

Nolan pulls back; his fingertip still focused on the scar. "Believe my words, Ellie. Every word I say to you, believe me."

I look into his eyes. I want to believe him, but this is fleeting. We have this one night. I don't expect more even if I want it. "I'll believe you tonight."

He shakes his head. There are words there, on his tongue, but they don't leave his lips. He scowls as if he's going to reprimand me for not having faith in him that this thing between us will still be alive tomorrow. It might smolder for a week or two, but I have to stay grounded. I can't let myself want what I can't have.

Disappointment has been as much a part of my life as breathing. I don't know what it feels like to get the things you desire. That's why I stopped wishing for anything I don't already have.

He kisses his way down my neck. His lips are plush and soft as they leave a trail of desire that heats my skin. I squirm when he reaches my shoulders, and his fingers push aside the small, thin straps of material that hold my dress in place.

I'm hit with a rush of frustration when his mouth stops as it reaches the top of my breasts. He squeezes them, his fingers plumping my pebbled nipples through the thin fabric.

He's on his knees before I realize what's happening. His hands slide over the back of my legs from my ankles, up my calves and then to my thighs. He fists the hem of the skirt of my dress into his hands, pulling it up as he goes.

I shiver when my almost bare ass is exposed to the air conditioned room. I feel the smile on his lips against the skin of my thigh. "Your body is beautiful, Ellie. It's so fucking beautiful."

I believe him. I don't know if it's because I need to or want to. I don't care. I want to be beautiful to him. I want to be the only woman he wants or needs, even if it's just right at this moment.

He moves then. His lips search out that one spot of skin on my outer thigh that his fingers were so focused on. He kisses my scar, softly and tenderly. Reverently.

"You saved a life."

I nod, unable to form any words. It's just a kiss, but the sensation and the words combined overwhelm me.

"The next time I fuck you, I'm going to spend hours licking your pussy." His mouth moves across my thigh to the edge of my blue lace panties. "I'm going to pull you onto my face and you'll ride me until you come over and over again. Until your taste is imprinted on my lips and until the only thing I can smell is the scent of you."

RISK *Deborah Bladon*

My knees buckle from his fevered words. I stumble only for a second before his strong hands grab hold of me, leveling my balance.

"Tonight I'll sample this," he rasps as his right hand fists the edge of my panties before they snap apart under his touch. "A taste and then I need to fuck."

I reach down to steady myself, my fingers tugging on his hair. My eyes close when I feel his lips on me. He parts my folds with his tongue. I moan softly as he hones in on my pulsing clit. The pressing need to come chases everything else away.

"Please, Nolan," I murmur as my hips circle slowly. My body finds its own rhythm, desperate for the release that his lips and tongue promise.

He answers my plea with a finger. One long, expert finger glides inside of me, its path clear as it seeks out that spot that I sense will send me reeling. I've never been with a man who knew how to eat me this way, with just the right balance of slow, smooth lashes of his tongue and the voracity of his lips as they suck on my swollen nub of nerves. No one has ever slid a finger inside of me and crooked it at just the right angle, so my body reacts without thought.

I'm so close that I whimper. I can't control it. I want the release so desperately that I dig my fingernails into his scalp, grinding myself on his mouth, aching for him to take me there. I crave more. I need more as much as I need my next breath. I don't care what I look like or sound like. I just want to come.

"I have to fuck you," he whispers against my flesh. "The first time you come for me I want to feel it around my cock."

I close my eyes at the heat in his words. It's there in his voice, the raging need to be inside me.

"Christ, Ellie."

I feel his breath on my neck, sense the movement of his hands, and hear the unmistakable rattle of a belt buckle and a zipper lowering.

I open my eyes to the darkened room. There's enough light from a small lamp in the corner to illuminate us both. I see his cock. Beautiful. It's long and thick, jutting out from his body. He pulls a condom package from the front pocket of his pants. I watch silently as he sheaths himself, slowly and meticulously. His large fist pumps over the barrier that is now the only thing separating the two of us.

He kisses me again, but this time the tenderness is buried beneath a layer of measured aggression. His tongue tangles with mine, teasing and taunting. I push my body closer to his, wanting to feel every part of him that's exposed.

He's as dressed as he was when we got here. His shoes are still on. Only one button is undone on his pressed shirt. His pants hang open, enough that his cock has the room it needs, but the rest of him is hidden away.

I try to unbutton his shirt but his hands are on mine, tugging them behind my back. "Your hands. I can't. If you touch me, I'll blow apart. I fucking swear I will come apart, Ellie. Don't."

I whimper. "Fuck me then."

"That mouth," he hisses. "That goddamn mouth of yours makes me so fucking hard."

I try to move but his grip is too tight. I lean forward and run my tongue over his jaw, across the stubble that's now taken root on his skin. I bite him softly. "Don't wait. Take me now."

He grinds against me, one hand cupping the nape of my neck, the other circles my waist. His movements are precise, quick and fluid. He spins us both around, lowering me onto my back on the leather couch.

"I've thought about this a million times," he says darkly. "You like this. Spread open, wet, aching for me."

He moves and my body does too, seamlessly my legs part and he settles between them. His cock is resting against my thigh. It's heavy, needy.

He palms it as he looks down at me. His eyes are hooded and filled with lust. "You tell me if it's too much, Ellie. You tell me to stop if that's what you need."

"Yes," I breathe, my body pulsating with need. "I will if it's too much, but I like when it hurts."

He circles my clit with the head of his cock before he slams himself into me in one solid thrust.

I scream because it's uncontainable. The bite of pain wrapped around so much pleasure bows my back. I grab onto his shoulders, my nails digging through the fabric of his shirt, trying to etch a mark into his flesh. I want to own a piece of him, just as he owns me right now.

He pumps, lightly at first as if I'm a doll who will break into a million pieces if she's fucked too hard.

"I want this," I purr through a moan. "You won't hurt me."

He pushes deeper, my body adjusting to him, not easily, but eagerly. He pumps harder, each movement of his hips in tandem with a groan from his lips.

"Fuck," he growls as he kisses my neck. More words are there, but they get lost in his breath on my skin.

I moan when his hand tugs the front of my dress down. I whimper when he bites my nipple between his teeth, and then I come. I come hard as he relentlessly drives his cock into my core.

He kisses me through my orgasm, his teeth scraping against my bottom lip. "Give me another, Ellie. Let me hear that again."

I do. I lick my index finger, slide it down my stomach and rest it against my still throbbing clit. I circle it slowly as he watches, his cock pulsing inside me, even though he's as still as the air that surrounds us. My hips move, seeking more. I grind up and into him, brazenly taking what I want. I get it when I feel the rush of the next climax, potent and fierce as it rolls through me.

"I could come just from the sight of that." He rests his forehead against mine as we both look down at our bodies connected. "That was so fucking hot."

He bucks, grinding into me. His hand moves, trailing soft fingertips down my stomach, to my hip. His touch changes as he grips my skin. He presses, holding me down as his untamed need to come takes over again.

His mouth roughly claims mine as he pumps deep, long strokes that spike heated pleasure through me before he finds his own release. My whispered name on his lips is the only sound in the room as his chin drops and his heavy breaths stutter.

Chapter 21

Ellie

"Tell me what I can do for you, Ellie."

I stare at him. He's standing now, his pants still hanging open, his cock tucked back inside his boxer briefs. He kissed me softly after his orgasm, telling me over and over again how good it felt when I came around his cock. When I asked for a glass of water, he tied off the condom and walked into the kitchen. I took a deep breath. It did nothing to steady my nerves or to slow my rapid heartbeat.

"Can I use the bathroom?" I ask quietly. "I need to put myself back together."

"You could let me take you apart again," he says with a smile.

I could. I will. First, I need to find out if my legs still work. "The bathroom first, please."

He holds out his hand, and I reach for it. I'm acutely aware of his every touch now that he's been inside of me and I've heard the way his breath catches when his hips pump.

The man can fuck. Even with his clothes on and his polished shoes still neatly tied, he tore me apart. My pussy aches, my heart is thrumming a beat that I can hear vibrating in my ears and my dress is a twisted mess.

Yet, he looks like someone who caught a sprint on his way out the door after a late shower. His hair is tousled from where I ran my fingers through it.

His shirt is slightly askew. Beyond his still open pants, he looks every inch the successful businessman. A few quick fixes and he would captivate an entire boardroom of Matiz executives without anyone knowing what he just did.

I'm tempted to ask him to strip so that I can savor the sight of his nude body and take that memory home with me to bed. I don't. Instead, I squeeze his hand and push myself up from the couch.

"You tore my panties," I accuse as I smooth out my skirt. "Now, I have to go home without them."

His eyes search the floor for the small bunch of lace that used to cover me. "That's not a complaint, is it?"

How could it be? It's been awhile since I've been fucked. It's been never since I was fucked like that. He could have ripped my dress to shreds and sent me on my way with just my purse and my shoes, and I would have politely thanked him for the orgasms and dinner.

"I should take my purse with me," I say aloud, even though the only reason I need it is so I can fix my makeup. I'm not sure why. He just told me he wants me again.

He leads me across the room to the piano and the spot I left my purse when we first arrived. I follow quietly, watching him move. He stalks the space with the familiarity we all do when we're in our home. He inches around the piano bench without looking down at it. He maneuvers slightly to the left when we reach the corner that leads down a hallway with three white doors.

RISK   *Deborah Bladon*

"The guest bath is the second door on the right."

I nod as my gaze skims over the two dark wooden frames hung on the wall in the hallway. They're both pictures, each capturing a sailboat on a body of water. The photograph farthest from us is taken from a distance. The pink stained sky of early evening gives way to blue water and a lone sailboat, peaceful as the sun sets, not a soul in sight.

The second picture is more defined. The sailboat is different. It's larger. The sails crisp and white, too tall to fit in the frame. A group of people stands on deck, all smiling with their hands in the air as if the photographer caught them mid-wave. There are two children and five adults. A black and white dog sits in the middle of the shot, eyes trained on whoever is holding the camera.

"Is this your family?" I look up at Nolan and smile. "Are you sailors?"

He takes a step forward, his expression pained. "This was taken a long time ago. It was a very long time ago."

I lick my lips. My throat is dry and my regret is high for bringing it up. "It looks fun. I've never been on a sailboat."

"It's exhilarating." He tilts his head as he studies my face. "I haven't been on one in years myself. You never forget the rush of the air or the feeling of freedom."

"They're beautiful pictures," I say slowly. "Are you one of those kids?"

It's a natural assumption. One of the men bears a striking resemblance to Nolan. His chin is set

134

RISK   *Deborah Bladon*

the same and the shape of his eyes is identical, but there are differences too. His hair is sun-streaked. It's a combination of golden brown with blonde streaks. The wrinkles around his eyes and mouth are more pronounced because of the bronze color of his skin. He's tall, but the other men in the photograph are taller, their shoulders broader.

The children's faces are shadowed with the wide brims of hats and their torsos covered with red and yellow trimmed life jackets. They look like pure sunshine, with smiles that reek of privilege and hope. I never smiled like that when I was their age. I'm not sure I've ever smiled like that.

"You're right. They are beautiful pictures." He skips past my question as he steps toward the washroom. "You can use this one. I'll use the one attached to the bedroom."

I nod as he hastily crosses the hall and disappears into the shadows of his bedroom.

***

I smooth back my hair as I listen to Adley's panicked voice in my ear.

Finally, I get my first chance to speak since calling her when I noticed she texted me more than a dozen times. "You locked yourself out? I thought the party you were having was inside our apartment, Ad."

"It was." Her voice trembles. "I drank too much and I have to work early tomorrow, so I went to the café around the corner to get a cup of coffee. I forgot my keys. I'm tired, Bean."

"We have coffee," I say even though it's a useless reminder at this point. "Did you call Tori to see if she could let you up?"

"She's in Oregon for a family thing," she replies quickly. "I called her first. She'd let me in if she weren't clear across the country."

Tori lives in the apartment above us. She and Adley used to be roommates before Tori fell in love on the elevator with a fireman who just moved into the building. It was a whirlwind romance that left Adley with an orange bridesmaid dress she hates and an empty bedroom.

The timing couldn't have been better for me, though. Tori moved out just over two months ago and since Adley was slow to start the search for a new roommate, I was able to move in.

"I'm still at the coffee shop, Ellie." Adley clears her throat. "I tried standing in front of the building for more than fifteen minutes but no one came home. Besides, even if I get inside the front door, I can't get into our apartment. It has that automatic lock on it."

I know exactly what she's talking about. When I left to get shampoo on my first night back, I realized I'd forgotten my wallet as soon as our apartment door closed behind me. It was locked tight when I turned back to open it. I had to pound on it loudly to steal Adley's attention away from the program she was watching on her laptop. It's a great security feature for hotel rooms, but for apartments it's more annoying than anything.

"I'm with Nolan," I whisper even though I haven't heard any movement at all in the hallway. "I don't want to leave yet."

"Can't you just come home for two minutes to let me in?" She sighs heavily. "You're not that far away, Bean."

I shake my head as I stare at my reflection in Nolan's bathroom mirror. My makeup held up better than I thought it would. Those free Matiz samples I get to take home from the store are worth it. "You should call the building manager to let you in, Ad. When Nolan called him about the air conditioner, he was at our place in no time. Nolan's place is across town."

"How is that possible?"

"How is what possible?" I press my free ear against the bathroom door, but still, I hear nothing.

"I distinctively recall you telling me that Nolan lives close to Cremza. That's four blocks from here, Bean. You could walk here, let me in, and be back there in less than twenty minutes."

I watch my smile give way to hesitation in the mirror's reflection. He did say that. He made a point of saying he was a regular because he lived near the ice cream shop, but the definition of *near* varies depending on who you're talking to.

Nolan has a private driver at his beck and call which means that everywhere in Manhattan is close to here. For those of us who depend on our own two feet and public transportation, it's far. When we were done eating our burger earlier, Nolan called the driver and he quickly pulled up next to the curb, by the street cart. We hopped in the air conditioned car and he brought us here. I know if we took the subway or the bus, it would have taken infinitely longer. "Give me ten minutes, Ad. I'll call you back."

"Are you coming to save me?" she asks overdramatically. "I can't sit in this coffee shop all night, Elinor."

I don't laugh the way I usually do when she uses my full name. Instead, I end the call and swing open the washroom door, intent on asking Nolan if I could borrow his driver so I can help out my friend before I crawl into bed with him.

Chapter 22

Nolan

J'ai envie de t'embrasser.

The words themselves weren't meant to impress Ellie. I wrote them on her palm because I have yet to meet a woman who wasn't enamored with the fact that I can speak rudimentary French.

I had to learn the basics of the language when I went to Paris after my sophomore year in college so I could fuck around France with Crew. His family has an estate there, and when he invited me, I packed one bag and renewed my passport.

I'm not fluent, but I know enough to get by, including how to tell a woman I would like to kiss her. When I wrote it on Ellie's palm, I fully expected her to ask me what it meant. I didn't expect her to press her gorgeous lips to mine in response.

She knows French. She also now knows that my family loves to sail.

Loved to sail.

It's been years since I've been on the water, but when I looked at that picture, the memories rushed back. It was taken on a day I'd waited weeks for and promised myself I'd never forget. The image is about more than a particular moment in time. It's a capture of the last time we were all together.

It hangs here now, in this apartment, the frame collecting dust, the pure beauty of that scene unappreciated. No one sees it. I rarely look at it, but I keep it hung on the wall because I've kept every promise I ever made to my grandfather.

I want to ask Ellie where she learned French, but that treads on ground I don't have a place on. I have no right to ask her anything when I have something to tell her that could alter her entire perception of me.

I have to savor tonight. I need her again. The first time I held back, trying desperately to get her off not once, but twice, before I let the thirst that was burning inside me take control. I fucked her recklessly on a leather couch. It's not what I envisioned when I planned tonight, but when she kissed me with those full lips and I felt the heat radiating from her body, I was gone.

Lost in her.

Drowning in a need that consumed every part of me.

"Nolan?"

I hear her hushed voice from the other side of the bedroom door. I'd pushed it almost shut when I entered the room so I could make a quick call. Then I toed off my shoes, removed my socks and my shirt and stood by the open window hoping to catch a breeze that would cool me down. It didn't happen.

My phone rings. I try to ignore it. I want to ignore it, but I can't.

I tug it out of the front pocket of my pants.

I pull open the door as the phone continues to ring.

"I need to take this, Ellie." I look down at her. Her lips are plumped and bruised from the roughness of my kiss. Her skin is glowing from the rush of her

RISK *Deborah Bladon*

orgasm. She looks ready for another round, but first, I need to tell someone to fuck the hell off.

"I'll wait." She stands in place, her eyes skimming over my bare chest.

I nod, inching around her to cross the hall to the home office. I flick the switch and the overhead light flickers on.

"Nolan Black," I say into my phone. "It's late. Start talking and make it quick."

The man on the other end of the call delivers bad news. My gaze is still locked on Ellie and where she's now standing at the entrance to the office. I don't turn my back or shoo her away. I don't give a fuck if she overhears this conversation. I just want to stare into her eyes.

She breaks the connection when her gaze travels around the room.

"The shipment is already overdue." I even my tone, cutting the man I'm speaking to off mid-sentence. "Unless it's delivered by noon tomorrow, you'll be facing a hefty fine per our original contract."

I listen half-heartedly as he tries to excuse away the delay. Ellie smiles before she turns her attention to a calendar hung on the wall. The image on display is familiar to me, but judging by the way Ellie's staring at it, she's never seen anything like it before.

It's a beach in Hawaii. Maui, I believe. I picked the calendar up from a youth group. They were selling them in the parking lot at the airport in Honolulu. I had just finished a business trip in Lahaina and when a guy approached wearing board shorts and a ripped T-shirt with a message

141

summoning for a change in the world, I handed over a twenty dollar bill and shoved the calendar into my carry-on. I hung it up when I got home as a reminder of the tranquility of the islands.

"I'm putting this on my bucket list," Ellie murmurs before she snaps a picture with her phone of the calendar. "I'm going to Hawaii before I die."

I tuck my phone next to my chest, blocking my voice from the guy who is now telling me that they lost track of the truck carrying the first shipment of our new products. That's a quarter of a million dollars worth of missing lipstick, eye shadow, and mascara. "If you pack that bikini you were wearing last night, I'll go with you."

She looks as surprised as I feel by my words. Why the fuck would I invite myself along on a future trip to Hawaii with her?

I bring the phone back up and catch the tail end of the guy explaining that they are sending out several men to track the truck down since the driver isn't picking up when they call. I don't give a shit if they send out a full-on search party. The product needs to be at our warehouse when promised. Simple.

"Find him and call Crew Benton," I grumble. "Do not call me back. Your contact is Crew for the rest of the night. Not me."

I end the call and immediately direct my attention to Ellie.

"I have an emergency too." She sighs. "My friend locked herself out of our apartment. I need to go home so I can let her in."

"Can't she call someone else?"

She shrugs her shoulders, her hair falling away from them. "I told her to call the building manager, but she just sent me a text telling me she couldn't reach him. I can't leave her locked out. I need to go help."

"I'll call Crew." My gaze drops to my phone. "I'll get him to call the manager. He'll have him at your place with a key in hand within minutes."

"Are you sure?" She takes a step toward me. "Because I can run down there and be back here in no time."

"You live miles from here," I point out. "Even if my driver catches every green light, it's not a quick trip."

She studies my face before her eyes sweep over my desk. "I guess it's not that close."

My phone starts ringing again. "No, it's not close at all."

"You should get that." She shifts restlessly on her feet. "I'm going to text Adley."

"I'm not getting it," I say just as I see the incoming number. "Shit. I have to take this, Ellie. I'm sorry."

Silence hangs in the air between us before I breeze out of the room and cross the hall back into the bedroom, shutting the door behind me.

Chapter 23

Ellie

"You don't want me to come back?" I ask to clarify what he just said. "You think I should go home, let Adley in and stay there?"

Disappointment doesn't even begin to describe what I'm feeling right now. It's there in my voice. I can hear it. Nolan sure as hell can too. I don't care.

I was prepared to tell him to him go ahead and call Crew so he could help Adley before he came walking back into the office. I could sense immediately just by the expression on his face that our date was over. I had known it before he explained that the last call was a pressing matter that had to be dealt with immediately. In simple terms, it means I need to haul ass out of his apartment right the fuck now, even if I'm not ready to.

"I'm sorry, Ellie."

You'd think he'd have the decency to at least tear himself away from his phone while he half-heartedly apologizes for ending our night early. He doesn't though. He types away, sending someone a text message or an email. For all I fucking know, it's a sext message.

I skim my fingers over the screen of my phone. "I'll take off now. I have an Uber coming to get me. He's only six blocks away."

"I could have called for my driver."

144

He could have, but he didn't. Instead, he focused on something on his phone the same way he is now. I want to talk to him. I have questions that I need answers to.

To begin with, I want to know why he said he lives near Cremza when he obviously doesn't. I'm assuming he said it as a way to break the ice when we saw each other there. I'd like to hear him clarify it for me.

I'd also love to know why he has a yellowing copy of the New York Times from a day in May five years ago open on his desk. The calendar on the wall is stuck back at that month too. I noticed the date when I was drooling over the picture of a sandy beach displayed for that particular month.

The dust-covered, open packaging from a smartphone sits atop his desk. The model is obsolete. The only value it would have to anyone at this point would be as a paperweight, even though it was in high demand a few years ago. It's been replaced several times over by newer, more streamlined versions.

The phone Nolan is holding is the same model as mine. It's just two months old and already there's a promise from the tech company that produces it, that a better phone is on the horizon.

It's as if we stepped into a time machine when we crossed the threshold and entered this room.

Maybe I'm paranoid because of what happened with Tad. Maybe I'm just reading more into Nolan's home office than is there. I can't tell. I just know that something feels off and my intuition rarely fails me.

"I'll call you in the morning, Ellie."

Again, his eyes are glued to his phone's screen. *Seriously?*

"Sure, whatever works," I say because, at this point, I just want to leave.

I wait for him to offer to walk me out, but that would require some attention being thrown my way and that's obviously not happening.

"I'll get my purse and my shoes and then I'll go," I grumble as I step to the side. "I can find my way back to the lobby on my own. Can I ask you something first?"

As if on cue, his phone rings again. He stiffens, his hand reaching to scrub the back of his neck. "Fuck, just fuck."

It's enough of an answer to send me toward the office door. "Good night, Nolan."

He catches me by the elbow, his chest pressing into my back, his voice thick in my ear. "If this were anything else, I would bury it until tomorrow. I would completely ignore it and take you to bed."

But… I wait for it.

"But, I can't. I fucking can't."

I turn back to look at him. "I'll catch up with you soon."

He kisses me softly on my forehead as his phone continues its cruel reminder that his attention is no longer mine. "Tonight was amazing. It's just the beginning."

Of what, I want to ask, but I don't. I can't. He brings the phone to his ear and he brusquely tells the

RISK   *Deborah Bladon*

person on the other end to hold as he waits for me to leave the room.

***

"Ellie Madden?" he literally screams my name at me. "Are you fucking kidding me right now?"

I wish I were. There are a lot of Uber drivers in Manhattan. What are the chances that the one that I get is the boy I used to sit behind in eighth-grade geometry class? It's the same boy who was in virtually every one of my calculus classes in high school. He's not a boy now. He's a man with thinning light brown hair and hazel eyes. "It's me."

"You remember me, right? Rick Jones. You don't look the same."

"Neither do you," I counter. From what I can remember he does look the same, except for the hair that is trying to grow on his chin. Those few whiskers are determined, but they're apparently losing their battle. Rick is still the same hairless wonder he was when we graduated high school.

"I drive an Uber for a living."

"Really?" I scratch the top of my cheek. Of course, he drives an Uber. It's the only reason we're having this mini high school reunion in his car outside of Nolan's apartment.

If he takes twelve minutes to pick up every customer he has waiting for him, he might not be driving people around for money much longer. I got so frustrated after waiting on the sidewalk for ten minutes that I almost canceled the ride so I could flag down a taxi. That's when I saw him finally creep

147

around the corner at a speed I could beat while hopping on one foot.

"It's a temp thing. My goal is to be a surgeon."

"Are you studying for that?"

"I'm pacing myself," he begins, and then it ends. He doesn't add to that. I don't ask because I don't care. "So you're headed uptown?"

I glance at the GPS unit of his car. The address for my building is already programmed into the screen. I look carefully at the red line that is charting the technology calculated route Rick will take. "It's faster if you go through the park."

"There's only one filly I follow and it's this beauty." He taps his finger on the corner of the GPS monitor. "We'll take her lead."

I type out a quick text message to Adley telling her I'm finally on my way. When I look up, we still haven't moved.

"Are we heading out soon, Rick?"

"You could have sat up front with me, Ellie." He cranes his neck so he can stare at me. "It would make it easier for us to talk."

"I'm in the middle of an emergency right now." I gaze out the car's window at Nolan's building. "I'm not all that talkative."

"Is there anything I can do for you?" he asks with actual emotion in his tone. "I've had it rough at times too. I get that we all need a friend once in a while."

I smile at the offer. It's kind, even if the look in his eye is making me uncomfortable. "If you could just get me to that address as soon as possible, that would help a lot."

RISK   *Deborah Bladon*

"That I can do." He waves his left hand in the air. "Consider this your chariot, Princess Ellie and I'm your trusty stead."

Um, no thanks.

I look back at my phone and the message Adley just sent telling me to hurry. Since I can only travel as fast as this chariot moves, I don't text her back. Instead, I open my phone's camera wondering how I can snap a stealth picture of Rick to send to her. I know she'd remember him but the last thing I want to do right now is prompt him to say cheese and smile for me.

I sigh as the car finally starts to pull away and he focuses on the road.

We don't make it three feet before he slams the brakes on. Luckily we were moving at a snail's pace, so the abrupt stop barely registered.

"Is something wrong?" My head snaps up in time to see a black Mercedes Benz pulling up to the curb directly in front of us.

"New York traffic," Rick mutters. "That idiot cut me off."

The driver side door of the Benz opens and a man in a dark suit steps out. I know him even though we've never met. I wasn't introduced but I recognize him immediately. He's Nolan's driver and just as he rounds the back of the car, Nolan Black himself comes out of his building, dressed just as he was when we went in hours ago.

149

Chapter 24

Ellie

"You have to speed up, Rick." I tap him on the shoulder. "We're going to lose them."

The car jolts as he gives it some gas. "We can't get too close, Ellie, or they'll make us."

Make us? Rick's giving his all for this adventure I coaxed him into.

Truthfully, it didn't take much more than a plea to get him to follow the Mercedes. He hesitated briefly before telling me that old friends have to stick together. Since I never once considered Rick a friend when we were in school together, I took it as a compliment, and I thanked him for ignoring his car's GPS and throwing caution to the wind.

"Who is he to you?"

How the hell do I even answer that after tonight? Is Nolan just a one night stand? I can't say there's potential for anything more at this point because I don't know. I go with the only logical answer I can think of. It's the truth. "He's my boss."

He keeps his eyes trained on the road. "You work for that guy? I thought you'd be a detective working for the NYPD by now."

So did I. "So did I. How did you know I wanted to work for the NYPD?"

"Your senior class career day speech." He flicks on the left turn signal as soon as the driver of the Mercedes does. "Is that what this is? Are you on some kind of undercover mission right now?"

I'm on some kind of fucked up, post orgasm, curiosity fueled mission right now. Nolan made it clear that his night was going to be swallowed up by whatever emergency kept his phone busy. No more than fifteen minutes after telling me that, his driver is at his place, whisking him off to who the hell knows where.

"You know that he's headed straight for your place right, Ellie?"

I know that he's headed in the direction of my apartment, but Manhattan is vast. We're also moving toward many bars and restaurants. For all I know, Nolan rescheduled his fancy dinner to include another woman and she's going to be his second course.

"He's not going to my place." I stare out the window. He didn't have the decency to maintain eye contact with me for more than ten seconds after we fucked. I doubt like hell he's chasing me down. He has my number. If he wanted to finish our conversation, he would have called me by now.

"How long have you been working this job?" Rick takes a hard left and I skid across the vinyl seat. "I get it if you can't give me any details. I know there's a strict code of silence when you're tailing a suspect."

What's the code when you're following a really great fuck? I shake off his assumption. "Not long."

"When we get close do you want me to hang back?" He flashes me a quick grin over his shoulder.

"I can let you out down the block from him so you can follow on foot."

Rick is a man with a plan. I don't want to confront Nolan tonight. I can't. Adley has texted me twice since we pulled away from Nolan's apartment, asking where I am. It's friends first in my world, so this ends wherever the Mercedes stops. I just want to see where Nolan is going. I know it's not his office. We didn't turn right onto Fifth Avenue.

The taxi in front of us slows, so Rick goes around it to keep the Mercedes in our sight. "We're getting close to your place, Ellie. You're sure that's not where he's headed."

I watch as we pass Cremza, the doors shut, the lights dim. It closed hours ago, the large sign in the window a reminder that tomorrow is *two scoops for the price of one'* day.

I send another text to Adley telling her I'm only three blocks from the coffee shop now. "Adley wants me to say hi."

"Adley York?" He eyes me in the rear view mirror. "You two are still tight, hey?"

"Best friends forever." I smile at his reflection. "We live together now."

"I can't say I'm surprised." He turns on the right signal blinker. "He's pulling over. I'll hang back."

I want to tell him to pass the Mercedes and take me home. I thought I wanted to know where Nolan was rushing to after he sent me out the door, but now, my stomach is tied in thick knots and my palms are clammy. He didn't promise my anything. We had sex and the night ended. I shouldn't be doing

RISK   *Deborah Bladon*

this. I shouldn't let Tad's asshole ways turn me into something I'm not.

I don't stalk men. It's not who I am.

Still, I don't protest when Rick maneuvers his car to the curb and stops. I look out through the windshield as Nolan's driver opens the rear passenger door and Nolan steps out. The doorman from the building he's in front of approaches him. Nolan shakes his hand and pats him on the back and then they disappear together through the glass front doors.

His driver gets back in the Mercedes and merges seamlessly into the traffic. I sit in the backseat of Rick's car staring at the luxury residential high-rise, wondering what, or more likely who, inside that building is worth ditching me for.

***

"He's not in this morning," Nolan's assistant says briskly, her firm tone cutting, but patient. "As I told you when you called thirty minutes ago, Ms. Madden, I don't know when he will be in his office. He's unavailable at the moment."

That's probably a good thing. I'm running on spite and a couple of hours of sleep at this point. When Adley and I finally got back to the apartment last night after Rick dropped me off, I thought she'd be ready for bed, but the four cups of Italian roast coffee she had, while she waited for me, kept her bouncing off the walls.

I got in my bed after I showered, washing away the last of Nolan's touch from my skin. I bunched my dress into a ball and threw it in a basket

153

destined for the washing machine at the laundromat. My intention was to rid myself of every physical reminder of the night, but the ache in my body wouldn't go away.

Adley came into my room as I was replaying my conversation with Nolan in my head. She didn't ask me how my date was and I was grateful. Instead, she launched into an animated speech about her thirty-year plan. I was all ears as she talked about the veterinary clinic she wants to open and I heard, in fine detail, what her future husband looks like.

It's Crew Benton. Adley described Crew Benton to a tee, even if she didn't realize it.

She finally ran out of steam shortly after four this morning, when she collapsed onto my queen size bed and fell asleep with her head on my shoulder. I slept too, but it was marred by the image of Nolan walking into that building just a few blocks from here.

"Miss Madden?"

I shake my head when I realize I'm still on the phone. "Can you tell him that I'd like to see him once he's in? It's important."

"Certainly," Eda says briskly. "There's another call coming in."

With that, she hangs up. I tuck my phone back into the front pocket of my red pants. Nothing screams stealth Matiz security guard like red pants and a white and red striped shirt. It's bold, but it was the first pieces of clothing my fingers touched in my closet, so I tugged the outfit on, pulled my hair into a tight bun and came to work.

"Excuse me."

RISK   *Deborah Bladon*

That voice is too sweet for it to belong to anyone who works here. It's melodic, like an angel. A sweet little angel who isn't old enough to understand that boys, and eventually men, have the ability to make you feel like a rare jewel and the gum on the bottom of their shoe, all in the space of an hour.

I turn and look down. She's as precious as her voice. Perfect almond shaped green eyes and hair as red as mine. She's dressed in a pink T-shirt and matching skirt. Her lilac painted toenails on display in her little leather sandals.

"Can I help you, Miss?"

Her face brightens with a broad smile. "You called me Miss."

"Little girls are Miss." I crouch so I'm looking directly at her face.

"What are little boys?" She brings her hands together in front of her.

"Trouble. Little boys are nothing but trouble." A deep voice interjects from the left.

I turn toward it. It's Nolan Black with the slightest hint of a smile on his face and an attractive brunette at his side.

Chapter 25

Nolan

"Don't lead her astray, Nolan. Boys aren't trouble. It's just certain men that are."

Gretel Gallant is only saying that because I've turned her down, twice. The most recent time was six months ago when I went to her apartment to meet with her husband. She answered the door wearing only a diamond necklace after she sent her husband to pick up their daughter from after school care. She's as hot for my dick now as she was back then. She made that obvious when she approached me the second I walked into the store.

"Cat got your tongue, Nolan, or are you silent because you know I'm right?"

Jesus. You'd think she'd keep the snarky attitude at bay in front of her child.

"What brings you and Leila into the store today?" I tap her daughter on the head. "You're too beautiful to wear makeup, Leila."

"So is my Mommy."

Ah, the innocent eye of a child.

"Is there something I can help you find?" Ellie directs her attention to Gretel.

"I'm a regular," Gretel says it like it matters. It grants her no special privileges. She's in the store at least a few times a week, often asking the staff if she can see me. She can't. I keep a fair distance between

RISK   *Deborah Bladon*

my cock and Gretel at all times. "We were just leaving."

Ellie eyes Leila. "Is there anything I can help you with, Leila?"

She shrugs, her hands disappearing into the pockets of the skirt she's wearing. "I just wanted to tell you that I like your hair."

Ellie smiles softly, her fingers leaping to her bun. "Thank you. Your hair is really pretty."

"Mommy says I can change it if I want when I'm older."

Of course, Gretel would say that to a six-year-old. She's had more work done than most of the women in Manhattan combined.

"I think you're perfect exactly the way you are," Ellie says the words that are dangling from the tip of my tongue. "There's one thing I think we need to talk about, though."

"What?" Gretel barks, her hands leaping to Leila's shoulders. "Don't tell her that you like her nose."

"I like it better than your nose, Gretel." I turn toward her, raising a brow. "I like the last nose you had better than this one too. The one before that not so much."

She shoots me a look that says *shut the fuck up,* or it might be *fuck me.* Either way, it's not happening.

"Did your Mommy pay for anything for you today, Leila?"

Ellie's voice is soothing and calm. Gretel stands in silence as Leila shakes her head from side-to-side. "Not for me. She bought all those things in the bag for herself."

"Did you bring any of your own money with you today?"

Leila giggles, her hand darting to cover her mouth. "I don't have money. I have to earn it, and I don't like chores."

Like mother, like daughter.

"I can see that you have something in your pocket." Ellie points to the left pocket of Leila's skirt. "It looks like a tube of mascara. Is that what it is?"

Leila looks back at Gretel before her eyes settle on Ellie. "Yes. It's mascara. I want it."

"If you want to take something home from the store, you need to pay for it." Ellie's gaze slides over Gretel's face before she looks at Leila again. "Sometimes it's hard to resist taking whatever we want, but we have to earn money to pay for those things."

"Mommy says she earns every dime she spends listening to Daddy talk."

Ellie sighs, her hand darting out in front of her. "Can I have the mascara back?"

"I guess," Leila whispers as she tugs it out of her pocket. "Daddy says I can't wear makeup until I'm twenty."

"Your father can say what he wants, but I set that rule." Gretel snatches the mascara from Ellie's palm. "Mommy will buy you this, princess, and anything else you want."

Ellie's jaw drops as Gretel grabs Leila's hand and they walk away.

"That woman makes me crazy," she whispers as she watches Leila's face light up at the lipstick counter. "What lesson is she teaching her daughter?"

"One she'll hopefully regret one day." I exhale roughly. "I'm sorry I missed your call earlier. I was in the middle of something."

"No problem." She looks toward the entrance of the store, her eyes tracking a customer who just walked in. "I get it. You're a busy man."

"We need to talk, Ellie." I take a deep breath, trying to steady my voice." I have a meeting soon. Can you come up to my office at two?"

Her eyes drop to the plain white watch on her left wrist. "Is it business or personal?"

"You work for Crew," I point out. "It's about last night."

She looks at my hands, her teeth scraping at her bottom lip. "I'd like to talk about that too."

"I'll see you at two o'clock sharp." That's only four hours from now. Four fucking hours for me to figure out how to tell this gorgeous woman that I'm not the man she thinks I am.

"I might be a little late." Her gaze drifts to where a group of customers has gathered around a perfume display. "I'm having lunch with Liam at one fifteen, but I'll be sure to come up to your office as soon as I'm done. I need to get back to work now."

She tosses me a look, but unlike Gretel's there is no ambiguity in Ellie's hidden message. It clearly says *your loss, jerk. Your fucking loss is Wolf's gain.*

Well, shit.

***

"Ellie Madden wants to talk to you," Eda announces as she blocks my path when I step off the elevator and approach my office door.

"I just spoke to her."

"In the last ten minutes?" She eyes me carefully. "She's called twice since I've been in, Mr. Black. It's obvious that she has an issue she wants to discuss with you."

The issue is why I was such a raging asshole to her after we fucked. I got a business call last night when I was with her, then a personal call and before I could stop the runaway train of fate, Ellie was on her way out the door.

I didn't need to hear from Eda that Ellie was trying to hunt me down this morning. The one missed call to my cell from her less than an hour ago and her body language downstairs inside the store said it all. Eyes in every direction but at my face, her hands fisted at her side, her stance wide. She looked like a kickboxer ready to hit the ring.

I was tempted to shield my balls with my hand to keep them intact if she decided to unleash a roundhouse kick. The woman can drop me to my knees in an instant. No violence needed. A taste of her lips and a second inside her tight body is all it will take. The body I want again, and again. The body that belongs to the woman I wish I could spend all day talking to. The same woman who is having lunch with Liam Wolf and probably dinner with River Whatever-The-Fuck-His-Surname-Is.

"What are you thinking about?" Eda nudges her glasses back up her nose.

"Clowns."

"Cute clowns or scary clowns?" She furrows her brow.

I enter my office with Eda right on my heel. "Neither."

"Clowns are one or the other, sir."

Is she seriously schooling me on clowns right now? "These two clowns don't fall into either category."

"Are they circus clowns or the kind of clowns that you can outsource to attend a party or whatnot?"

I had no fucking idea that Eda knew so much useless information about clowns. "I'd like to outsource them both to a raft in the middle of the ocean."

"I know a guy." She finally pulls the pencil from behind her ear and taps it against her chin. "I know a guy who could take care of that for you."

"Take care of that for me?" I unbutton my suit jacket as I take a seat behind my desk. "Are you suggesting what I think you are, Eda?"

"If the clowns you've met don't fit the bill, I know someone with floppy shoes and a red nose. He's great with kids and adults. His rates are reasonable too."

"I'll keep that in mind." My gaze moves to the corner of my desk and a small ceramic elephant. A gift I'd purchased more than a month ago, but always forget here in my office. I scoop it into my palm. "I'm not in need of a clown right now, but thank you."

"Anytime." She takes a step closer to my desk. "She likes you. You know that, right?"

"Who?"

"Ellie Madden."

My head pops up at the mention of Ellie's name. "Why would you say that?"

Her lips curve up into a smile. "I have four daughters, Mr. Black. I know when a young woman is sweet on a man. I heard it in her voice when she called."

"You think she's sweet on me?" I cock a brow.

"Almost as sweet as you are on her, sir. Almost."

It's something. I want more, everything, all of Ellie, but for now, I'll settle for it.

RISK   *Deborah Bladon*

Chapter 26

Ellie

"You followed me to lunch," I accuse as Nolan shuts the door of his office. This time he sent his assistant on a mission to find the marketing notes for an online campaign for a skin care product that launched last year. She eagerly took on the challenge, telling him she'd be back in ten minutes. He told her if she did that she'd need to find a new job.

His hand goes to my waist, edging me back against the closed door. His breath, laced with the lingering aroma of a midday shot of something thick and strong, maybe whiskey, blows over my lips. "Let's call it even since you followed me last night."

I try to look away, surprised that there's a flush creeping over my cheeks. His hand jumps to cup my chin. His eyes, dark and unyielding, stare into mine.

"I did," I admit. "I didn't mean to. It just happened."

"It never just happens." He slicks his tongue over his bottom lip. "I didn't just happen to arrive at the restaurant three minutes after you and Liam did. I was on the sidewalk outside Matiz when I saw him wave to you as you left the store. I watched you greet him. One kiss from him on your left cheek and a hand, your right one, on his forearm."

I swallow hard trying to suppress all the anger I'm feeling. I'd noticed Nolan almost immediately

163

when he took a seat four tables over from where I was sitting with Liam. I felt his eyes on me until he left the restaurant five minutes before I did. I was tempted to skip our meeting, but curiosity wouldn't let me. "You had no right to do that. I was having lunch with him to talk about something important to me."

"You had no right to follow me last night." His eyes drop to my chest before they trail back to my face.

He's right. I didn't have a right, but I had a need. An overwhelming need to see where his driver was taking him.

"I was curious. I wanted to know where you were going." I try to jerk my chin free, but his grip is too tight. It's firm, tender, the promise of that touch on my body keeps me in place. I ask the question that's been silently haunting me since last night. "Did you go there to meet a woman?"

He looks directly at me, his voice calm and in control. "No."

"Did you fuck someone else last night after you fucked me?" My heart is racing with the uncertainty of how I'll feel if he tells me he did.

"No, Ellie. Absolutely not."

"Why did you go to that building?"

He pauses. "I live there."

I shake my head, curbing my urge to push him away from me. "You live in the apartment you took me to. The one we fucked in."

His chin drops faintly. It's so slight that it's barely noticeable. "I own the apartment that I took you to. I used to live there. I don't anymore, but some of my things are still there."

164

"You made me believe that you live there now." I stare into his eyes. He can't win this. I won't let him. I'm not going to be made a fool of by a man again. Ever.

"I let you assume that I live there now, Ellie," he says roughly.

I clear my throat. "So you don't have a hotel room that you take women to? You have an entire apartment?"

His phone buzzes in the pocket of his suit jacket. "I haven't taken any other woman there recently."

"Recently?" I spit out a laugh. It's a joyless sound inflated with bitterness. As much as I haven't admitted it to myself, I wanted to be different. I didn't want to be just one of many to him. Not to him. "What is recent to you? Two days ago? Three? A few hours? When's the last time a woman was there with you?"

"Five years, three months, fourteen days."

The precision of his answer jars me enough that it catches my breath. "What?"

"It's been a long time." He skips past the oddity of his last reply as if it means nothing. "I take women I want to fuck to an Executive Suite at the Bishop Hotel."

"You didn't take me there."

He leans in, pressing his lips to my temple. "I want more than to fuck you, Ellie."

"What do you want?" I look up and into his eyes. They've softened, transitioned from defensive to open.

"I want to know you. I want you to know me."

***

"You already know me." I push my hands against his chest, but the man is solid. He's a wall. "You commissioned a complete background check on me when you hired me."

"Is that so?" He smiles.

"Yes." I nod toward his desk. "You had a file with my name on it on your desk when I came in that morning with my list of security improvements."

He doesn't flinch. "You're very aware of everything around you. I was surprised you didn't realize a car was following you last night while you were following me."

Shit. I didn't think of that. Why would I think of that?

"Was it a security detail?" I scan his face, looking for some subtle reaction but there's nothing.

"Yes. That's exactly what it was."

"Why?" I hesitate a moment, then ask. "Why would you need that? You own a cosmetics company. It's not like you're the President of the United States."

That draws a smile to his lips. "A man doesn't need to run a country to require extra security sometimes, Ellie."

"Elaborate on what that means."

"It means that people, other than the President, need security."

"Why do you need personal security?" I press my hands against his chest again, but there's no movement on his part. He won't budge. "Are you in trouble?"

RISK   *Deborah Bladon*

"Define trouble." He dips his chin, the grin on his lips widening.

"You think this is funny?" I shake my head, frustrated and embarrassed. I didn't expect this at all. I felt victorious in some twisted post-fuck sense when I followed him last night. It was as if I'd caught him doing something before he could hurt me.

It still hurt, though, not in the same bone-numbing way that it did when I realized that Tad had cheated on me with who knows how many women. When I saw Nolan leave his apartment last night, I felt a sense of loss over what could have been.

"Not funny." His smile disappears, replaced by calmness. "There's an occasional threat directed my way. I'm never sure if it's a disgruntled customer or an actual lunatic. If it has any weight, I have security personnel who follow me until things settle."

"I didn't know."

"Now you do," he says, his voice low. "I think it's interesting that we both felt compelled to follow the other."

"Why did you follow me to lunch?" I ask hoarsely.

"I consider Wolf a threat. A much different threat than those that require extra security, but still, a threat."

I'm buoyed by the answer as much as I am irritated. He doesn't own me. He fucked me once. That doesn't grant him a ticket into my soul. "A threat? Because you think he wants to sleep with me?"

167

"He doesn't want to sleep with you, Ellie. He wants to fuck you and I'm not about to let that happen."

Chapter 27

Nolan

Following her to lunch was a spontaneous, cock driven decision. I was coming back from a meeting with Kristof when I saw Liam on the sidewalk in front of Matiz. I waited, in plain view, until Ellie emerged from the store, her face beaming as she approached him.

She held back when she got close. The only contact a quick brush of his lips across her cheek and her hand sweeping across his arm. They walked side-by-side, not touching, to an Italian place around the corner that serves overcooked pasta and sauce from a jar.

I could have easily stopped there and turned back toward the office. I didn't. I took a table, ordered a whiskey and spent the next hour trying to read their lips. It was useless. She knew I was there. Her face gave way to what was going on inside of her.

Conflict. The anger from my presence combined with her confusion about last night.

I didn't know she followed me until Kristof mentioned it during our brief meeting right before I saw Ellie with Wolf. She watched me come out of the building she thought I lived in before seeing me walk into the building I actually live in. It's not how I wanted her to find out, but I'm pleased it's out in the open. I'm glad that she knows at least one of my secrets.

"Liam doesn't want to fuck me." There's irritation in her tone.

She pushes against my chest and this time I take a step back. It surprises her enough that she doesn't move immediately. So I take another step, to the side this time. She passes me and moves to sit in one of the chairs in front of my desk.

"I saw the way he was looking at you, Ellie. He clearly wants to fuck you."

She looks up to where I'm standing next to her. There's defeat in her eyes. "Liam is trying to help me get a job. His brother is going to help me."

"Nick?" I tilt my head. "Nick writes crime novels. What could you possibly do for him?"

"No. I'm not talking about Nicholas." She pinches the bridge of her nose. "It's Liam's oldest brother. Sebastian. He's a detective. He works for the NYPD. He might be able to help me get a job."

Shit. She was having lunch with him because of his brother.

"You want to work for the police department?"

She nods, vigorously. "I do. I will. I just need a chance to get my foot in the door there."

I race through my mind trying to determine who I know who holds a high enough rank in the NYPD that they could pull the necessary strings to get Ellie a job. There's no one. It's one of the few organizations in this city that my family has no ties to.

"Liam will talk to his brother," she goes on, "I'll meet with Sebastian later this week."

I want that job for her, even if it means I won't see her every day. "I'm sorry I jumped to the wrong conclusion, Ellie. I thought there was something personal between you and Wolf."

"What if there was?" Her blue eyes flick up to mine. "We had sex, Nolan. We didn't promise each other anything last night."

She's right. No promises were made, at least not verbally. It's obvious that the actions that we've both taken since then say otherwise. "We can remedy that now."

Her gaze follows my every movement as I sit in the chair next to her. "Remedy it how?"

"Clearly I was concerned that your lunch with Liam was going to lead to something more."

"Clearly," she quips.

I smile. "It's just as clear that you had some questions about where I went last night after you left my place."

"I was curious when I saw you come out of the building we'd been in together." She carefully dances around defining the space as the place we fucked. "You said you had something to take care of. I just assumed that meant that you'd be in all night."

"I want to you to understand something, Ellie." I lean forward, resting my forearms on my knees. "I'm the first to admit that I can be an asshole. I don't play nice in business. I will cut a man off at the knees if he threatens anything that I hold dear, but I will never, ever be like the man who hurt you."

"What makes you think a man hurt me?" Her arms cross over her chest.

I want to throat punch the idiot who put her on the defensive like this. "I know a man hurt you. A fucked up bastard named Tad Darling had a ring on your finger when he took half of the women in Vegas to bed."

She blinks at me as if she's trying to absorb every single syllable of what I just said. She's processing it, just as I was earlier when Kristof gave me the rundown on Tad Fucking Darling and how he treated Ellie. That goddamn son of a bitch.

"Is there anything you don't know about me, Nolan?"

I don't know if you're the girl who I saved a decade ago. The beautiful girl with the red hair who didn't want anything from me, but gave me more than I ever deserved. The angel who was face down on the pavement in a pool of her own blood the last time I ever saw her.

I swallow back the urge to ask if she's Kip or if she recognizes that I'm Rigs. Instead, I say the only thing I can. "Many things, Ellie. There are many things I don't know about you, but I want to learn everything."

***

"I'd like to know things about you too, Nolan."

Her words aren't unexpected. How could they be? I just told her that I want to know everything about her. I want her to be curious about me. I want to be the only man she thinks about.

"My favorite color is blue. I hate spiders, and I tried to take piano lessons last year, for the eighth time, but I quit. I fucking quit because my piano teacher was a hard ass."

"You hate spiders?" She smiles at me. "Or you are afraid of spiders?"

"Don't rub it in, Ellie." I sigh. "I know you're not scared of anything. You probably wrestle alligators on your days off. I get that you're brave. I am too, but when there's a spider within twenty feet of me all bets are off."

My phone buzzes in my pocket again. I ignore it. If it's anything important, Eda will knock. She'll disturb me if need be.

"I want to discuss something." I meet her gaze. "I'd like this to be exclusive, for now. I'd very much like if we could agree not to date other people."

"You mean you want me to agree not to date Liam and River."

Of course, I mean I want her to stay away from those two clowns. They're both circling her waiting for a chance to pounce. I want a barrier in place that they can't cross. I need to explore this without the added anxiety that their presence will bring.

"I mean any man who wants you."

"I just got out of a serious relationship a few months ago." She takes a deep breath. "Jumping into something exclusive might not be the best thing for me right now."

"My cock is the best thing for you right now." I square my shoulders. "The rest of me too, but you have to admit, the sex was stellar last night."

"That ego, Nolan." She waves her finger in the air at me. "You need to tame that down."

I laugh. "I'm just telling it like it is, Ellie."

She chuckles softly, her hand smoothing back her hair. "So you want us to date only each other for now?"

"Yes, that's exactly what I want," I tell her without a beat of hesitation.

"When was your last serious relationship?" She glances toward my office door. "Was it with Shelby?"

"Shelby? That wasn't a relationship. That was a mistake that never qualified as anything."

"So it was before her. When did your last serious relationship end, Nolan?"

I scrub my hand over the back of my neck. I've never been ashamed to admit this. We all have strengths, each of us owns a weakness or two. Mine happens to be relationships. "I've never been in a serious relationship, Ellie. I've only ever had two girlfriends in my life and both of those were when I was fifteen-years-old. When they found out they were both my girlfriend at the same time, I stopped having girlfriends."

She doesn't laugh. There's no rush to scold me for teasing with her. Instead, she purses her lips.

"Why make this exclusive? We can date each other without labeling it."

No, we can't. That leaves the door open for any other man to come strolling into her life and that's a complication I don't want. "I have no interest in dating other women right now. I'd like to date only you with the understanding that you're not seeing other men."

There's a long pause. A fucking long pause as she stares right at me, into me. "I'll agree to date only you, Nolan if you agree to date only me. I can't promise how long I can do that for, but for now, I'd like to try."

Great. Good. Ellie Madden is dating me. She's only fucking me.

She stands and I follow. I reach for her, wanting a kiss, a touch, anything before I open my mouth again to tell her the one thing about me that defines who I am.

I cup her delicate face in my hands. I lean down and kiss her. It's soft at first and then urgency rushes over the connection and before I realize what I'm doing, my hand is on the back of her neck, insistent, coaxing, pushing her lips into mine. My body wants to seal the deal and cement her to me before she learns the truth. I want this and I want what I have at home. I want it all. I need it all.

She circles my waist with her hands, her fingers crawling under my suit jacket to clench the fabric of my shirt. I'm erect, hard and wanting. I want too much. I need to stop. I have to fucking stop.

"Ellie." I pull back from the kiss, but only enough that my lips skim over her lips when I say her name. "You have to know. I need to tell you."

"Tell me what?" She pops up to her tiptoes to claim my mouth again.

I give in because the need to taste her lips is stronger than my resistance. I run my hands down her back to cup her firm ass. I squeeze it, pulling her against me so she can feel what she's doing to me.

"You're hard." She smiles against my mouth. "You're right. The sex was stellar. Your cock is too. I admit it."

"Wait until you taste it." I tug her even closer, the hard ridge of my erection pressing against her. "I want to see these lips around it."

My pulse races when her hand drifts lower and then lower still. She grazes her fingers over the front of my pants, the touch electric. My dick throbs from the promise of her touch. "Now, Nolan?"

Yes, now. Get on your knees and take it down your throat. All of it, until your eyes water and your pussy is on fire from sheer need.

I want to say it, but I stop. I fucking stop and step back, my hands firmly rooted to her shoulders.

"We can't," I breathe. "Ellie, we can't."

"Why not?" she whines. She whines like she wants it as much as her next breath.

"I need to tell you something." I cover my mouth with my hand. These words aren't easy. I don't say them often. Only a few scant people in my life know what I'm about to tell her.

My phone rings again. The sound is a lure to bide me more time. If I answer, I can think. I can fucking think without a raging hard-on about what I want to say to Ellie.

"What do you need to tell me?" She holds my gaze for a moment before her eyes drift to my office door. "Did you hear that? Was that a knock? Is someone at the door?"

I heard it. Eda knows better than to disturb me when I've asked her not to. There's only one situation

RISK   *Deborah Bladon*

that would warrant the incessant phone calls and the interruption by my assistant.

"Eda," I call out, hoping she can hear me. "What is it? Is it her?"

The double glass doors of my office open in one fell swoop. Crew stands directly behind Eda, his phone in his hand. He ends the call and my phone stops ringing, just as he brushes past Eda to stalk toward me. "Mayday. Now, pal. Let's go."

Ellie holds Crew's glance for a moment before she turns back to me. "What's going on? What is it, Nolan?"

As my eyes find hers, I say the words I've never said to a woman before. "It's my daughter. My daughter needs me, Ellie. I'm sorry. I have to go."

She lowers herself back into the chair in front of my desk as I follow Crew out of my office and sprint to the open doors of the elevator. I didn't want her to find out like this, but now it's out there. She knows. Ellie knows that I'm a father and the most important thing in the world to me is my five-year-old little girl and her broken heart.

Chapter 28

Ellie

A daughter. He has a daughter.

I didn't bother to ask his assistant any questions after Nolan left his office with Crew. I doubt she would have told me anything. Eda doesn't strike me as the type to gossip about her boss behind his back. Besides, this is something that I need to discuss with Nolan. It's a child. He's a father to a little girl.

I got up from the chair in Nolan's office after what felt like four hours. It was only a few minutes. I went down to the store and finished my shift. I spent the entire afternoon glancing at my phone, hoping to hear anything from Nolan. Nothing came. Not a text or a call.

I took a detour on my way home, walking past the building that his driver dropped him off at last night. It's a luxury high-rise that caters to some of Manhattan's elite. You don't secure an address there without a trust fund or a successful business in your portfolio.

The doorman gave me a curt nod as I passed by. I didn't stop to ask him if I could go up to see Nolan. I haven't been invited. I understand why now.

"He told you that he's never had a girlfriend and yet he has a daughter?" Adley dips her spoon into the container of cookie dough ice cream she pulled out of our freezer. "This has to be one of those broken condom babies."

I scowl as I look at her. "It's Nolan's daughter, Ad. Even if she wasn't planned, she's his daughter."

She quiets, her lips thinning as recognition brightens her eyes. I'm a baby that was the result of a mistake. My mother told me as much before she died. My father said otherwise after we'd buried her. I knew it was my mom telling me the truth. They never lived in the same house. I don't recall a time the two of them were together in a room, other than at the funeral home when he paid for her service and kissed the dark wood of her coffin as tears streamed down his face.

"When they talked about Crew's niece they must have been talking about her," I murmur. "That's why he had the hay on his shoulder and the earring on his ear. It was because of her."

"They seem close enough to be brothers," Adley offers. "Kids are fun, Bean."

They are fun. Every moment I ever spent with Jayce, Tad's seven-year-old son, was a treasure to me. I didn't think I'd love him when I first met him, but the deep love I developed for him drove me to beg Tad to move his company headquarters to Las Vegas so we could be closer to Jayce after Tad's ex-wife remarried.

Our visits with him were limited to every Wednesday night and alternating weekends, but I made the most of the time. When Tad dumped me, I lost Jayce too. I never saw him again even though I held tightly to the faint hope that Tad would let me say goodbye to him. That never happened.

"I know they are." I cover my mouth with my hand. I don't want to say Jayce's name because it hurts so much when I think of him. Adley knows that. She's shied away from talking about him since Tad left me.

"Your nieces are a blast. You love them like mad."

I do love them. All three of them are unique, even though the two eldest are identical twins. I can tell them apart because I've known them since the moment they were born seven years ago. Megan has a freckle on the tip of her nose that her twin sister, Melrose, doesn't have.

"I haven't seen them since I've been back," I admit. "I miss them."

"Queens is a subway ride away." She rests her spoon on the table. "We can go see them this weekend. I'd love to see them again."

The slight change in subject is helping, but not enough to make me forget that the man I had sex with last night has a child. "Why do you think he didn't tell me about her?"

She places the lid back on the ice cream container. "Can I get real, Bean?"

"I guess?" I shrug my shoulders. "Have you not been real up to this point?"

Her eyes drop to the table before she looks at me straight-on. "I don't think he tells most of the women he's fucking about his daughter. If I had a kid, I don't know if I'd tell a random guy I hooked up with that I was a mom. Actually, I know that I wouldn't. It's private. It just seems to me that it's one of those things you tell a person you know has potential."

Her words mirror the thoughts that have been playing on a loop in my mind all afternoon. I've tried to reverse the roles and placed myself in Nolan's shoes. I doubt like hell I'd tell a man if I had a child unless I knew it was something he needed to know because our relationship warranted it. I know, without a doubt, that I wouldn't let him meet my child until I knew there was a foundation with some strength between us.

With Tad it was different. We'd known each other for months before we ever hooked up. I knew about Jayce long before I fell in love with Tad. I sometimes wonder if my love for Jayce skewed my feelings for Tad.

"What about her mom?" Adley goes on when I don't respond. "Has he said anything at all about who that might be? He has to have a relationship with her, even if it's just a cordial passing off of their daughter during parental visits."

"No, not a word." I open the ice cream container back up and dip in my spoon. I didn't take Adley up on her offer to indulge when she pulled it out of the freezer. Now, with the added stress of thinking about the mother of Nolan's child, I can't resist the temptation. "He's never mentioned a woman to me other than Shelby."

"The thief he was having dinner with at Meadow?"

"That's her." I let the ice cream melt on my tongue before I swallow. "I don't know who he had a child with."

"You'll find out soon enough." She raises her spoon in the air as if to toast. "Here's to Nolan's baby mama. Let's hope she's everything he never wants again."

I laugh to bite back the anxiety I feel. My parents thought they hated each other for years and yet, my dad died still as in love with my mom as the day I was conceived.

***

"You're sure it's not too late, Ellie?" Nolan takes a deep breath.

I stand at the doorway to my apartment, dressed in only a pair of shorts and my NYPD T-shirt. The shirt was a gift from Adley when I graduated from college. She knows I hope to replace it with a full uniform one day.

"I told you it wasn't." I did say that when he called fifteen minutes ago. That was close to midnight. I'd brushed my teeth and gone to bed when my phone started to ring. I answered immediately and was relieved when he said that everything was okay. I agreed to let him come over because I know that all the questions I have for him will keep me wide awake.

"Where's your roommate?" His eyes scan the interior of the apartment. "Her name is Adley, right?"

"Yes." I step aside so he can enter. "She works at a vet clinic. She was called in for an emergency."

"She's a vet?" The cock of his brow doesn't hide his surprise.

Adley is too often mistaken for a typical blond with big tits. She owns that but only because she's confident in her intelligence. She knows she brings a lot to the table and to any person who spends the time to get to know her. "She will be. She's an assistant right now."

He nods. He skims his hands over the jeans he's wearing. "Can we sit down and talk?"

I like to pace when life throws me a curveball. More often than not, I walk. I can put miles on my running shoes in a day if I feel stress. I already did that tonight after I ate too much ice cream.

I took on the paths of Central Park when the sun was setting. It was filled with people, but with my earbuds in and my favorite songs on repeat, I was able to find my center again. It feels out of reach again now that Nolan has walked through my door.

"Do you want anything?" I stand when he takes a seat on the fabric couch that came with the place. "I only have water or juice. I can make coffee if you want."

"No." He takes a deep breath. "Please sit, Ellie. Let me explain."

I sit far from enough from him that I'm satisfied he can't reach out and touch me. I don't want that. I can't feel his skin against mine as I listen to this. "What's your daughter's name?"

He looks surprised. He swallows before he answers. "May. Her name is May."

"May," I repeat it quietly. "It's pretty."

"She's pretty." His brows are drawn. "I'd tell you that she's the prettiest girl in the world, but I'm her dad, so my perception is skewed. Aside from that, she is the prettiest little girl I've ever seen."

"What does she look like?"

He moves. His legs spread as he reaches toward his front pocket but then he stops. "I could show you some of the pictures I have on my phone but I'd much rather you see for yourself in person. I'd like you to meet her."

I'd like that too. I think. At some point, I would like it. Not now. Not yet.

He looks at me pensively. "I don't tell the women I spend time with about May. I haven't until now. I'm protective of her. I need to be."

"Aren't all fathers protective of their daughters?" I ask with a smile.

"I suppose they are." He studies the room we're in. There's nothing notable about it but his gaze slides over every piece of furniture and the framed pictures of Adley's family.

He's waiting. Waiting for me to say something. Anything.

"I meant what I said in my office earlier, Ellie." He shifts in his seat, moving closer to where I am. "I'd like us to date exclusively. I realize I made the suggestion before you knew I was a single dad, but I still want us to spend time together."

I nod, but what comes out of my mouth isn't fueled by my desire to date him. It's driven by my need to know more about his daughter, and her mother. The woman he made love to and created a life with. "What's your relationship with May's mom like? Is it civil? Do you see her often?"

Closing his eyes, he bows his head, his hand scrubbing over the back of his neck. "I don't see her. I don't know her. I have no idea who May's mother is."

Chapter 29

Nolan

She looks at me the way you'd expect a woman to look at a man who she believes is throwing bullshit in her direction.

I brace for the question. It's the same question I've heard from my family, from Crew, and before his death, even my grandfather sat me down and looked me in the eye before he asked it.

"You don't know who her mother is? How is that possible, Nolan?"

When you fuck so many women that you can't remember names or faces it suddenly becomes possible.

When you look into the face of a baby and see only yourself reflected back, it becomes possible.

"May was left just inside the lobby doors of the building I took you to last night. She was an infant. There was a note with her addressed to me. It was handwritten but untraceable. There was nothing else left with her other than a blanket and the diaper she was wearing."

Her eyes flick across my face at lightning speed. "Someone just left her all alone?"

I nod. "The doorman found her once she started crying. He called me and I called the police."

"The police?" There's no judgment in her tone. It's a simple question.

"I didn't know what to do. I knew that I needed to make sure she was all right, so I called 911."

She moves slightly, closer to me, although her hands remain stiff in her lap. "What happened then?"

It's a blur, but it's not. I was floating on something back then. It was fear and joy. Hope and disbelief. "I demanded a DNA test and that I be allowed to take her back home with me."

"Were you able to?" she asks, running her hands over her knees. "Did they let you take her home?"

"My lawyer fought hard, but yes." I sigh. "There were stipulations including my sister and her husband agreeing to become May's temporary guardians. They'd adopted a boy a few months before so the court saw that as a plus. The three of them needed to move in with me temporarily, but their presence guaranteed May could stay."

"That's why you moved to another apartment," she breathes. "You needed the room."

"I negotiated a rental agreement the day May was released from the hospital and the nursery was fully equipped within hours. I bought the place a week later."

"She was in the hospital?"

"A precaution," I explain. "There was no record of her birth. We had no idea if there were complications, but thankfully she was fine. A bit premature, but fine."

"When did you know for certain that she was your daughter?" The first sign of a smile tugs at the corners of her mouth.

RISK   *Deborah Bladon*

"The first time I held her." I look directly into her eyes. "In that lobby, I picked that baby up and looked down at her and I knew. I knew she was mine."

***

I asked for a glass of water to chase down the lump in my throat. It did little good. It was worth it, though. Ellie sat closer to me when she brought me the glass. So close that I can reach out to touch the bare skin of her legs. I haven't, but the temptation is there.

"What happened today?" Her eyes catch mine. I see her genuine concern. It was there when I left my office in a mad rush earlier and it was still there when she opened her apartment door to let me in. "Is she all right?"

Yes.

No.

She's perfect except for her shattered heart.

"She'll be fine." I lean back into the couch. "May's dog died a few weeks ago. It was her first loss. She's having a difficult time adjusting."

"Losing a pet can be very hard." Her lips turn down until she's frowning. Her brows pinch together. "I had a dog once. I remember how deeply I mourned that loss."

Kip had a dog; a feisty little Yorkie mix. She'd give it some of the food I would bring her, making it sit at attention before she'd pull off her mitten and feed it from her hand.

187

"What kind of dog was it?" I hone in on the opportunity to connect Ellie to Kip.

"A sweet one." She segues effortlessly into her next question. "What kind of dog did May have?"

"A beagle. Old and crotchety but she loved that fool with everything she has."

"Was it your dog before May arrived?" Her eyes brighten.

"What do you think?" I relax, resting my arm on the back of the couch.

Her brows shoot up with the question. She cradles her chin in her hand, studying my face carefully. "I think not. You don't seem like the kind of man who would have a dog unless his little girl wanted one."

"You're right," I say slowly as I lean closer to her. "She wanted to adopt a dog, so we went to the shelter and Barney gave her those old doggy eyes and she fell in love."

"You'd give her the moon if she asked, wouldn't you?" Her mouth curves into a soft smile.

"I'd hold her up and let her take it from the sky." I would. I can give my daughter everything she wants, but I can't give her one single detail about her mother.

Chapter 30

Ellie

"I'm such an idiot," I mumble to myself while he talks on the phone. He doesn't race off to another room to make the call. He does it right in front of me. I like it. I like hearing him asking a woman named Tilde how May is. This is his life, and he's let me inside.

He ends the call with a brief reminder to Tilde to call him if May wakes up. It's the third time he's told her that. "That was one of May's nannies. Now, explain the idiot comment, Ellie."

I wish I could. It's not about one thing, but I'm not going to tell him that. I'll just go with the obvious because dammit I should have put the clues together and realized that he didn't live in that apartment he took me to last night. "When we were in the office of your fake apartment, I knew something was up."

"That apartment isn't fake." He sits next to me again. He'd risen to his feet when he called Tilde, but he hadn't walked but a few inches from the couch. "It's real."

"You know what I mean," I say flustered. "It's not where you live."

"I own it. Many of the things I hold dear are still there."

I know he's referring to those photographs of the sailboats in the hallway. I've thought about those since he told me he moved out of that apartment. If they meant anything to him, he would have taken them with him to his new place. For some reason, they're hanging in an apartment he's left virtually untouched for years.

"The calendar was stuck at the month of May five years ago and the newspaper on your desk was open to a day from that month too. Is that when May was left in the lobby?"

The month of May. The baby named May. Wait.

"Did you name your daughter after a month?" I ask, without thinking the question through. Does it sound judgmental? I don't mean it that way. I've given some minimal thought to what I might name my kids when I have them. I'm leaning toward vintage names.

"She's named after my mother," he answers evenly. "Her maiden name was May."

I nod in understanding. "I should have realized you didn't live there when I was standing in the office. I knew something wasn't right. I wanted to ask you last night why you have the packaging from a smartphone that hasn't been sold in years on your desk."

His eyes drop to where his phone is resting on his leg. "Before last night I hadn't been to that apartment in more than a year. I have someone go there to check on it every two weeks. They dust and wash windows and do whatever else needs to be done. I gave them very strict instructions not to touch anything in the office because there are still some personal items in there. That's why it looks like a shrine to a day five years ago."

"The day May arrived?"

"Yes." He stiffens slightly. "I didn't put much thought into the move. I had other things on my mind."

An unexpected child and an entirely new life. I can't imagine being thrown into the role of parent and protector without a moment's notice.

"Why do you keep it?" I lean closer to him. "If you don't live there anymore, why keep the place?"

He shrugs as his hand slides from his leg to mine. "You could say that I'm keeping it for sentimental value."

I nod with a smile. "That makes sense. You keep an entire apartment because it has sentimental value while the rest of us just keep our mementos in a shoebox under our beds."

"Is that where I would find all of Ellie Madden's secrets?" His hand moves higher, edging the hem of my shorts. "Do you have a shoebox under your bed with all your keepsakes in it?"

"I'm not telling," I tease as I rest my hand on his leg. "I don't like showing my hand. It's much more interesting if you learn all about me piece by tiny piece."

"I'd like to learn more about what's beneath this tiny piece of material you apparently think passes for a pair of shorts?" His hand moves higher until his fingers inch beneath the leg of my shorts. They skim the tender flesh of my pussy.

I feel the weight of arousal instantly just from the softest touch of his fingertips.

"You're wet, Ellie." His voice dips, lower, throaty. Lust is there woven around the words.

I move my hand higher until it's brushing against his erection through his jeans. "And you're hard. It seems that we're even again."

"You have condoms."

I can't tell if it's a question or a statement. "You have assumptions."

"I have a raging need to fuck you." He pushes my hand around the outline of his cock. "Do you have condoms, Ellie?"

I straighten my back and huff out my answer. "No. I haven't bought any since I've been back."

"Good." He moves closer, his hand parting my folds under the tight material of my shorts. "You weren't planning to fuck either of those clowns."

"What clowns are you talk…oh, oh my God," I stutter when his index finger circles my clit.

"Spread your legs," he growls in my ear. "I'll get you off like this. I want to watch you come."

"My roommate," I whimper. "She might come home."

"It won't take long. You're close. I can feel it." His breath is hot on my neck, his lips kissing a trail to my ear. "Spread your legs, Ellie."

I do it. I know I shouldn't. If Adley walked in I'd be horrified, but his touch and the words. All of it makes me want the release his fingers promise.

He pulls his hand out and within the next breath it's down the front of my shorts. He runs his fingertip over my clit, rubbing, teasing, pressing. Every stroke of his finger, each movement is in perfect concert with my body's need.

I close my eyes as I near the crest. My hand darting to cover my mouth, to muffle the sounds I know I'll make without thinking.

"Look at me." His voice is controlled, an edge of roughness in his tone. "Let me see what my touch does to you."

I come, quickly, violently, my legs moving off the couch, my ass curving as my body seeks more. He gives it when he yanks his hand free of my shorts, tosses me over his shoulder and takes me to my bed.

RISK   *Deborah Bladon*

Chapter 31

Nolan

I haven't eaten pussy for that long since, truthfully, never. When I go down on a woman, I have one goal in mind. I want her to orgasm as quickly as possible. I generally settle for just one and then my pleasure becomes my priority. I'm a selfish bastard. I know it.

The lesson I learned when I first started on my personal sexual path was that you need to give the woman you're with what she wants first and then you can take. It's my prescription for success in the bedroom or any other room I fuck a woman in.

Last night it was in Ellie's bedroom. She told me which room to enter and when I left over an hour later it was with her smell and taste all over my face and hands. I licked and sucked her beautiful pink cunt until she was quivering and told me it was too much and that she couldn't take anymore. Then I kissed her goodnight and me and my hard-as-nails dick walked home hungry for more of the taste and those fucking sounds she was making. It was a squeak and a moan and a chorus of words that make no sense, but I could have listened to that all night long. I wanted to slide inside of her, but I didn't. I couldn't.

I had no qualms about fucking her without a condom. She's too aware of her surroundings not to be tested regularly. She had sex with the scummiest man whore in Las Vegas for months. She's been tested since. I'd bet everything I own on that. I'm clean too and I'm in no position to knock her up, so it's safe.

Extra safe.

It's a-vasectomy-a-week-after-May-arrived-kind-of-safe.

I was clipped for good measure after I realized that those statistics on the side of a box of condoms are real. They do fail. My daughter is proof of that.

I always played safe before May was born, always. I wouldn't touch a woman unless my dick was wrapped and she was using birth control, but obviously one of those women, one with the same shade of blonde hair and brown eyes as May, lied to me.

The onus was as much on me as her. I fucked whoever the hell she was with full knowledge that regardless of what we used to prevent a pregnancy, there was a slim chance of conception. I'm grateful for the latex failure now, but back when I became an instant dad when I was twenty-three-years-old, I was fucking panicked. I decided that I'm a one-kid-only kind of guy and went to see my doctor.

A week later the problem was taken care of. I still use condoms, every single time, but I have the reassurance of knowing that I'm not going to wake up with another baby on my doorstep.

I bit my tongue last night when I undressed Ellie and crawled on top of her while I was still fully clothed. I wanted to tell her that I trusted her and that she should trust me. I wanted to fuck her raw with nothing between us, but I want the trust that comes with time. I'm not going to pressure her into anything. I'm in no hurry.

"You look like a cat that just ate a canary and enjoyed every last bite of it."

My head snaps up to see Crew standing in the doorway of my office. I've been here alone since early this morning.

I fell asleep once I got home from Ellie's, but then a soft touch on my shoulder woke me. It was May with tears in her eyes and a hand-drawn picture of Barney in her hands. My daughter isn't an artist although it's her goal to be one. That's the plan this week, so I bought her a package of markers and a sketch pad. Her mission before this was to be a farmer. That's why we visited a petting zoo an hour upstate. I'm all for her chasing her dreams, all of them.

My job as her dad is to make sure the route is safe while she does the exploring.

"What time is it?" I scrub my hand over my face. I didn't shave. I showered just before five this morning when May finally went back to bed.

"Time for me to break the bad news to you." He strolls into my office, stopping short of the chairs in front of my desk.

"What bad news?" I glance down at the screen of my phone. No Mayday messages have come in. It's a code Crew came up with for the three nannies I employ after May took a tumble and split her lip when she was a toddler. If they type it in a text, it means it's an emergency. If I don't respond, they contact Eda and Crew simultaneously.

It doesn't take the edge off the panic I feel whenever I see it or hear it, but it does convey the message that my daughter is in trouble in an inconspicuous way, regardless of who else is in the room.

Very few people know I have a child and her existence isn't fuel for public consumption. I don't want her picture online or her image sold to the highest bidder. The vague promise that was in the note left with May when she was an infant has kept me wary of letting anyone near her.

"You're fucked." He chuckles as he takes a seat in one of the chairs. "You're royally fucked, pal."

"In what sense?" I lean back into my chair.

He smirks. "In the sense that you have never, to my knowledge, told any woman about May. Yesterday I was here when you just put it all out there in front of Ellie."

I did do that, without a second thought. "I wanted her to know. I want her to know May."

"Since when did that become a good idea?"

Since I decided that I want her to see me in a way no other woman ever has and since I want my daughter to spend time with the most perfect example of a strong woman I know. Every other woman I have ever met is inferior to Ellie in every conceivable way. I can't deny that. I wouldn't try. "I like her, Crew. May will like her too."

"I get that." He taps his shoe against the floor. "What's going on between you two is new. It's early, Nolan. You need to wait for a beat before you take Ellie home to May."

RISK   *Deborah Bladon*   ·

I don't take offense. He loves May just as much as I do. To her, he's Captain Crew, her uncle. He's been there every step of the way, but she's my daughter. I get to call the shots. "When the time is right, I'll introduce them."

"There's no rush," he points out as he stands. "If this thing between you and Ellie has legs, you have all the time in the world to introduce the two of them. Pace it right, pal. Give it time. Think about what's best for May."

He's right. I know he is, but right now, after spending half my night with Ellie and the other half with my baby girl in my lap drawing pictures of our life together, all I want is for my daughter to meet the woman I can't get enough of.

Chapter 32

Ellie

"What's going to happen to all these pastries?" I sigh heavily. "What do you do with them?"

"I assume the cleaning crew takes care of it." Eda picks up a mini donut and pops it in her mouth. She chews rapidly. "I have no idea what they do with them."

I scan the large cloth covered table that was set up by the catering company hired to feed the Matiz executives who came to the meeting that just ended. I was required to sit in so I could listen to their individual concerns regarding security. One person brought up the fact that sensitive files are being emailed through the company's internal system. I'm not equipped to address that so Matiz's cyber security expert handled it.

I only had to speak once when a woman who runs the nail polish division had a question about the new protocol I put in place regarding self-samples. I told her that the reason I outlawed them is that too many customers were helping themselves to the sample bottles. When one went missing, the sales staff used to replace it immediately with a new bottle of polish. It wasn't uncommon for the store to run through two or three bottles a day to replace those taken.

Now, when a customer wants to paint a fingernail to see if they're purchasing the right shade, the person working the polish counter does it for them and then places the sample bottle back behind the counter. If a customer does decide they like the color, the sales associate will hand them a bottle from the display case and then either ring their purchase in or direct them to the main check-out area which is only a few feet away. It's a very simple way to cut down on the theft of the polish but one that apparently no one thought of until now. Since Matiz polish ranges from twenty to thirty dollars a bottle, the savings is significant.

"Why do you ask, Ellie?" Nolan asks as he stalks toward me. "You can take as many as you like home. I know you have a sweet tooth."

I have a sweet spot on one of my teeth, not an entire tooth. It's likely going to take me the rest of my life to work through that gallon of ice cream he brought to my apartment. Adley and I have eaten a few spoons a day since he brought it over and there's barely a dent in it. Pastries are the last thing I need.

"I wasn't asking for me."

He nods at Eda which immediately sends her on her way out the door with another donut in her mouth.

He waits until she leaves us alone in the boardroom before he touches my cheek. "Who were you asking for?"

"Do you think the cleaning crew throws them in the trash?" I count just the tarts on the table. There are twenty two. There are at least twice as many small donuts and an entire chocolate cake that no one bothered to cut into. Most of the people at the meeting took a cup of coffee from the self-serve station beside the pastry table and sat down. They didn't even look in the direction of the tarts, donuts, cake or the delicious looking muffins that appear to have candied walnuts on top of them.

When I turn to look at him, he's studying me. There's a question in his eyes, so I wait for it, but he shakes his head faintly before he looks at the table. "They don't throw them out. I take the extra food after our meetings."

"You must really like donuts and cake." My voice is soft. "You also must work out like a madman to look as good as you do if you're eating ice cream and pastries all the time."

"I don't eat them all the time," he quips.

"You ate both the butter cookies we got from the street cart."

"I did?" He pops a donut in his mouth and chews. "Jesus, I'm a rude prick sometimes."

I raise an eyebrow. "They're very good cookies. I don't blame you."

"Blame me, Ellie." He taps his chest. "Tell me that I need to make it up to you."

"You don't." I reach out to cover his hand with mine. "Just tell me what you do with all this food. I'm curious."

He lifts my hand to his mouth, feathering his lips over my palm. "It's sent to a mission in Midtown. They distribute it to the people who need it. If we only deliver pastries, like we are today, I'll arrange for something more substantial to be brought in, so the people they help will have a well-balanced meal and dessert too."

His words bring a smile to my face. "You're not rude. You're one of the good guys."

"If you see me as a good guy, I'm doing something right." His voice is quiet. "Your opinion of me matters a great deal. I like knowing that you see that in me."

"I think a lot of people see that in you." I tug my hand away from his when I look toward the corridor beyond the open door. Matiz corporate employees stream past at a steady clip, each turning to glance our way. There's a grin on every face, just as there was during the meeting. "Everyone who works here seems very happy."

"I pay them to look happy." He raises his hand, jerking his thumb back in the direction of the door. "The second I'm out of earshot, they're bitching about me."

"You don't know that." I meet his eyes. "I think people who work for you genuinely like you."

"Including you?" He lowers his hand to my waist, his fingers pressing through the thin blue blouse I'm wearing causing my nipples to furl into firm points. "Do you genuinely like me?"

I nod as his gaze falls to my blouse. "I work for Crew, but, yes, I genuinely like you."

"I can tell. We're alone so feel free to show me how much you like me." The tone of his voice lowers as he steps even closer. My body heats, the flush racing over me. The need to touch him winds through me from my core. He's taunting me with my own desire for him.

RISK   *Deborah Bladon*

I lean in, not wanting anyone passing the room to catch my words. "I'm not sucking your cock in this conference room, Nolan."

He stares at me, first my eyes and then my lips. His fingers bite into my skin through the blouse. "Don't tease me with that mouth, Ellie. You've made me hard."

I glance down. The outline of his erection is straining against his pants. "Don't tease me with that."

"I'm not teasing," he hisses the words out. "Don't think for a second that I won't lock that door and strip you naked. I'm not opposed to fucking you on the conference table."

"I thought we were talking about you fucking my mouth."

"Jesus." He runs the pad of his thumb over my bottom lip. "Come to my place at nine tonight. The place I took you to."

"You mean your shoebox?"

A soft smile crosses his lips. "Is that what we're calling it now?"

"You said it has sentimental value, so it's your shoebox."

"I suppose it is." He steps back as someone clears their throat in the doorway behind him. "That's Miller from Marketing. We have a meeting. If he's lucky, he'll have a job when it's over."

"Don't pretend you're not a nice guy, Nolan Black." I inch back on my heels. "I'll see you at the shoebox at nine."

"Nine sharp. I'll be there waiting for you."

"I'll try not to touch myself before then," I whisper. "No promises, though. You look extra hot today in that suit."

"That mouth," he growls under his breath as I walk past him and smile at Mr. Miller on my way to the elevator.

Chapter 33

Nolan

"Mr. Black, I need a moment," Kristof Hellaman says as I step off the elevator after my meeting with Miller.

I spared the Marketing Manager my wrath today. It wasn't because Ellie had insisted that I'm a good guy. It was because I believe that second chances can yield tremendous results. He has one last opportunity to impress me with his vision of the campaign for our new skin care line. If he fails to knock it out of the park the next go-round, he'll be leaving the building with only his pride and a box of his belongings.

"My office." I walk quickly. He follows me in silence, waiting when I tell Eda to hold my calls.

"What's this about?" I ask as soon as the door is shut. I trust Eda, implicitly. She's one of the few people in my life I confided in when May arrived. She's never questioned anything she's overheard. She wears her loyalty on her sleeve, yet there are still conversations that aren't her concern. Typically, that's any discussion that Kristof and I have.

"Tad Darling, sir."

Anger crawls through me at the mention of his name. He's the man Ellie loved. She promised to marry him and he tossed her trust aside like a piece of dirty trash. I'm grateful in a twisted way that he's an asshole. It set her free so that when she fell in my lap, she wasn't bound to him in any way.

"What about him?" I perch a brow.

He clears his throat. "You wanted an eye kept on him, sir. I've done as you asked."

"And?" I shrug off my jacket, hanging it on the coatrack by the door.

"He's coming to New York."

"When?" I shoot back, irritated by the idea of the man being in the same city as Ellie.

He looks at the view of Manhattan on display through the window behind my desk. "He'll be here at the end of the month. He's arriving at LaGuardia on a private jet. I've sent the details of his itinerary to you."

I tug my phone free of my pocket. I skim the email, noting the hotel Tad's staying at and his departure. "Is there an official purpose for this trip? Does he have business here?"

"My contact in his office assured me they'd forward any details of any meetings he has planned." He crosses his arms across his chest. "Right now, it's classified as a personal trip."

That fucker is coming here because of Ellie. He must have realized she's no longer breaking her back for minimum wage at a casino in Vegas. I haven't overstepped the boundary that would grant me access to the notes from a meeting attended by both Tad and Ellie in a Vegas law office months ago. It's information I can buy with a healthy check and a signature from the person willing to trade their moral code for a price.

RISK   *Deborah Bladon*

The curiosity may be killing me, but it's Ellie's business. I don't want our relationship to veer off course because of my thirst to know the finer details about something that happened before we met. I've already crossed too many lines, but it's for a good reason. Tad Darling mistreated her. He disrespected her in a way that compromised her safety. It's unforgivable.

Ellie is more than capable of taking care of herself, but I can be available for support if need be.

"I want you to track his movements while he's here. If he approaches Matiz or Ellie's apartment, you're to get in touch with me, immediately."

I don't have a plan for what I'll do if that happens. I won't interfere. I'm not going to wait on the sidelines while they discuss their former relationship and its death by Tad's hand. I just want to be aware and informed. Control comes with knowledge and the more information I have on Tad Darling, CEO of Darlux Media, the better.

***

"The pictures that were on the piano are gone."

Ellie stands in place in the middle of the living room. Her eyes are locked on the spot on top of the piano where a handful of scattered photographs were the last time she was here. They were brought here by Crew a few days after May was born. I was already packing my things so I could move. The pictures were taken at the hospital hours after May was left in the lobby. I'd forgotten them here in the mad rush to get

RISK   *Deborah Bladon*

to my new apartment and get everything in order for my baby girl.

"I came here earlier and picked them up." I hand her a bottle of chilled water. "I took them to my place."

She draws a quick breath. "The place where you live with your daughter?"

"Yes," I answer simply.

She nods. "What time do you need to be back there tonight? Is dad curfew a thing?"

I chuckle just as I bring the water bottle I'm still holding to my lips. "Dad curfew is indeed a thing. I'd like to be back before midnight. She's been waking up every night since Barney died."

She opens the bottle of water in her hand and takes a large sip. Her throat moves with the motion, her head tilting back slightly.

I want her like that on the bed. Naked and on her back, her head hung over the side with my cock in that mouth and her throat working to swallow every last drop I give to her.

"You're staring at my neck, Nolan. I don't have to ask what that's about."

She hands me the bottle of water. Her hands make quick work of the sash that holds her green wrap dress in place. It drops to the floor at her feet, revealing the creamy pale skin of her body, almost all of her body. She's wearing nothing but a black lace bra, matching panties and a pair of heeled sandals.

"Your body is beautiful," I say hoarsely, my voice caught somewhere between my cock and my throat.

"From what I've seen of your body, it's beautiful too but I want to see all of it." Her hands leap to the front of my dress shirt. She opens one button and then another before I reach up and still her. I hold her fingers to my chest.

"I didn't ask you here just so I could fuck you."

She looks up and into my eyes. There's a trace of innocence in her expression, but there's more. The promise of pleasure that's all-consuming is there. "You did ask me here so you could fuck me. I came because I want to fuck you. We're adults, Nolan."

"We are adults," I confer. "I like fucking you, but I also like talking to you. You're going to let me take you to dinner at my favorite restaurant. I want that soon, Ellie."

"I'd like that." She tugs her fingers from my hands, watching my face. "Tonight I'd like something else."

"What would you like?" I ask because I want to hear the words. I want to know that this breathtakingly beautiful woman wants the same thing I do.

"I want you. I just want you, Nolan."

The answer undoes me. It's not just my dick that reacts this time. There's more. It's inside of me. An ache to give her everything she wants and needs.

"Come here." I take her hand in mine, tugging her close before I crush my lips against hers.

Chapter 34

Nolan

I kneel on the bed just as she requested after she slowly, so fucking slowly, undressed me. She insisted and who the hell was I to argue with her? She took her time, revealing every inch of my body as if it was a gift for her. Her smile widened when her fingers trailed over my abs. Her breath stalling as her hand gripped my cock and pumped it.

I almost pushed her to her knees just inside the door of the room, but that wasn't what she wanted.

She got on the bed after sliding off her panties and bra. I followed when she asked, and now as we face each other, I know what she wants. The slick of her tongue over her bottom lip gives it away. She wants my cock in her mouth. I want that too.

"This is the first time I've seen this," she whispers.

"A cock this big?" I palm my dick. It's big. I've had enough women tell me as much. I have nothing to judge by. I keep my eyes trained ahead whenever I take a piss in a public bathroom.

She smiles. "Your ego is as big as your cock."

"My ego isn't this big." I stroke the length of my shaft enjoying the way her eyes follow the path of my hand.

"I meant that I've never seen you completely nude until now." Her gaze jumps to my face. "We've been together twice before and you've kept your clothes on both times."

"I don't know how I managed that." I laugh. "I'd be naked all the time around you if it wouldn't get me arrested."

"You should be naked all the time." She reaches forward to graze her fingers over my chest. Her touch is tentative, soft. "Your body is incredible for someone who eats cookies and donuts."

I like the teasing, both in her words and in touch. Her fingers crawl lower, slowly burning a path over my stomach. "Your body is perfect, Ellie."

I see the hesitation before she nods. "I like that you think so."

Every man she's ever been with should have told her how perfect she is, but they haven't. I've known that since the first time we were together and she tugged at the top of her dress after we'd fucked. She tried to cover herself, shield her body from my eyes after I'd come.

That's why I stripped her of her T-shirt and shorts in her apartment the other night and feathered kisses all over her bare skin. I want her to know that I covet her and that her body is worthy of worship, by me. I don't want another fucker near it.

"I've thought about how I'll suck your cock."

I groan. I fucking groan aloud when those words come out of her mouth. "Show me, Ellie."

She does. She leans forward on her hand and knees, her bare pussy and ass in the air as she takes the crown of my dick between her lips. She kisses it gently at first. Her lips surrounding it with a flick of her tongue over the tip. Then it deepens and the kiss

RISK *Deborah Bladon*

becomes a suctioned slide. She hollows her cheeks, her mouth working on me as she purrs. Tiny echoes of pleasure that vibrate off my dick.

My hand knots in her hair as she glides me between those lips and across that wet tongue.

She moans around my dick, loudly. Not a sound that says she's enjoying the fisted hand in her hair, but a sound that screams that she loves having my cock in her mouth and the movement of my hips as I pump into her. I fuck that sweet, sinful mouth leisurely, easily.

She adjusts her knees and I wish to hell there was a mirror behind her. I want to see her. I want a view of that wet pussy that I'll lick as soon as I blow my load down her throat. Then I'll fuck her, hard and recklessly against the wall. I want it all. I want more.

"I could do this all night." Her breath races across my thigh as she licks the length of me, her tongue lashing against my sac. "You taste so good."

"Down your throat," I rasp. "I need to fuck your mouth."

"Yes," she hisses before she shifts again, her ass moving, taunting me.

I take control because the need is too strong. I use my hand to set the pace on the back of her head and I thrust and I thrust. Long, easy strokes give way to fast, frantic pumps until I come hard and intensely as she takes every last drop.

***

"You don't have to leave, Ellie." I kiss her forehead. Her hair is damp, her skin covered with a

RISK   *Deborah Bladon*

sheen of sweat. We've been at each other for hours, licking, sucking, touching and fucking. It's a miracle that I have the energy to stand straight.

I got dressed because I had to. I put my shoes on because I need to leave. I did it all while she drifted to sleep with her hands tucked next to her face, her nude body sprawled out on the bed. That image is a picture of her confidence in my words. She knows I hunger for her body, every angled curve and inch of her.

She squints at me with one eye. "Did you miss curfew?"

"I did," I admit. It's closing in on one in the morning. "I called the nanny. May's asleep, but I have to go so I can be there. She might wake up and need me."

She rolls onto her back, her breasts coming into view. Her arm moves to cover them. "I'll get dressed. I need to go home."

I trail my lips along her forearm before I push it down with my chin. I suck her right nipple into my mouth, swirling my tongue around it, bringing it back to a stiff point. "I want you to stay. I wish I could too, but you should. Sleep here. Spend the night."

"I can't." She rests her hand on the back of my head; her eyes open now looking into mine under heavy lids. "I can't stay here."

"You can," I insist as I rest my chin on her arm. "I brought some bottled water and fruit. That's in the refrigerator. I stocked the main bathroom with some Matiz shower products. There are towels there for you as well. I want you to stay and rest. You're exhausted. You can go home tomorrow."

213

Her hand slides to my cheek. "You're a good guy. I knew it when I first met you in Vegas."

I study her face. I see less of Kip each time I look at Ellie. I might have thought Ellie bore a resemblance to the little redhead I used to know because they share the same spirit. They're generous and kind, but Ellie has a light within her that Kip didn't possess.

"Sometimes you look at me and I can't figure out what's going on in your mind." She traces my brow with the pad of her thumb. "Tell me what it is. What are you thinking about when you look at me that way?"

I can't tell her. The questions that follow will have the expectation of a truthful answer attached to them. I won't lie to her. I never want to skim over the truth with Ellie. If I tell her about Kip I'll need to explain what happened the last night I saw her. I'll have to confess what I've done.

The way she touches me will change. Her eyes won't widen the way they do now whenever she looks at me. She won't crave me anymore.

I risk losing her if I answer that question, so I don't.

"I need to go, Ellie." I kiss her cheek. "I want you to give some thought to meeting May."

Her eyebrows draw together. "You want me to meet her? It seems soon, Nolan. Isn't it too soon?"

It is soon. A few weeks ago I couldn't imagine wanting my daughter to meet any of the women I've slept with, now the idea of the two of them not meeting feels wrong. "It's soon, but I know you'll like her and May is going to be crazy about you."

She likes that. It brings a smile to her mouth. "Are you worried about what will happen when we aren't seeing each other anymore? Isn't it hard to explain to a child when someone just drops out of their life?"

Her words slice into me. She's convinced herself that this is short term. She doesn't see the potential because the asshole she used to be involved with stole all sense of certainty away from her. He also took his son away from her. I have no grasp on the extent of her relationship with Jayce Darling but I sense that's where her hesitation about meeting May stems from. "I want my daughter to know you. Regardless of what happens between us in the future, I know it will benefit May to know such a strong woman."

She sighs, her body visibly relaxing. "Can I think about it? It doesn't have to be tomorrow or the next day, does it?"

"It can be whenever you like." I smooth my fingertips over her cheek. "I'll call you in a few hours. Be as late as you want to be for work tomorrow."

"I work for Crew, not you. I'll be on time. I've never been late for work a day in my life."

Chapter 35

Ellie

"What the hell is that bed made of? The feathers from angel's wings and the sighs of babies?" I whisper to Nolan. "I fell fast asleep after you left. I was an hour late for work, Nolan. One whole hour."

"You like the bed?" A grin ghosts over his lips. "Do you like it enough to meet me in it tonight? Say at nine?"

That sounds like a pattern. The place we're meeting at may not be a hotel suite, but it's only a step up. I know he can't take me to his apartment, but I have a place. I also have a roommate but Adley's planning on pulling the evening shift starting tomorrow at the vet clinic. She says it's for extra money. I say it's because of the new vet who just started working there.

Dr. Donovan Hunt.

She showed me his Instagram page early this morning when I stopped at home to change clothes. The good doctor has more than a million followers and a smile that can light up a room. Adley's plan to work the late shift with him means an extra two dollars an hour in pay and a man who has at least one thing in common with her. Judging by all the pictures on his Instagram feed of him holding puppies, he loves animals as much as Adley.

RISK   *Deborah Bladon*

"I'm meeting Wolf's brother tonight," I say casually because it's business. "We're going to talk about the NYPD."

I don't need to clarify it. Nolan knows that Sebastian Wolf may be a major career contact for me. Liam sent me a text message early this morning to ask if I was available tonight. If this is my only chance to talk to someone with some influence in the NYPD, I won't pass it up.

"What time is that?" He raises his hand to wave at a customer. "It's not going to take all night, is it?"

No, but I need to catch my breath.

"I don't know how long it will take, Nolan." I lower my voice, trying to keep our conversation between only us. "I was planning on going to sleep early. We can see each other another night."

For a moment, he doesn't move or say a thing. "Last night was incredible, Ellie. If I made you uncomfortable when I brought up you meeting my daughter, I apologize. I want it, though. It's something I'd like to see happen."

I'd forgotten about that part of the night until now. He wants me to meet her. I want to make sure it's the right thing to do. I can't tell if this mutual attraction and infatuation between us will last. I don't want to get attached to his daughter only to have to walk away when we end. "I'm still thinking about it."

"No pressure," he says as his gaze travels over my head. "I hope your meeting with Nick's brother goes well. I'll hang out with May tonight."

I nod. "I'll look forward to seeing the artwork on your hands tomorrow."

"I want to kiss you, but I won't." He stares into my eyes. "I'll save it for the next time we're alone together. Until then, Ellie."

"Until then," I whisper with a nod of my chin. Until then, I'll wonder if this is too good to be true because it feels like the best thing that's ever happened to me.

***

"I'm sorry, Ellie." Adley pulls on the corner of a package of frozen carrots. "I know how much you want to work for the NYPD. You'd make a great detective."

I smile at the compliment. Adley's always been my biggest cheerleader, although she's never understood why I want to be a police officer. I stopped trying to explain it to her years ago. "We could just grab something at the all-night deli, Ad. You don't have to cook dinner."

That's code for *please don't cook dinner tonight.*

Sebastian Wolf suggested we grab a bite to eat, but I declined. I don't think it was an offer for a date, although I'm not the best at reading a man's interest. Sebastian is handsome in an entirely different way than Liam is. He looked every bit the part of a homicide detective, complete with suit, tie and a dark shadow of late day scruff over his jaw.

When he told me that he could help me get an administrative job within the department, I thanked him. He reiterated what I was told when I was turned down by the NYPD the last time I applied for the program. If I didn't make the cut the first time, I need to try again. I will. I just need to decide when.

"You're sure about dinner?" She slams the freezer door shut. "This is my only night off this week and to tell you the truth I wasn't really in the mood for whipping up a gourmet meal."

She may be delusional, but I like her confidence in her cooking skills. Besides, I'm currently the only one eating the food she prepares, and I haven't gotten sick, yet.

"I'm positive, and it's my treat."

I hold up my hand to ward off the argument I know she's about to launch into. Adley's had my back for years. She helped me when I didn't have two dimes to rub together. I made sure to keep track of how much money she loaned me so when I was finally in a position to pay it back, I did. That was just a few months ago and when she got the courier package with the check made out to her inside of a handwritten thank you note from me, she was in tears.

I love Adley and I know that she didn't expect any of that money back, but I needed to give it back. It was one of the easiest decisions I've ever made.

"I already know what I'm getting." She slips her feet into her low heels. "They have this meatloaf sandwich that I could eat every single day for the rest of my life."

I look down at the floor, to shield my smile. Meatloaf was the first meal we ate together. That feels like a lifetime ago. "A meatloaf sandwich for you and macaroni and cheese for me."

"You'll share with me. Won't you, Bean?"

I will. I always have. We've shared almost everything since the day Adley's family took me in and made me feel like I finally had a home.

Chapter 36

Ellie

"Are you going to eat all of that?" Gretel points at the food in my hands.

I admit it looks like a lot for one person. I'm holding a meatloaf sandwich and a bag of potato chips for Adley. I also grabbed a medium size container of macaroni and cheese for dinner and a bagel for my breakfast. I must look like someone who hasn't eaten in months.

"My friend and I are sharing it." I look beyond her shoulder to where Adley is standing near a display for a new flavor of coffee creamer. "How are you, Gretel?"

I'm not asking because I care. I don't care how she is. I thought if I ever saw her again it would be inside Matiz. I never imagined that I'd run into her and her daughter at a deli at ten o'clock at night.

"Hi, Ellie," Leila says brightly. "Your hair looks pretty again today."

"You look lovely, Leila." I smile down at her. "That's a beautiful dress you're wearing. Is tonight a special occasion?"

Before the child has a chance to open her mouth, her mother interrupts. "We went to a musical. Leila insisted we go to see that new musical that opened last week. It's no more than a three out of five, but I suppose if you're a kid, it's a home run."

"I loved it." Leila claps her hands together. "I want to go again."

"Your daddy will take you." Gretel pats her daughter on the head. "Go find a snack you can take to daycare tomorrow."

Leila scoots to the side where an assortment of fruit and cheese boxes are arranged in a refrigerated display case.

"I should pay for all of this and get home." I dip my chin. "It was good seeing you again, Gretel."

"You're not going to believe who I saw tonight."

Since the only person Gretel and I have in common besides Leila, is Nolan, I stop. I know I shouldn't. It was obvious when I stood next to her at Matiz that she'd be all over Nolan if given a chance. I have no idea if she could sense that something was going on between us and this is her way of stirring up trouble, but I'm frozen in place. It's not only curiosity keeping me here. It's self-doubt. I haven't been able to accept that Nolan might actually be serious about me because I'm still tainted from what Tad did. I'm aware of it. I'm working on it, but I'm still not strong enough to walk away from Gretel or what she's about to say.

"Who?" I ask with a playful lift of my brow. "Who did you see?"

"Your boss." She elbows me, almost causing the meatloaf sandwich to roll out of my hands. I grip the food tighter.

"Crew?" I ask with a glimmer of hope. "You saw Crew Benton?"

"I wish." She winks. "I made it with him before I was married. We did it in a photo booth in a

RISK   *Deborah Bladon*

restaurant in Times Square. Dirtiest sex I've ever had. The mouth on that man is wicked."

TMI, Gretel. That is way too much information about Crew Benton that I will never be able to erase from my memory now.

Since I don't want to hear any more details about what went happened in that photo booth, I ask the obvious question. "Was it Nolan that you saw?"

"Who saw Nolan?" Adley walks over and taps my shoulder. "Is he here?"

Gretel gives Adley a quick once over. "I'm Gretel Gallant. Are you Ellie's friend?"

"I'm Ellie's best friend." Adley touches the middle of my back. It's a signal we developed years ago for whenever our *bitch or bastard radar* signals when a person is bad news. "Adley York."

I look at Adley and wink. "Gretel is a Matiz customer. She's here with her daughter."

Adley glances at Leila, who has now wandered over to where the yogurt is. "It's good to meet you, Gretel. Are you wearing Matiz's Beach Blush lipstick?"

Gretel's entire face transforms with a genuine smile. Her eyes brighten and her cheeks redden. "You noticed? It's new for me. What do you think?"

"I think if Matiz is planning a promotional campaign for it, you're the model. Hands down."

I look at Adley. I can't tell if what she just said came from the heart or not. Regardless of its source, it made Gretel happy.

"Speaking of models," Gretel lowers her tone as she glances toward Leila. "I saw Nolan and Shelby Leon having a drink tonight."

I immediately see Adley's gaze drop to her phone. Her fingers skim over the screen. She's doing a search for Shelby Leon to see if it's indeed the woman who was having dinner with Nolan in Vegas. I already know that it's her. I heard her say her full name to the head of security when they arrived at Meadow to escort her out.

"I couldn't tell if it was business or pleasure." Gretel raises an eyebrow. "I'm guessing it was both. Matiz is looking for a model for the launch of some of their new products and Shelby would be perfect. Have you seen her cheekbones? I'd pay good money for those."

"You saw Shelby Leon in person?" Adley shrieks. "Oh my God, Gretel. You can't be serious. I don't believe it."

What the fuck? What the actual fuck is Adley doing?

Gretel grins with pride. "I saw her ten minutes ago."

"Where?" Adley doesn't look at me even though I'm staring intently at her.

"It was at Normand's," Gretel says casually as she glances at Leila.

"Normand's Pub?" Adley asks excitedly. "The place that is four blocks from here?"

"That's it." Gretel nods. "Left corner of the patio, small table, she's sitting with Nolan Black."

"She's my all-time model crush." Adley jumps in place, her hands clapping together. "Let's go, Ellie. I have to see her in person. This may be the only chance I ever get."

RISK　　　　　　　　　　　　　　　*Deborah Bladon*

"Hurry." Gretel gives my shoulder a push. "You better hurry and just for the record, if you two eat that trash on a regular basis, you'll never look like Shelby Leon and me. That's just a piece of friendly advice from one woman to another."

I shake my head as I walk away and head toward the check-out line. I stop before I reach it and pick up a candy bar just as I hear Adley tell Gretel her left eyebrow is larger than the right.

***

"If he were my boyfriend, Bean, I'd be at Normand's right now asking him what the fuck he's doing."

I fall in step beside Adley. As soon as we left the deli, she set off storming in the direction of Normand's Pub. I stood in place until she realized I wasn't next to her. By the time she walked back toward where I was, I'd made up my mind that I wasn't going anywhere near Normand's.

I told her as much. I appreciate the fact that she was able to get Gretel to tell her where Nolan is without being too obvious, but it doesn't change how I feel.

If I have to sneak around after a man, he's not the man for me. I did it with Tad. It was after we'd already broken up but it taught me that no man is worth that degree of stress. If Nolan chose to have a drink with Shelby tonight, that's his prerogative. Mine is to ask him about it and then end whatever's been going on between us.

He was the one who wanted us to be exclusive. If he can't hold up his end of the deal for more than a few days, I'm done.

"I'm not going to confront him while he's with her." I walk at a steady pace. "I'd rather eat dinner with you, get a good night's sleep and talk about it with him tomorrow."

She sighs. "He's going to tell you that Gretel was seeing things, Bean. He'll come up with a believable excuse. Men do that when they're caught doing messed up shit to a woman."

I stop and face her. "He can come up with any excuse he wants, Ad. That doesn't mean I'll believe him. He ended things with Shelby in front of me in Vegas. He's told me since that she meant nothing to him. If he's on a date with her tonight, I don't want to see him again."

I won't want to see him, but I'll have to. I work for him. This is the main reason why I had reservations about getting involved with him. It'll be uncomfortable and awkward now, just as it was with Tad when our relationship ended. I had to quit my job as security coordinator at his company, Darlux Media, because he made it impossible for me to work. I wasn't given notice of essential meetings. I couldn't make deadlines for reports because the dates were constantly changed. I was set up to fail and I did.

"I'll talk to him about it after work tomorrow. I can handle this and still keep my job." I'm not sure if I say it aloud to convince myself or Adley. It doesn't matter. By this time tomorrow, I'll be in the very same position I was in Las Vegas just a few months ago. I'll be working for a former lover and trying to hold onto a job I want and need.

Chapter 37

Nolan

"You know I'm not one for eavesdropping, Mr. Black, but I swear I heard you talking to someone on the phone just now about becoming a police officer." Eda stands in the doorway of my office. "Are you considering a career change?"

"If I were going to change careers at this point, I'd chase after your job, Eda."

She purses her lips as she surveys me over the frames of her glasses. "My job? Why is that?"

"You're paid five times as much as any other assistant in this organization, and you show up to work whenever you get the urge. You're late today." I look down at my watch. "Two hours late to be exact. You made it here just in time for your coffee break."

She smiles. "I have a good reason for being late today, sir."

"The reason better be Miller in marketing."

"Mr. Miller?" Her face flushes bright red. "I don't know what you're talking about."

"I had a meeting with Miller the other day. He brought up your legs three times, Eda and he's always hanging around your desk." I resist the urge to grin. "Why do you think I keep sending you to marketing? Your husband died more than four years ago. It's time to get back in the game."

She fans herself with her hand. "I did have coffee with Mr. Miller yesterday."

RISK   *Deborah Bladon*

"Coffee?" I arch a brow. "You two are moving at a snail's pace. If you weren't with Miller this morning, where were you?"

"I went to the airport."

I tilt my head, studying her face. She looks like she's about to burst. "Do you want me to ask why, Eda?"

"Yes." She nods vigorously.

Three of her four daughters live out of state. If one flew in for a visit, I'm giving Eda the week off. I'm not going to limit her time with her daughters. Since becoming a parent, I now understand why my assistant uses her allotted vacation days to spend when her kids are here. "Which one of your girls is here?"

"I haven't been called a girl since I got sacked in the Super Bowl back in seventy one," a deep voice says from behind her.

"Jersey?" I stand when I see him walk up behind Eda. "What the fuck are you doing here?"

"Watch the mouth, Rigs." He closes the distance between us before he pulls me into a warm hug. "Your granddad would take you to task for that language."

He's right. Jersey was my grandfather's closest friend for most of his life and is more like him than anyone I know. I never heard a curse word leave my grandfather's lips. He'd threaten to wash my mouth out with soap if he heard me doing it. "When I saw you in Vegas you didn't say anything about coming to New York. Is the family all right?"

"I'm back for a shotgun wedding." He steps back and rests his hands on my shoulders. "You're looking at an almost great-grandpa."

"Congratulations." I tap his chest. "Who's having a baby?"

"Caroline." He shakes his head, his deep blue eyes filling with tears. "Can you believe it? My sweet Caroline is going to be a mom."

"She'll be a great one." I bite back the urge to tear up too. My grandfather, Emmanuel Black, held May only twice before he suffered a fatal stroke. He would have been a defining force in her life. I wish every single day that she could have known him the way I did.

"That she will." He turns to look over his shoulder. "Janine called Eda to pick us up so we could surprise the kids. You're treating Eda well, aren't you?"

"I couldn't ask for a better boss, Wally." Eda leans against the doorjamb. "I'm still grateful that you and Janine got me this job."

"We may have got your foot in the door." He pulls back and reaches out to Eda. "You've kept it there."

She takes his hand and squeezes it. "You've kept my sister happy for most of her life. You're the best brother-in-law a woman could ever ask for. We're both lucky."

"That we are." He kisses the back of her hand. "Janine brought you a gift. She picked up a handbag at an auction. I don't get the appeal, but she's got one and said you'd love one too. That's a surprise, Eda, so don't blow it."

RISK   *Deborah Bladon*

"You just blew it." She drops his hand. "I'll act surprised. Janine spoils me."

"That's what big sisters are for." He turns back to me. "I got May something too."

"You got May something?" I scratch my chin. "You don't need to bring her a gift every time you're in the city."

"I do, Rigs."

I would never tell Wally he can't give my daughter a gift. He's an important part of her life. Since he moved to Vegas, we don't see him as often, but when he's in New York, he makes time to see May. He tells her stories about the great-grandfather she'll never know and answers her questions about whatever she's curious about that day. Their bond is special and important to my little girl.

"I was at a magic show on the strip and they had junior magic kits for sale." He chuckles. "The cape, top hat, magic wand, the whole nine yards. She's going to love it."

She will. It'll mean the world to her and her dream job will morph from artist to magician in the blink of an eye. I grab my jacket from the coatrack. "We can head over to see her now if you've got the time."

"I'm here until my great-grandchild arrives. I've got all the time in the world for May." He pats my cheek. "For you too, Rigs. You ever need anything, I'm here for you. Rain or shine; night or day."

Rain or shine. Night or day.

Those six words are what my grandfather said to me every time I saw him. Until the last time when he told me he loved me and that he was proud of the man I'd become.

***

"Tell me why you didn't want to meet at the shoebox, Ellie." I clench my hands together in front of me on the table. "This café is hopping for this time of night. I had no idea so many people drank coffee before bed."

"Maybe they aren't planning on going to bed," she shoots back with a straight face.

Apparently, we're not going to bed together tonight either. It was an easy conclusion to jump to after she called to ask me to meet her at this coffee shop less than a block from her place. I suggested the shoebox apartment, but she was adamant that it had to be here. I wanted to see her, so I jumped on board and walked over.

"What's going on?" I lean back in the solid wooden chair I sat in while I waited for her to arrive. I'd stood to greet her with a kiss, but she bypassed me completely. She headed straight for the counter and ordered herself a mug of hot fruity tea.

She blows on the steaming liquid, her tongue darting out to touch her top lip. If she's trying to remind me of what I'm not getting tonight, it's working.

"Ellie?" I prompt with a pat of my hand on the top of the table. "Is everything okay?"

She sets the mug down without taking a sip. "I'm not the jealous type, Nolan."

I am. I'm so fucking jealous that I spent much of my morning calling anyone I could think of who works for the NYPD. I was looking for someone that might be able to score Ellie a place in the Police Academy. I pulled up profiles on social media for three guys I haven't spoken to since high school, but who all wanted to be police officers. I struck out, three for three.

Foolish pride may be the driving force behind my actions, but I want to be the one to help her get her dream job. Sebastian Wolf is a homicide detective, and from what Kristof dug up, he's not well liked on the force. The guy has broken every rule in the book so if Ellie's hoping he'll be her ticket to securing a uniform; she's got a long wait ahead of her.

"I know you were with Shelby last night." Her voice is tinged with sadness.

Fuck. Just fuck.

I try to keep it together. My gut instinct is to accuse her of following me, but I want that. I want her to want me all to herself. I need Ellie to feel as compelled to know everything about me as I am to know everything about her.

"Gretel saw you," she offers, her chin high, her eyes focused on mine. "Adley and I were picking up dinner at a deli and Gretel was there getting snacks for Leila. She said you and Shelby were at Normand's Pub having a drink."

"Shelby had lemon water. I had a scotch, a double."

She stares at me for a minute, her eyes darting from my face to the mug of tea. "I don't care what

RISK   *Deborah Bladon*

either of you ordered. I care that you were there with her."

Somewhere inside of me I feel elation at knowing that. I feel hope seeing the pained expression on her face. It matters to her that I was with Shelby. What matters to me is that she understands why.

"I went out for a drink with Crew after May fell asleep."

"Gretel didn't mention seeing Crew and I'm pretty sure she would have if he were there." She shrugs. "She was specific when she said that she saw you and Shelby talking."

"Shelby showed up and Crew moved to another table so we could talk." I'm not going to try and hide what's going on. My intention after I spoke to Shelby last night was to talk to Ellie. I want her to know what Shelby said to me. I want her to understand before Shelby follows through on her threat to sell her story to the most popular gossip site on the internet. I told her to do it. I have no idea if she was serious but I want Ellie to hear Shelby's fucked up accusations from me, not read about them online.

"Talk about what, Nolan?" She asks incredulously, her hands shakily reaching for the mug.

I lean forward to stop her hands in place. I cover them with mine. I can't risk her burning herself, or me, when she hears what I'm about to say. "Shelby is pregnant, Ellie. She says the baby is mine."

Chapter 38

Ellie

This was not how this conversation went in any of the dozen scenarios I played over in my head since last night. Not once would I have guessed that they were sitting on that patio talking about a baby. He's going to have another child. This time with a supermodel who moonlights as a petty thief. Good for him. I don't want any part of this.

"I'm leaving." I try to stand, but his grip on my hands is too tight.

"You're going to sit here and let me explain, Ellie."

I've been waiting all day to talk to him. I went up to his office right after lunch to see if he was available, but Eda told me he'd left for the day. I was tempted to call him, but I wanted to respect his time with his daughter. Maybe he wasn't even with her. He was probably with Shelby picking the furniture for a new nursery.

"I don't need an explanation, Nolan." I move to the edge of the chair and tug my hands away from his. "What you had with Shelby was before we met. I understand that. I'm not leaving because I'm mad that she's pregnant. I'm leaving because you obviously have a lot on your plate that you need to deal with."

He pulls back, his right hand scrubs his forehead. "I don't blame you for wanting to bolt, but

RISK   *Deborah Bladon*

I'd like a chance to explain things. I want you to understand something very important."

I already know what the next words out of his mouth are going to be.

The new baby won't change anything between us.

I can handle a relationship with you and a co-parent arrangement with Shelby.

Let's meet at the shoebox tomorrow night at nine and celebrate that I'm going to be a dad again with a few hours of fucking.

I might be wrong about the last one but I know I'm right about the first two.

"I don't give a fuck if Shelby is pregnant." He squeezes his eyes shut for a second. "Don't get me wrong. I'm not a cruel bastard. I hope the best for her but that baby has nothing to do with me. There is no chance in hell I'm the father. No possible chance, Ellie."

Isn't that the tune every man sings when he's caught by the balls, literally, caught by the balls? "How can you know for sure you're not the father? When we were in Vegas, I heard you admit to sleeping with her twice. You know from experience it takes one time, just one time."

"It's not physically possible for me to be the father of that child." He looks around the café. "Do you understand what I'm saying, Ellie?"

"You're saying that you don't think the condom failed." I sigh heavily. Is he that dense? He's gone through this before. If any man should be aware of the slim chance that a condom can fail to deliver on its promise, it's Nolan Black. "You need to rethink

RISK   *Deborah Bladon*

the brand of condoms you're using or maybe you need a lesson on how to roll one on the right way."

I roll my fingers in the air for good measure.

"I'm perfectly capable of putting on a condom."

"Apparently you're not." I straighten my shoulders. "Condoms aren't foolproof, Nolan. Neither is the pill."

"Vasectomies are. I've had one, so there is zero chance the baby that Shelby is carrying is mine."

***

A vasectomy? He had one. He can't have another child, ever.

"Did you hear what I said, Ellie?"

I lift my head when he asks the question. I look at him. He's young. He's older than I am by a few years but he's not even thirty yet and he's made the decision not to have another child. Logically, I understand why but still it seems drastic for someone his age.

"Yes." I pick up the mug of tea. "You had a vasectomy."

It shouldn't bother me. It's not as if he just proposed marriage and then dropped that bombshell on me. We're dating. We had sex; very safe sex which is a plus I didn't know about until now. Still, it tugs at the corner of my heart to know that he can't ever be a dad again.

"Does it bother you?"

Why should it? We'll date for a while, and then he'll move on to someone new and I will too.

237

Eventually, I'll meet a guy I fall in love with and we'll get married and have kids.

"No." My voice is barely more than a whisper. "Maybe. I'm not sure."

He presses his lips together as he studies me. Then he licks them, quickly. "I had it done a week after May arrived. I didn't want to risk having another baby."

"Are you glad you did it?" I ask. "Do you think you'll ever regret it?"

He opens his mouth and then snaps it shut. He gazes across the café at a couple with a baby in a stroller. The baby is fussing. The mom and dad, taking turns handing it toys and a bottle filled with milk. "I'm glad I have May. She's the only child I want."

It's honest. It's also finite. A long term relationship with Nolan Black means no children of my own. I shake off the thought. "I guess I'm safe to assume that Shelby didn't know about it before last night."

"She didn't," he concurs. "I explained to her last night that she's barking up the wrong tree. She insisted that she'll still get a court order for my DNA to prove I'm the father. I told her to call my lawyer."

A child's life is being broken down into legal briefs and blood samples. That's not how I want it to be when I become a mom. I want my baby to feel loved and wanted. I want every second of my pregnancy to be filled with hope and promise.

"Tell me what you're thinking, Ellie. What's going through that beautiful mind?"

RISK   *Deborah Bladon*

"A million thoughts." I pick up the mug and then put it back on the table in the next breath. "It's a lot to take in."

"I know," he says firmly. "I didn't anticipate us having this conversation yet. I didn't know it would be this soon."

His words suggest that he was planning it at some point. He sees potential where I see nothing but utter confusion.

Do I keep dating a man who can never be a father to my children?

What happens if I fall in love with him and realize that having children of my own means more to me than he does?

"Do you see yourself having children one day, Ellie?"

I nod my head while a grin pulls at the corner of my lips. "I think so. It's a distant concept to me at this point, but I think one day I'd like to be a mom."

He takes a deep breath. "I understand if this changes things for you. I still want to see you, but if you need to walk away, I promise I'll only chase you for a few weeks."

I let out a laugh. I'm not sure if there's anything genuine in it or not. I'm also not convinced that ending this is the right thing for me. I like him. I like him so much that the thought of walking away from him, makes me pause.

What harm is there in seeing where this will go? If it gets too serious, I can stop and take a breath to think about what I want.

239

"I still want to see you," I reassure him. "No promises, Nolan. We need to take this day-by-day. Date-by-date."

"We can take this whatever way you want it, Ellie."

I pick up the mug of tea and take a sip. "I want it slow and steady."

"We're still talking about dating, right? You're not talking about…"

"No," I interrupt with a small smile. "I'm not talking about fucking. I'm talking about going home to my place and you going home to your apartment."

"So I can think about all the things I wish I were doing to you?" he whispers as he leans forward on the table.

So you can be there for your daughter if she wakes up. The only daughter you'll ever have.

I don't say it even though it's the only thing I can think about. Nolan Black comes with a ridiculous amount of baggage, yet I can't walk away. I know I should but somewhere deep inside me it feels like there's a link to him that is too strong to ignore.

Chapter 39

Ellie

"I'm the expert, Bean." Adley taps her fingers on her chest. "I'm your resident expert on vasectomies. Ask, and I shall answer."

I apply mascara to my lashes never once looking away from the mirror. "I don't have any questions."

"None?"

"One," I acquiesce when I turn to look at her in the doorway of the bathroom we share. "How exactly are you an expert on vasectomies?"

"We do them at work all the time." She spoons some cereal in her mouth.

"You neuter dogs at the vet clinic," I point out as I skim the edge of my fingernail under my bottom lashes to pick up a clump of the black mascara. "That's not the same as when a man has a vasectomy."

"It's close enough." She grimaces. "You're making more of a mess by trying to clean it up with your finger. You can't go to work at Matiz looking like a rank amateur."

I laugh. It's the first time I've laughed since I got home from the café last night. Adley was up watching an episode of her favorite sitcom when I walked through the door. I sat next to her eating cold microwave popcorn that she'd over salted, which she chuckled at every lame joke the actors exchanged.

241

I didn't bring up my conversation with Nolan until this morning because I wanted the night to think. I appreciate Adley's opinions but sometimes I have to give myself time to process things before I ask her to weigh in.

"I'll clean it up before I go in." I turn to the side and lean my hip against the yellowed laminate countertop. "Would you date a man who could never have a child?"

"He has a child." She taps the spoon against the side of the ceramic bowl. The sound that emanates from it punctuating what she just said. "He has a daughter. That means that if you two get serious, you'll be a stepmom to his kid and never a mom to your own kids."

I realize that. I've been thinking about it all night. "He had a good reason to have the vasectomy. I understand why he did it, but it's so final."

"Not necessarily." She steps into the bathroom, resting the empty bowl on the counter next to me. "A skilled surgeon can reverse a vasectomy. It doesn't always work but there's a good chance."

There's a good chance if the man wants that. Nolan made it clear that May is the only child he sees himself having. It sounded like a non-negotiable point to me. "I'm worrying way too much about this. I haven't known him for that long, Ad. We haven't been dating that long."

She picks up my hairbrush and taps it against her palm. "If that were true, you wouldn't look like you haven't slept a wink, Ellie. You like this guy and he just dropped a life bomb on you. It's okay to question if this is right for you. The more time you spend with him, the more chance you'll fall hard and then what will you do?"

"I'll cross that bridge if I get to it." I tug the brush away from her and run it through my hair. "I can have fun with Nolan and not fall hard. I know I can do that."

She moves so she's standing right behind me, her face peeking out over my shoulder in the mirror. "You're already falling for him. Watch your heart, Ellie. You only have one and it's already been broken."

***

"The heart on your palm is more heart shaped than the last one." I gesture toward his left hand. "Your daughter has some major talent."

He smiles as he flips his hand over revealing his colorful palm. "She cracked open the entire marker package this morning and immortalized Barney on my hand. I didn't have the heart to wash it off before I came in."

I don't think I would have either if any of my nieces did that to my hand. Not only is there a heart drawn in blue ink near his thumb, there's also a pink square shaped happy face with two triangles on top that I assume are ears. On each of his fingertips are letters written in a kaleidoscope of colors. B A R N E.

"She ran out of space for the Y?" I ask with a grin.

"May's determined." He wiggles the index finger of his right hand in front of me. "Here's the Y."

"How's she doing?" I look over at where Eda is shuffling through a pile of magazines. She was the one who came down to the store to tell me that Crew wanted to see me. Once I got up to the floor where the executive offices are, I spoke to him about my update on employee theft and when I turned to leave his office, Nolan was waiting for me.

"She's coming to terms with Barney's death." He motions to the two chairs in front of his desk. "We can sit if you have the time."

I'm on his dime right now, so I make the time. I sit and cross my legs while he shoots Eda a look. She scurries out of his office, the door clicking shut quietly behind her.

"I thought about you all night, Ellie." He lowers into the chair next to me. "I know that you didn't expect to hear what I told you last night. It had to have been a shock to you."

"It was." I sigh with a faint shake of my head. "I don't know what I expected you to say about Shelby. I never thought you'd tell me that May is the only child you'll ever want."

"Until I saw May I didn't want any children," he confesses. His hand grips the arm of the chair. "Once I saw her I knew that my heart didn't have room for another. It's May for me."

I don't know what my heart has room for. Maybe it's a foster child. Maybe it's a son I'll have with the man I marry. Maybe it's a girl named May who belongs to a man I can't stop thinking about.

"I want you to meet her, Ellie." He leans back in the chair, his shoe tapping on the floor. "I'm not going to push you to do it soon, but you'll like her.

She'll like you. When you're ready, you just give me the word and I'll set it up."

I smile with a silent nod of my chin. I'm not ready. I'm not sure when I'll be but I am one hundred percent sure that I'm not ready to walk away from Nolan just yet.

RISK   *Deborah Bladon*

Chapter 40

Nolan

"I had no idea you still owned this place."
Crew stands in the foyer of the apartment Ellie coined
as my shoebox. I didn't share that tidbit with him. I
won't. That's something that I want to exist between
only Ellie and me.

"He gave it to me on my twenty-first birthday.
I can't sell it."

I don't have to define who *he* is. Crew knows.
My grandfather handed me the keys to this apartment
the day I turned twenty-one. I didn't appreciate it at
the time. I thanked him but not in the way I should
have. I knew the gift was coming. He'd given my
sister, Sarah, a one bedroom in Chelsea on her
twenty-first birthday. It was two years prior to the day
I got my keys. I hugged him, looked at the views and
then took off to hit a string of bars with my friends.

I christened the place later that night with a
woman I can't remember. I nailed her on the foyer
floor. Our clothes were a twisted mess as we went at
each other while we were both still riding the high of
the tray of tequila shots we'd shared.

The day after my birthday I ordered furniture
and equipped the apartment with all the essentials.
The piano arrived a month later. It belonged to my
grandmother when she was alive. She wanted me to
learn to play. I never have.

246

RISK   *Deborah Bladon*

"You can sell it." Crew walks to the windows and stares out at the view. "You'd make some nice coin on this, pal. We can use my new listing agent. She's got her finger on the pulse of the market. She'll get you top dollar and have it sold in a week."

"I'm not selling." I run my fingers along the keys of the piano. The sound is rough and out of tune. "I want this place to stay in the family."

"You think May is going to want to live here when she's a grown-up?"

"It's an option." I push back the mental image of my daughter as an adult. I can't think about it. The concept is so far-fetched that it's out of my reach. "If she doesn't want it, maybe one day her kids will."

"Emmanuel would be fine with you selling it." He looks up at the high ceilings. "You made memories here. Life moves on, Nolan. He'd get that."

He might. I don't know that for sure.

When he handed me the keys, he told me to make the most of it. He brought me the framed pictures of our sailboat. It was the boat he'd purchased for the two of us when I was May's age. I learned how to rig the sails by watching him and when I could finally do it myself, he called me a true sailor and gave me the name Rigs. I loved the name almost as much as I loved the man.

We hung those pictures in the hall together. His eyes watered when I told him I'd never move them from that spot and I haven't. I can't. His hands touched the frames as I stood back eyeing them so he could level them.

"The apartment stays as is," I say with a dismissive wave. "I need to grab some things from

247

the office. Once I do that, we can get those beers you promised me."

"You've got a deal. If you need help, let me know."

I turn to leave the room, my eyes catching on the couch and something shiny wedged between two of the cushions. I walk over and tug it free. It's a pendant attached to a thin gold chain. It's Ellie's. She was wearing this the first night we came here.

Earlier today when she was in my office she had a string of fake pearls around her neck. She'd fingered them as we talked about last night. I wanted to invite her out for a late dinner, but her body language said it all. She needs time to digest the fact that I've made the conscious choice to never have another child. It may be a deal breaker for her. If it is, I have to accept it. I chase the thought away with a shake of my head.

"Who does that belong to?" Crew eyes the necklace.

"Ellie," I say under my breath as I hold his gaze. "I've brought her here a few times."

"You're inching closer to taking her home to May. You still think that's a good idea?"

I pinch the bridge of my nose. I don't know what to think anymore. Ellie is young and ambitious. She wants to be a police officer, and eventually a mom. Her life plan is carved out in her mind and I doubt like hell it includes a man with a kid who refuses to have another.

The chime of my phone saves me from trying to piece together an answer to Crew's question. I read the text message that pops up on the screen.

"I need to bail on those beers, Crew."

"Mayday?" he asks as he stalks the room toward the apartment door. "Let's go. I'll get an Uber."

"May's fine," I say as I tuck the necklace in the front pocket of my jeans. "I'm meeting Ellie."

"You're ditching me for her?" He blinks, a smile ghosting his mouth.

I look down at the screen of my phone and the next message that pops up. "I'm meeting her for half a burger in thirty minutes."

"You want me to grab the stuff you need from the office here and drop it by your place later?"

"It's just some pictures of me and my grandfather. I want to show May what I looked like at her age."

"She's going to love those." He opens the door to the apartment. "I'll head home."

I move past him and wait until the door shuts behind us both. "Are you good with sitting in on that marketing meeting in the morning? Miller needs to step it up. I want eyes on him as he presents his new ideas to the team."

"I'll be there." He walks ahead of me, pushing the call button as we reach the elevator. "I need to say one thing, pal. This is it, and I'll shut the fuck up about it forever."

I shrug. "Go ahead. Say it."

"Don't lose sight of the big picture. May is your priority. She just lost old Barney. Don't set her up for another loss."

"That little girl is my world." I step aside when the doors to the elevator open and a woman steps out. "I'd step in front of a train for her. You know that."

"I do." He motions for me to get on the lift first. "You may not see it right now but you'd step in front of a train for Ellie too. Think about whether she'd be willing to do the same for you."

Chapter 41

Ellie

"Move." I fist the material on the front of Nolan's T-shirt giving it a firm tug. It's solid enough that he can't help but take a heavy step in my direction "Get out of the way! Now!"

"What the hell?" he mutters under his breath as a man on a bicycle whizzes past him.

"Slow down," I call after him. "You're going to kill someone."

He flips me the bird without turning back to look at either one of us.

"That's not permitted," I huff as I look past where Nolan is standing to make sure there isn't another reckless cyclist on their way. "You can't ride on the sidewalk unless you're a child. He's not a child. He's a fucking asshole."

I scream that last sentence in the hope that the light wind picks up my voice so the cyclist can hear me. I know he can't though. He's likely weaving around the pedestrians crowding Eighth Avenue by now.

"Are you all right?" I run my hand over his chest to smooth away the wrinkles on his shirt. "You definitely feel all right."

He grins before he leans down to kiss my forehead. "I just had the pleasure of being rescued by the beautiful Ellie Madden. I've never felt better."

"I didn't rescue you," I argue with a pout. "I gave you a heads-up."

"You tore my shirt," he challenges. "It's a small price to pay so don't mistake it for a complaint."

I study the front of his shirt. It's worn. The logo that used to be emblazoned across the front has faded. There's a small hole in the center, but I doubt I made it. "This shirt has seen better days. Since when do you dress like this?"

"You're saying you don't like how I'm dressed?"

I love how he's dressed. The T-shirt is the same color as his eyes. The jeans he's wearing are faded to perfection. He's wearing polished black shoes which look completely out of place yet perfect at the same time. "I never said that."

"So you like this look?"

"I don't mind it," I acquiesce. "It's the laid back version of you."

"Is this the laid back version of you?"

I look down at the white shorts and pink blouse I'm wearing. "It's semi laid back. I had a date before I called you."

He glares at me, the entire expression on his face shifting instantly. "We only date each other, Ellie. Please tell me you haven't forgotten that."

Of course not. We haven't discussed it since he brought the subject up in his office. That was before I knew about May or his vasectomy. I could argue that those life changing realizations void our agreement, but they don't. I promised him exclusivity. I intend to keep that promise until it's no longer what I want or until he tells me the same.

RISK   *Deborah Bladon*

"I went to Queens for a playdate with my nieces."

I see the relief wash over his face. His shoulders relax and the tightness in his jaw disappears. "You have nieces?"

"Three of them," I admit. "I haven't seen them since I've been back in the city, so I went to Queens and hung out with them."

"How old are they?" He glances over his shoulder before his gaze settles back on me.

"The twins are seven and their sister is six."

"Twins?" he chuckles with a swipe of his hand across his brow. "Are they identical?"

I nod. "They are, but I can tell them apart. Aunties have ways of doing that."

"I've heard that." He straightens, his arms crossing over his chest. "What about the rest of your family? Can any of them tell them apart?"

"I don't have any other family. My parents aren't here anymore." I shift on my feet. "They're both gone. They're dead."

"I'm sorry, Ellie." He reaches for my hand. I let him take it. "I didn't know."

That surprises me. With all the information he's known about me, I'm shocked that he didn't uncover the truth about my mom and my dad.

"Do you want to talk about what happened to them?"

It's the question I always dread. It's not easy to answer. My mom died from cancer. Her inattention to her own health was her death sentence. She felt ill one morning and by the time the doctor at the free clinic by our apartment in Boston was done his

253

examination the news was grim and she was on her way to the hospital in an ambulance.

A week later the news was worse. They gave her three months to live but her will was lost in the hospital room when a doctor she'd never met before told her that the cancer that had started in her lungs had overtaken her body.

That was when my dad came from New York City. They talked and cried, and then hours later she died. Life changed then and again on a cold winter evening when my dad, weakened from his addiction to anything that could numb the pain, died in a park in Manhattan, while I waited for him on a bench less than a mile away. He never came and my life was never the same.

"We don't have to talk about it tonight, Ellie." Nolan's voice breaks through my thoughts. "I'll order us a burger, two fries and a bottle of water. You can have the butter cookies this time."

I swallow. I want him to know about my parents but the words aren't there. "We'll split the cookies."

"Not tonight," he says under his breath. "You just saved my life. I owe you, Ellie. The cookies are just the start of my repaying you for that."

***

"We're even." I crawl across my bed, looking back at where he's sitting. "You can stop, Nolan. Please stop. We're even."

He wipes his lips against his shoulder as he reaches out to grab me. "We are not even close to being even. Sit on my face, Ellie."

"Oh my God." I try to pull my leg free of his hand. "I came twice already. You don't need to do it again."

"I do." He grazes his fingers over my calf. "I love it, Ellie. I fucking love the taste of you and those sounds you make. If you'd let me, I'd record the audio of you coming on my phone so I can listen to it when I jack off in the shower."

"No." I laugh as I shake my head. "No recordings. I don't want those surfacing after we break up. I'll never live it down."

"Stop," he hisses as he moves up me. He grabs my waist flipping me over until I'm beneath him. "Don't talk about this being over. You don't fucking know how I feel, Ellie."

I chuckle. "I know exactly how you feel. Your cock is hard. It's going to crush my thigh."

"I'm falling, Ellie." He rests his forehead against my cheek. "I'm falling so hard."

My chest tightens. It's the sex that's driving his words. We kissed on the street after we ate the burgers and he fed me the cookie. When I asked him to my place, he flagged down a taxi and held tight to my hand until we closed my bedroom door and stripped.

"Don't." I push against his chest. "Don't say it unless it's real."

He moves so his hands are bracketing my face as he stares down at me. "It's real. What I feel is so fucking real that it scares me but I crave it. I need it. I need you, Ellie."

I need him too. It's not just the sex and the fun. It's more. When I'm around him I feel my heart binding to his in a way it never did with Tad or any man I've ever dated. This is more. This is real and I'm terrified that if it ends, I'll never get over him.

"I want you to make love to me," I whisper into the still air between us. "I've never had that. I want you to show me what it's like."

He bites his bottom lip as his throat works on a deep swallow. "I've never had that either. I never wanted it until now."

I watch in silence as he rips open the condom package he brought with him. He sheathes himself before he leans down to kiss me tenderly. "Let me fall for you, Ellie. Let me show you what you mean to me."

RISK   *Deborah Bladon*

Chapter 42

Nolan

"I think I fell in love last night."

Eda stops in place right in front of my desk, the cup of coffee in her hand shaking. "You what, sir?"

"Sit." I point at the chairs in front of my desk. "Have a sip of that coffee. You look like you could use it."

She lowers herself into one of the chairs. "This is your coffee. I bring you coffee every morning."

"Why?" I rest my elbows on my desk. "It's not part of your job description."

"I bring you coffee because you send me flowers every second Friday." She takes a sip of the steaming liquid. "You think I don't know it's you, but I do."

"Before Harold died he asked me to arrange a flower delivery for you every second Friday of the month for a year. It was important to him, so I continued the tradition."

She absorbs that, her eyes a clear window into her emotion. "He started doing it when we first married. Back then, it was a bouquet made up of flowers he'd pick from other people's gardens on his way home from work. The professional arrangements came years later, but it was always every second Friday, no matter the season."

257

RISK   *Deborah Bladon*

"I'll stop when you tell me to stop," I half lie. I'll tone it back to one delivery a month if she asks me to stop but I'll never give it up completely. I see her gazing at the elevator when she knows a delivery is coming. She waits and as soon as it arrives, she packs up her desk, takes the flowers and leaves for the day.

"I won't tell you that." She rests the coffee mug on the corner of my desk. "Did you say you fell in love last night, sir?"

"I think I did, yes."

"You think you did?" She tilts her head to the side, her eyes scanning my face. "You're not sure if you did?"

"No." I exhale sharply. "I don't know if I fell or not."

"It's not typically like a cliff, Mr. Black." She teeters on the edge of the chair. "It's not often that one just falls in love in an instant and is completely aware of it. It takes time."

"How much time?"

She scratches her nose, her finger pushing on the frame of her glasses. "It depends. How long did it take the last time you fell in love?"

"There isn't a last time," I respond quickly. "I'm a novice at this, Eda. This is my first time at the rodeo."

"Miss Madden is a lovely first love."

"She is." I scrub my hand over the back of my neck.

She studies me. "The first time she came to the office and you sent me to marketing I knew there was something special about her."

RISK *Deborah Bladon*

That doesn't surprise me. Eda anticipates everything before it happens. She's the one who told me darker shades of lipstick would be the big ticket items last fall. She was right. She's also the person who warned me that Shelby was trouble when she showed up at my office unannounced. That's how we met. She marched into my life because she wanted to be the face of the summer line. I took her to bed instead, not heeding any of Eda's words.

"Don't try and make sense of falling in love, sir." She picks up the mug and stands. "Just enjoy it. Let your heart feel what it wants to and trust that Miss Madden feels the same about you."

I do trust it. I saw it last night when I made love to Ellie and she clung to me for an hour after. It was there in her eyes when she kissed me goodnight and held my face in her hands. She's falling in love with me too and I'll do everything in my power to make certain that doesn't change.

***

"The background check brought up nothing on a sibling." Crew keeps his eyes trained on where Ellie is standing next to the entrance of the store. "The information Kristof pulled listed Ellie's mother's name and her date of death. He found nothing about her father or a sibling."

"I had no idea her father was dead or that she even knew him." I stiffen as I survey the area near the skin care creams. "I wasn't surprised when she told me about her mother's passing. I wasn't prepared when she brought up her nieces."

"I'll call Kristof right now and get a new file on Ellie." He taps my forearm. "I'll get him to dig deeper. Any questions you still have will be answered."

"I don't want that." I look at him. "If I have a question, I'll ask Ellie myself."

"Ask me what?"

I turn at the sound of Ellie's voice. Her eyes dart between Crew and I before she finally settles on me. I wait a beat before I say anything. "Ask if you're free for dinner tonight."

"Not tonight." She shakes off the question with a two-word reply and a shrug of her shoulder. "I keep forgetting to ask if you've seen a necklace. I lost one. I usually keep it in my shoebox but I thought it might be in yours."

"Shoebox?" Crew huffs out a laugh. "You two are already at the cute code talk stage which means I'm out of here."

Ellie watches as he walks away. "The necklace isn't expensive, but it does mean something to me. I'm pissed that I didn't get the clasp fixed before it broke."

"It's being fixed as we speak." I tuck her hair behind her ear. "I found it at the shoebox yesterday. I was going to give it to you last night but it slipped my mind. I noticed the broken clasp this morning so I sent it to a jeweler in Chelsea. She does excellent work."

"You're kind of perfect." She tosses me a smile. "I'm sorry about tonight but I promised Adley we'd go to a movie."

Her devotion to her best friend is admirable. It's also annoying, but I'm learning that Ellie isn't the type of woman to alter her life for anyone.

"I'll hang out with May." I lean in to kiss her forehead. "Shoot me a text before you go to sleep."

"So I can talk dirty to you?"

"So you can text dirty to me," I correct her with a smug smile.

"Deal." She reaches for my hand and brings it to her mouth. She closes her eyes before she brushes her lips across my fingertips. "Keep your phone close, Nolan. You never know when I'll get the urge to message you."

I watch as she walks away, the swell of her ass under the tight red pencil skirt she's wearing moves with every step she takes.

My phone chimes. I look down at the screen and the message from Ellie.

You're so busy staring at my ass that you haven't noticed the woman standing behind you staring at your ass. I can't say I blame her.

I look up to see Ellie disappear into the stock room, her back straight, her focus forward.

I debate whether to turn but I do. I pivot on my heel and face the woman who apparently is checking me out.

"Nolan Black," she says my name before I register that I've never seen her before. She's petite with long dark hair and a tailored white suit. "I'm Thea Morgan. I'm representing Shelby Leon. We can do this the easy way or you can make it hard. I'm open to either approach."

RISK *Deborah Bladon*

Somewhere in there is a reference to my cock. I can tell by the way she's checking out the outline of my erection through my pants. I have Ellie's ass to thank for that, which I will do, personally as soon as possible.

"My eyes are up here." I tap my nose. "My lawyer is across town. He's the one you should be speaking with."

She slides her gaze up my frame until her eyes are locked with mine. "My office is half way between here and there and I have a press conference scheduled there in an hour with Shelby by my side. I thought you might want to discuss terms before that happens."

"The only thing I want to discuss is how misinformed you are." I tense. "My lawyer has undeniable proof that I am not the father of Ms. Leon's baby. If my name is brought into this in a public manner, there will be repercussions."

"I'll postpone until I review what your attorney has." Her gaze darts quickly around the store. "I use Matiz products. I have to tell you I've never used anything better."

I nod. I'm not opening my mouth to acknowledge the compliment. I don't trust her.

"This is completely off the record, but I'm available." She wiggles her bare left hand in the air. "My divorce was finalized last month and Shelby mentioned that you helped her forget about her ex. If you're interested, I'm free tonight. Say at seven? No strings. Unless you're into that because I'm open to trying anything."

262

It's been awhile since a woman threw herself at me this way, but I'm not catching. I'm not even in the fucking ballpark anymore.

"I'm not interested."

"I should mention that I'm double jointed and I was a backup for the Olympic Gymnastics Team eight years ago."

It's impressive but not for the reasons she's going for. "I'm involved with someone. I have no interest in continuing this discussion with you. If you have anything else to say to me, bring it up with my lawyer."

Her cheeks flush as she bows her head. "Fine but the offer is still open. I can do things on a set of uneven bars that will make your head spin."

I arch a brow. "There isn't a man alive who is worth this. Don't beg for it. Never beg for it."

"I'm not begging," she huffs out a laugh. "I was offering."

"I declined." I glance at Ellie. She's back from the stock room and now in deep conversation with another security guard. "Twice. There is nothing you can say that will make me change my mind."

"I guess it's my loss and her gain."

"Who?" I turn back to look at her.

"The woman you can't take your eyes off of." She gazes at Ellie. "You look at her the way my husband used to look at me. Ex…my ex-husband."

"I'll let my lawyer know that he should expect your call and I expect never to see you again." I take a step toward the door. "Tell Shelby I wish her well but she needs to let go. I'll never be a part of her life."

Chapter 43

Ellie

"I have an interview with the NYPD next Friday." I lick the ice cream that's dripping down my finger. "I wanted to give you a heads-up since technically you're sort of my boss."

"No sort of about it, Ellie." Nolan leans forward to run his tongue over the path mine just took. "I'm your boss, and I want you to get that job."

"It's not for the academy." I hand him the cone and the last bit of melting cookie dough ice cream that's left in it. "I'll be working an administrative job, but it's still an in. It would be a big deal to me to get my foot in the door like that."

"I admire you." He places the cone into a glass decorative bowl on the coffee table. "You go after what you want."

"You do the same." I grin at him. "I don't think that bowl is meant for ice cream. It looks like a piece of art."

He glances to the side, his eyes skimming the bowl. "It looks like a piece of art that's holding a melting ice cream cone now."

I survey the space around us. I've never been to the shoebox when there's been sunlight filtering through the windows. It's Saturday afternoon and when he called to tell me that May had a playdate with a friend and he was free, I jumped at the chance to see him.

We shared a sandwich on the patio of an upscale restaurant on the Upper East Side. Then we rode the subway to Cremza and finally we raced back here to the shoebox, trying desperately to eat our shared cone before it all melted under the sweltering heat of late summer.

"The paintings in here are originals, aren't they?"

His eyes stay focused on my face. "Both are originals, yes. They belong to my mom."

"Your mom trusts you with those?"

He furrows his brow. "What's that supposed to mean? My mom thinks I'm very trustworthy."

"What's she like?" I pop my feet up to the couch, wrapping my arms around my bare knees. "What's your dad like? I've seen pictures of them online but I'd like to know what they're like."

"Let's see." He crosses his long legs as he leans back against the leather. "My mom is an angel. She's as smart as a whip and beautiful. She loves my sister and me unconditionally. We can't do wrong in her eyes."

"She sounds amazing," I mutter. "What about him? Your dad?"

"Ernest Black is what you imagine every grandpa should be." His brows rise. "He's kind but tough. He'll take you to task if you cross him but he'll give you a hug with his next breath. He's the best businessman I've ever known. He has insight that I'll never possess. He taught me everything I know about Matiz before he retired and fucked off to Europe with my mom."

"They come back here, though, right?" I question. I read an article about Nolan's parents online. It said that they own homes on several continents but make a point of coming back to New York a few times a year.

"They show up when they want." He chuckles. "Usually at my place in the middle of the night. I have a bedroom for them there."

"It sounds like you're close to them."

"They're the best people I know." He taps his chest. "They've always stood by me. They love May fiercely. I couldn't ask for better parents."

It's what I always imagined a family should be. What I always wanted for myself.

"You'll meet them when they come home." He reaches for my hand. "I want you to meet them."

I don't point out the obvious elephant in the room. I haven't even met his daughter yet and every time we're together I think about that.

"I have a picture of my folks in the office." He drops my hand and stands. "You mentioned seeing a photograph of them, but I have one of when they first met. I'm going to get it framed for their anniversary. I'll grab it and show you. You'll get a kick out of the clothes they're wearing."

I can only nod as he takes off down the hallway. With every piece of himself that he exposes to me, I feel the weight of the imbalance between us. He's taking a risk by sharing his life with me. I need to start taking risks too.

***

RISK   *Deborah Bladon*

Ten minutes pass before I finally get up to see where he is. I hear his voice just as I round the corner into the home office. His back is to me. The chair behind the desk swiveled so he can look out at the city.

"May, you know that monkeys don't live in apartments," he says with a sigh into his phone. "When I said we would think about a new pet, I didn't mean a monkey."

I smile to myself. His voice is softer as he speaks to his daughter, the tone less abrasive. There's patience in his words as well as hints of happiness.

"I don't know what a monkey eats. I doubt that it's banana pancakes though."

I stifle a laugh with a swallow. My gaze falls to the open drawer of a filing cabinet. Dozens of pictures sit atop the cabinet and in the drawer. I pick up one. It's of two small children, a boy, and a girl. I study their faces, trying to find Nolan in the boy but his hair is a few shades lighter and longer. The girl is pretty. There's a ribbon tied into her long blonde hair.

"No, May. Bunk beds are not made for girls and their monkeys. Whoever told you that was pulling your leg."

I pick up one of the photographs. It's a small print of a man and a teenage boy with sun-streaked hair standing next to a docked sailboat. The boy is clinging tightly to the man's hand, the smiles on both their faces a testament to their love of each other. This had to be Nolan. The man is old enough to be his grandfather. This is his family. The pictures and memories and the phone call he's engrossed in are all parts of a life that I want a place in.

"I didn't mean that they grabbed your leg and pulled on it. It's a saying, sweetheart. I'll explain it to you when I get home," he murmurs. The amusement in his words is clear. "I'm visiting with my friend right now. I'll be home in a couple of hours."

I place the picture back with the others, my eyes lingering on the young boy's face while I finger the necklace around my neck. It's the one Nolan had fixed for me. He gave it back to me earlier and smiled when I told him it had been a Christmas gift from Adley.

"Yes, I'll make you pancakes for dinner. I need to go, sweetheart. I love you."

He waits for a breath before he ends the call.

I shuffle my sandals against the hardwood floor hoping the sound will be enough to turn his chair. It does.

"Ellie?" His smile is as warm as his tone. "I was gone for so long you must have wondered if I fell off a cliff."

"A cliff?" I lean toward him, my hands resting on the wall behind him. "Is that what happened?"

"Yes, that's exactly what happened."

I look for some understanding in his eyes, but there's nothing but calmness and contentment.

"If you heard any of that you know that my daughter wants a monkey." He pushes the chair back from the desk and stands. "She's persuasive but she can't win this battle."

"You sound so sure of that."

He scratches the light growth of beard on his jaw. "I'm good with another dog. A cat is fine. I'll get

RISK   *Deborah Bladon*

her an enormous aquarium for an entire school of goldfish but a monkey isn't moving in."

"A monkey who sleeps in a bunk bed and eats pancakes is pretty special," I say through a laugh. "I'd pay money to see that."

"I'll take you to the circus." He stalks toward me. "Only if you promise you'll stay away from the clowns."

"That's the second time you've brought up clowns," I point out as I gaze up into his face. "Are you as scared of them as you are of spiders?"

"Not scared." He leans down until his eyes are level with mine. "I don't like clowns. I don't want you to like clowns either."

"You can't tell me what I can like, Nolan." I feign a frown that quickly turns into a grin. "I might really like clowns."

"You might." He narrows his gaze. "You like me more though."

I like him more than most things. "Maybe."

"No maybes." He pushes his hands on the wall, so his arms bracket me. "Tell me what else you like, Ellie."

I know what he expects me to say. He thinks I'll tell him that I like his mouth, or his hands or his beautiful cock. I do but that's not what I want. I want something else.

"I like pancakes. I'd like to have pancakes for dinner."

His throat works on a large swallow. He blinks his eyes to chase something back. His voice has a rasp when he finally speaks. "You're sure? You're very sure, Ellie?"

"I'm positive," I say because I am. "I want to go home and change my clothes. After that, I want to come to your real apartment and have pancakes with you and May."

"Thank you," he says in a whisper before he kisses me. "Thank you for this."

Chapter 44

Ellie

I stand at the entrance to his building. I'm late. I promised him I'd be at his apartment door by five o'clock, but I had no idea what to wear. Adley wasn't around to offer her advice, so I tried on several different outfits before finally deciding on a pair of jeans rolled up at the ankles and an oversized light blue T-shirt knotted at my hip. It doesn't show too much skin. That's the look I was going for.

"Ms. Madden?"

I turn at the sound of a male voice saying my name. I know it's not Nolan. His voice is deeper with a clear timbre. This voice is higher. There's a pretense of something regal there.

"Hi, Dino," I say after glancing at his name tag. The only reference I have for how to speak to a doorman is my encounters with the man who worked in the building where Tad's condo was in Vegas. Paul was his name, and when he wasn't busy rushing to help the residents in and out of taxis, Ubers or their chauffeur driven cars, he was doing card tricks on the small desk he stood guard by.

My greeting takes Dino by surprise. He takes a step back and smiles. "Mr. Black told me to expect the most beautiful redhead in the world. He wasn't kidding."

Since Dino is cashing a paycheck partially funded by Nolan, I take the compliment with a grain of salt. "You're kind. I'm late. I should get up there I guess."

"It's your first time meeting Miss May, isn't it?"

The question is too personal, but it's welcome. I need a pep talk before I meet Nolan's daughter and since Adley was nowhere to be found, Dino is second best. "Yes. Do I look nervous?"

He holds his index finger and thumb an inch apart in the air. "Just a wee bit."

I suck in a deep breath and push my shoulders back.

"She's the sweetest girl you'll ever meet." He marches over to his desk near a bank of elevators. "She drew me this picture just this afternoon."

I look down at the sheet of white paper that's decorated with a tall semi-rectangular building, a stick figure wearing a large square hat and another figure next to it with enormous ears on the side of its head. "It's adorable."

"This is our building." He points out as his hand glides over the paper. "This is me in the hat and that's Montgomery, the monkey Miss May wants to adopt."

I giggle. "I heard about the monkey."

"If you smile like that, you'll win her heart." He moves to press the elevator call button. "They're on the top floor. Penthouse One. Just knock on the door and he'll be waiting."

"Thank you." I squeeze his forearm through his perfectly pressed uniform just as the elevator doors fly open.

RISK   *Deborah Bladon*

***

"Wow," I whisper under my breath when he swings open the door to his apartment.

It's not the view of the city that's visible on the far wall. It's not even the polished marble floors. It's him. Nolan is standing directly in front of me. A small girl with long blonde hair is next to him. They both smile at me and when they do the pink headbands sporting bunny ears sitting atop their heads move slightly in sync with each other. The fact that they're both wearing jeans and white T-shirts only adds to how perfect they are together.

"It's her." The little girl jumps up and down. "Daddy, is this her?"

He scoops her up easily with one arm. She leans her hands on his shoulder. "This is Daddy's friend Ellie. You should invite her in, May."

She nods and takes a deep breath. She mumbles something under her breath before she speaks, loudly and slowly. "Would you like to come in, Ellie?"

I stare at her. She's incredible. Her eyes are a rich shade of brown, her nose a perfect small replica of Nolan's. As she turns to look at him, I catch her profile. There's no denying she's his daughter. I see it in her smile.

"I brought you something, May," I say as I step inside. "I picked it up on my way over. That's why I was late."

"You're not late." She reaches for Nolan's wrist and looks at his watch.

"You can tell time?" I ask, trying not to sound surprised.

"Not yet." She shakes her head slightly, her bunny ears moving as she does. "Daddy is teaching me about the big hand and the little hand. He says no digital nine cents May."

She lowers her voice slightly as she tries to mimic Nolan.

"Nonsense, May," Nolan corrects her with a kiss on her cheek.

I reach into my pocket and pull out the small box that I asked the clerk at the store to wrap with a pink ribbon. "I hope you like this, May."

"I will. Presents are my favorite." She reaches her small hand toward me. "Thank you, Ellie."

I hand her the box and watch while she delicately unwraps the ribbon. She pulls open the box before her hand jumps to cover her mouth.

"Monkey earrings," she screams. "Daddy, look!"

Nolan shoots me a look that says that I'll pay for the gift later. I wiggle my brows.

She makes quick work of the packaging, pulling out both the clip-on earrings in the shape of a monkey's head. Nolan holds the packaging in one hand while he balances her in his arm.

"This one is for Daddy." She carefully clips the earring on his left ear, taking extra time to adjust it correctly. She softly kisses his cheek before she clips the other to her right ear.

"They're pretty, Ellie." She looks at Nolan. "Is she safety, Daddy? Can I hug her?"

"She's safe," he says quietly with a dip of his chin and an arch of his brow.

I answer the silent question he poses to me. "I'd love a hug, May."

Chapter 45

Nolan

"It's not L E, May." I write Ellie's name out on a piece of white paper sitting on my lap. "It's Ellie. See the letters I wrote here?"

May scoots out of Ellie's lap and crawls across the couch to land in mine. "Oh, Daddy. I see."

I look over at Ellie's colorful palm. May ran to her bedroom to get her markers as soon as we'd finished our pancakes. She set to work on Ellie's palm, drawing a picture of a monkey, a star and finishing it with Ellie's name written as it sounds, L E.

"It was a good guess, May." Ellie smiles at her. "It sounds like it's just an L and an E."

"My name has three letters," May announces proudly. "Daddy is teaching me the letters, so when I go to school, I'll be the smartie."

"I think you're great at writing the letters and drawing pictures."

May beams at Ellie's words. "I can draw you a picture of me. I'll get more paper."

With that, she bounces out of my lap and heads down the hallway toward her bedroom.

"You're fucking amazing," I whisper across the couch to Ellie. "She's crazy about you. I am too."

Her eyes light up. "She's a beautiful little girl, Nolan."

RISK   *Deborah Bladon*

I was fishing for an '*I'm crazy about you too, Nolan*,' but my apparently my bait game isn't strong enough.

"Do you need anything, sir," Tilde, one of May's nannies, comes out from the kitchen. "My shift ends in thirty minutes. I've prepped a bedtime snack for May. You'll find that in the refrigerator. She had tidied her room before you arrived home earlier. I think that's everything."

"You're free to go." I glance at Ellie before I turn back to Tilde. "I'm taking May to a museum tomorrow so I won't need you until four. You can let the staff know they have the morning off."

Ellie shifts uncomfortably in her seat. I was worried when she didn't arrive at five. By the time my watch signaled its daily alarm at five thirty I was convinced she wouldn't show. I was resigned to eating alone with May at six, as I do most days, but then the light tapping on the door erased all my doubt.

"Karen is here for the night." Tilde picks up an empty glass from the coffee table. "Enjoy your evening."

I watch Ellie as Tilde walks away. She follows her every step, not turning back to me until Tilde is out of sight.

"Tell me what you're thinking." I inch closer to her. "You look so serious. Something is going on in that head of yours."

She looks down at her hands in her lap. "It's a lot to take in. This apartment, your staff, May. It's so much, Nolan."

I know it is. Even though I was the one who cooked the pancakes, the chef I'd hired to prepare meals for May and I stood nearby. One of my housekeeping staff swooped in to clear the dishes even though I've asked them repeatedly not to do that. I want my daughter to take on more chores. Loading the dishes into the dishwasher is a task that May enjoys. The silverware is off limits for now, until she's old enough to understand safe handling of the forks and knives.

"It's just May and me that you need to worry about," I reassure her quietly. "You came here to see us. She's having a great time, Ellie. I want you to have fun too."

"I found some paper," May exclaims as she races around the corner from the hallway. "I'll draw you a picture of me that you can take home."

Ellie smiles as May climbs back into her lap. "That's the best gift in the world. I'll keep it forever."

***

"May will be asleep in a couple of hours, Ellie." I rest my hands on her shoulders. "I can give you the key for the shoebox and you can hang out there."

She looks over to where Dino is standing guard at his desk. "It's been a long day, Nolan. A great day but I'm exhausted. I think I should head home for the night."

I don't want that. It's not just because I'm aching to be inside her again. I want time alone with her after what happened today. She met my daughter. She stepped willingly into my life and didn't run in the opposite direction.

RISK *Deborah Bladon*

She hugged May as she was leaving my apartment. May hugged her back, tightly. She kissed Ellie on the cheek and told her that she hoped they could be friends. Ellie nodded because the emotion she was feeling was too much. I saw the tears beading in the corners of her eyes. I saw her knees shake as she crouched down to hold May close.

"You can rest at the shoebox until I get there."

"Until you get there?" She grins. "What will happen when you get there?"

"I can draw you a picture on your hand." I whip a purple marker out of my back pocket. "May didn't touch your right hand, so there's plenty of room for me to draw my…"

"Dino will hear you if you say cock." She leans close, her voice no more than a whisper.

"Dino's hearing isn't what it used to be." I pull her to my chest. "Besides, you like talking about my cock."

"No," she says with a laugh. "You talk about it way more than I do."

"That might be true but you think about it more than I do."

"I thought about it this morning," she admits as she kisses my cheek. "I've come twice today already, so I'm good."

"My cock wasn't involved in either of those," I point out. "I want in, literally, Elle, I want in."

She taps her finger on her chin. "I suppose I could go over the practice interview for the NYPD I found online while I wait for you."

"There's that fucking spirit I was looking for."

"You mean fighting spirit, Nolan. The expression is fighting spirit and it doesn't apply here."

"I meant fucking spirit."

"Because we'll be fucking?"

I nod. "That's the spirit."

She glances behind me. "Dino heard that. He's looking over here."

"That's because you're stunning." I kiss her lips softly. "I'll be at the shoebox by ten, Ellie."

She takes my key fob when I offer it. "I'll go there and nude study. I might order pizza."

I love when she teases me. I hope that she's teasing me. "Don't let the pizza delivery guy see you naked."

"You're the only man who sees me naked." She pops up to her tiptoes to wrap her arms around my neck. "I like it that way."

I love it that way, and I never want it to change.

Chapter 46

Ellie

"I had no idea that nude pizza was a thing." He pushes his jeans down his legs. "We should do this every Saturday night."

"I'm game." I take a bite of the large cheese pizza I ordered thirty minutes ago. "I hope you like plain cheese. It's my favorite."

"Mine too." He sits on the edge of the bed in his boxer briefs. "It's not technically nude pizza unless we're both totally naked, right?"

I look down at my pale pink bra and panties. I had taken off everything right after the pizza was delivered, but that only lasted three minutes. I pulled my bra and panties back on as I waited for Nolan to arrive.

"I'm a messy eater and I don't want any hot sauce to burn my nipples."

His eyes fall to my bra and the outline of my nipples. "If I haven't told you yet, your nipples are incredible, Ellie. They're pink and puffy and when I suck on them, they get so hard like they're aching for more."

"You make me feel really beautiful."

"You are a stunning woman." His fingers brush over my chin, tilting my head up to his. "I crave you. It's not just your body but all of you. Your mind and your spirit. There's this thing about you, Ellie. It's this sense of goodness that just is in the air whenever you're near. I feel it. I know other people can too. I just want to soak in that and in you."

I lean forward to cup his cheeks in my hands. "You have that too, Nolan. That sense of goodness. I felt it when I first met you. You protect the people you care about and you care about people you don't even know."

His eyes close for a beat. "I haven't always been a good person."

"You are now." I kiss him softly. "The past is the past. What matters is right now and you're a great dad and a wonderful lover and a pretty good boss."

He huffs out a deep laugh. "I'm a pretty good boss? I'm a fucking fantastic boss."

I kiss him again, harder this time, my tongue skimming over his bottom lip. "You were right. Your employees do bitch about you when you're not around."

"Tell me who." His arms circle me pulling me close. "Tell me their names and I'll fire every last one of them."

I gasp when he opens the clasp of my bra with one hand. "If I tell you all their names there won't be anyone left working for you."

He smiles against my mouth, his breath mingling with mine, his teeth brushing against my bottom lip. "Make me forget all of them, Ellie. Make me forget everyone in the world but you."

***

His mouth eats at mine, his tongue pulling, taking, making me want even more than he's already

RISK   *Deborah Bladon*

given me. He fucked me once on the bed before we took a shower together.

I took him in my mouth as the hot water beat down on us both. He was so close, but he stopped me, yanking me to my feet so he could finger my pussy. I came in the small space; his name stuck on my lips behind the moan that I couldn't contain.

"Safe," I groan into the kiss. "Are you safe?"

"You know I am," he growls. "I was tested last week. You're safe too."

He told me he wanted to fuck me without a condom when we were in the shower but I silenced him with a bite to his shoulder. He surged then, pushing two fingers into me while his thumb strummed over my swollen clit.

"Fuck me bare," I whisper with a smile against his lips. "Come inside of me. I want to feel it."

"Christ." He pushes me against the bedroom wall, lifting me up. "I've never done it."

"Never," I say breathlessly. "I'll be the first?"

"The first," he repeats as he moves his hands to cradle my ass. "My first bare fuck. The first woman I've ever loved."

I close my eyes to ward off the tears.

He loves me. I love him.

He thrusts hard, the entire length of him driving into me. I gasp as I claw at his shoulders, my legs wrapped around him, my back pressed against the wall.

"Jesus, this feels like heaven." His lips are on my neck. "You feel like my heaven."

I cling to him as he drives into me with long hard strokes. My back thumps against the wall, each of his groans shooting right through me to my core.

"I'm going to come so hard. This is way too fucking good." He clenches his jaw, his neck taut as he increases the tempo. The sensation of feeling him like this, inside me, raw and exposed is almost too much to bear.

"It's too good," I cry out. "So good."

He bores into me with solid thrusts, his mouth on my neck, on my cheek, his lips fluttering over my mine. "Take it, Ellie. Feel it. This is all yours."

"Mine," I repeat back. "You're mine."

"You better fucking believe it," he grunts as he digs his hands into my ass and fucks me, each stroke a promise; a pleasure filled vow that he belongs to me and I am his.

Chapter 47

Ellie

"You like cold pizza?" I scrunch my nose. "I would heat it up in the microwave."

"Las Vegas softened you." He takes another bite. "Real New Yorkers are good with eating cold pizza. Try it."

"I'm full." I lick my bottom lip. "I have to go soon."

"Where?" He tugs his T-shirt back over his head. "It's midnight. You're not going anywhere but home."

"That's exactly where I'm going." I slip my feet back into my sandals. "You should get home and I need to do the same."

"You liked her, right?"

I push my hair back behind my shoulders. "She's like a little princess. I really like her, Nolan. I'm glad I came over today."

"You'll come back." It's not a question. It doesn't need to be. He knows that I lost part of my heart back in his real apartment this afternoon. It's hard not to fall instantly in love with a little girl like May.

"I will. I'd love to spend more time with her."

"After you left she told me that I was lucky." He sighs. "I asked her why."

"Why?" I question with the hope that it's because of me. I want her to like me. A few days ago

I wasn't sure I wanted to know her, and now I want her approval. I want her to understand how important her dad is to me.

"She told me I was lucky because my best friend is better than her best friend."

"Are you May's best friend?"

"I wear clip-on earrings and get my toe nails painted. Of course I'm her best friend."

I glance down at his toenails. Two of them are painted bright orange. The surrounding skin is the same hue. "What color is that?"

"It's hideous."

I chuckle. "I was asking what shade of Matiz nail polish that is."

"A shade that will never be sold in any of our stores again. I'm pulling it tomorrow. My toes look like fucking pumpkins."

"You're such a good dad." I close the top of the pizza box. "Can I take this with me or do you want it?"

"I like that you think I'm a good dad. It's my goal to be the best at that I can be." He looks down at where my hand is resting on the box. "Are you going to eat that for breakfast tomorrow? If you are, don't put it near a microwave. You'll ruin it."

"No. I'm going to give it to a man who lives on the corner."

His fingers trace over the pizza place's logo on the front of the box. "You like helping people, don't you? You were going to give all those pastries from the conference room away too."

RISK   *Deborah Bladon*

His words aren't meant to make me feel uncomfortable, but they do. "I don't like wasting food."

He lifts a brow. "That's admirable and very responsible. There's some fruit in the refrigerator I bought the other day for you. You can take that for him too."

"I will." I smile softly. "Thank you, Nolan."

"I'll walk you out." He picks up the pizza box from the nightstand. "Text me once you're home so I know you made it safely."

"I can do that."

"You will do that."

I want to do that. I like the protectiveness. It makes me feel safe, even if I can defend myself with one hand tied behind my back. "I'll see you at work on Monday?"

"Unless you want to hang out with May and me tomorrow." He takes a step back. "She'd love to see you again."

"Thanks for the offer but I'm going to lay low tomorrow." I need some time to absorb everything that's happened today. I feel like I woke up with one life and I'm going to sleep with another, better, happier life. "Pajamas and Netflix for me."

"I wish I could join in on that." His voice is quiet. "I will one day."

He will. It won't be tomorrow or the next day, but I want it someday. I'm sure about that.

287

Chapter 48

Nolan

I told her I loved her last night. I was seconds away from being buried balls deep in her when I said it, but it left my lips. She heard it. Her body told me she did. She didn't say it back, and now I know why. Now I fucking know why she didn't say a goddamn word to me when I confessed what I felt.

"Daddy, that's Ellie."

Dammit.

I thought I could steer May out of here without her seeing what I'm seeing. It stopped me dead in my tracks when I walked through the door of this candy store.

A goddamn candy store.

On a Sunday afternoon.

Who meets their lover here? Who holds hands in a store filled with children?

I stare at where they're seated at a small table. Ellie's hand is wrapped in his. It's lost in there. Her eyes are staring at his face. The smile on her lips is a tribute to how much she's enjoying whatever the fuck she's doing right now.

"Ellie!" May screams her name loud enough that everyone in the place turns to look at us, including Ellie. She tugs her hand from his instantly, her eyes a window to the surprise she's feeling.

"May," she calls out, her voice cracking. "What are you doing here?"

RISK *Deborah Bladon*

What the fuck are you doing here, Ellie? What the fuck is he doing here?

I don't say a thing because I don't trust myself right now. I can't guarantee that I won't say something that will damage my daughter's perception of me, so I say nothing.

May rushes over to Ellie and reaches in for a hug. I follow, wanting to pull her back. I don't want to see them together like this. I don't want yesterday to be a mistake.

"Who are you?" May extends her hand toward him after she lets go of Ellie. "I'm May."

"Wolf," he replies with a smile and a brief shake of May's hand. "I'm a friend of Ellie's."

"Wow. Wow. Wow." May steps closer to him, her eyes skirting over his forearms and the elaborate tattoos on display. "You're way better at drawing than me."

"Drawing?" he asks with a chuckle. "What does that mean?"

I feel Ellie's eyes on me but I ignore her. I can't look at her. I don't know what she's doing but it's obvious this isn't pajamas and movies at home. The lemonades on the table and the open candy bar they're apparently sharing make this a date in my book.

May flips her hand over to show Wolf the picture of a monkey she drew on her palm this morning. "I draw like this and you draw like that."

He laughs. "Mine are a little different than yours are."

"Way different." She looks back at me before she takes another step closer to Wolf. "Is your name really Wolf?"

289

"It's Liam Wolf," he explains. "My friends call me Wolf."

"Can I be your friend?"

"We need to go, May." I tug on her shoulders. "Let's get your candy so we're not late for the museum."

She reaches for my wrist, her gaze scurrying over my watch. "We have until the little hand is at the two, Daddy."

"We're going now." I grab her hand. "Let's leave Ellie and her friend alone."

"Nolan," Ellie says my name softly as she stands. "Can I speak to you outside for a second?"

"No." I turn and look her in the eye. I see something there. It might be sadness or regret. It's definitely not guilt. "I'm spending the day with my daughter. If you have something to say to me, you can make an appointment with my assistant this week."

"You're serious?"

"Dead serious," I pull both words across my tongue slowly with an edge of anger. "Eda will handle any further correspondence between us."

"You're jumping to conclusions that are wrong." Her bottom lip quivers. "You have to know that. You must feel it."

"I want some candy hearts, Daddy." May tugs at my hand. "Let's get them before the little hand is at the two."

"I feel nothing." I pivot toward the line of people waiting to place an order. There's a burning pain in the center of my chest. "Let's go, May."

I don't turn back when I hear her tell Wolf she has to go. I keep my composure when she brushes

290

RISK   *Deborah Bladon*

past me as she heads out of the store. I do everything I can to smile when May tells me that today is the best day ever. It's not. It's one of the worst days of my life.

***

"Miss Madden called again to ask for an appointment to speak with you, sir." Eda stands in the doorway to my office. "Do you want me to continue to tell her that your schedule is full?"

"Yes." I look up from my desk. "I don't want to see her or speak to her."

"She's been up here three times today, Mr. Black." She pulls the pencil from behind her ear and twirls it between her fingers. "She can see right in here. She knows you're sitting in your office doing nothing."

"I'm working, Eda."

"You're staring into space." She taps the pencil on the edge of the doorjamb. "You're also wearing a monkey earring, sir."

I reach up and yank the earring from my lobe. "Thank you for pointing that out."

She rubs her hand over her face before cupping her chin. "Can I say something?"

"I'm not going to stop you."

"I don't know what happened between the two of you, but I do know that Miss Madden wants a chance to fix it."

"Some things can't be fixed."

"What happened, sir? I realize that this steps outside the boundary of boss and assistant but I have

291

a strong shoulder. I've counseled four daughters through the ups and downs of relationships."

I'm tempted to tell her. I've been avoiding everyone but May for four days. I dodged Crew's questions by telling him that I'm focused on the spring product line. I cut a phone call with my mom short when I told her that May needed me to read a story to her even though my daughter was fast asleep. I can't talk about it because it pisses me off. I gave her a part of me and she fucking threw it back in my face.

"I don't want to discuss it. Miss Madden made a choice. This is the result."

She takes a measured step closer to my desk. "You also made a choice when you started a relationship with her. Ending it with silence is brutal. Mr. Miller is doing that to me now."

"Miller is ghosting you?"

"Like Casper, sir."

"Get him in here so I can fire his ass."

"I just told you he's not accepting my calls or text messages, Mr. Black. How can I get him to come to see you?"

"Good point. I'm ignoring her because I don't know what to say to her, Eda." I don't. I don't want what I have with Ellie it to be over. I also don't want to give my heart to a woman who is spreading her love around.

"Anything you say is better than not saying a word." She shoves the pencil back behind her ear. "Trust me on that."

She may be right but I know there's nothing I could say or Ellie could do to change what I saw on Sunday afternoon.

Chapter 49

Ellie

"Four fucking days." I throw my phone on my bed. "What a complete ass. He's an ass, isn't he?"

"An asshole." Adley twirls her finger in the air. "You forgot the hole at the end of ass. He's an asshole."

He's not; not really. He's hurt. He saw something on Sunday and jumped to a conclusion that resulted in him diving inside a cocoon to protect his heart. Logically, I know that. Emotionally, I'm pissed as hell at him for ignoring me all week.

"His assistant told me he was busy and I could see him not ten feet away in his office counting the tiles on the ceiling."

"I wouldn't do it, Bean." She plops herself on her back on my bed, narrowly missing my phone. "I would tell the jerk to go to hell, and I'd move on."

I wish it were that easy. He told me he loved me and I felt the same thing. I didn't say it and I doubt it would matter at this point whether I did or not.

He saw me in a candy store holding hands with Wolf when I told him I was spending the day at home. I passed on time with him and May. He has to be thinking about all of that.

There's no way he could have known that I ran into Wolf when I went to the store to buy May a candy necklace. They were my favorite treat when I was a kid and I wanted to surprise her by taking one to their apartment. I had no idea Wolf's sister owns the store and he'd be there helping her out.

"You should have just told him on the spot why you were with Wolf." She bobs her foot up and down. "I don't understand why you didn't."

"May was standing right there." I sit on the edge of the bed. "I couldn't talk about it in front of her. It's a heavy topic. She's just a little girl."

"I forgot about the daughter." She scrunches her nose. "You were right to hold back, Bean. He was wrong to assume that you're boning Wolf."

"We were holding hands." I hold up both my hands in mock defense. "I know you're going to say that it's not an excuse for the way he's treating me. I agree completely but he thinks it means more than it does."

"It means that a kind man was consoling you. That's all it means." She cuts her hand through the air like a knife. "Nolan walked into that store at the exact second Wolf was comforting you. If his ego got knocked out of whack because of that, it's his problem."

"I thought about explaining things in a text or an email but I want to tell Nolan in person. I'm not wrong for doing that, am I?"

"It's not the kind of thing you just throw in a text, Bean." She half-shrugs. "You're not wrong for wanting to do it in person. I'm with you on that."

"What would you do if you were me?" I lay on my back next to her. "Seriously, Ad. Don't say what you think I want to hear. Tell me what you would do if you loved a man and he was ignoring you."

"You love him?" She rolls on her stomach. "Did you say you love him, Ellie?"

"Yes." I turn to look at her face. "He loves me too. He said it."

"Well, shit." She stiffens. "This changes everything."

"How does it change everything?"

"You fight for love." She smashes her fist into the blanket. "You defend it at all costs."

I look up at the ceiling. "How do you fight for something you're not even sure the other person understands?"

"You lost me."

I trace the outline of the light fixture with my eyes. "What if the person you want to fight for doesn't understand what love is? If you love someone, do you ignore them? Is that what love is?"

She rests her head against her hand. "I know this feels like what Tad did to you all over again, Ellie. I don't know Nolan very well, but he's a hell of a lot better than Tad."

I thought so too until a day passed and he hadn't returned any of my calls. Then another day passed and by yesterday I started to feel everything I felt when Tad stopped talking to me.

"When I called Nolan's assistant this afternoon, I promised myself it was the last time." I reach for my phone. "I'm not going to crawl after him forever. I tried. If he thinks I'm capable of cheating on him, maybe he's not the man for me."

"Maybe we need to turn our phones off and take a sick day tomorrow."

"I have an interview with the NYPD tomorrow," I point out.

"That's in the morning." She pops up to her knees. "Tomorrow afternoon the two of us are taking the train to Boston for the weekend."

"You want to go away for the entire weekend?" I stare at her. We haven't been to Boston together in years. "You can just leave work for two whole days?"

"I'm not on call this weekend." She palms her phone. "Dr. Hunt hasn't even asked for my number yet. I mean for his personal use. He has it if he needs me to hold down a dog while he cleans out its ears."

"Romance has to start somewhere, Ad."

"Maybe in Boston?" She looks around my room. "Pack some bikinis, Bean. We are hitting Beantown tomorrow afternoon."

"We don't need bikinis to go to Boston." I scoot to my feet. "I'm not walking the streets in next to nothing."

"You wouldn't get one complaint."

"You're ridiculous." I slap her shoulder. "You're also the best. This weekend will be fun, right?"

"This weekend will be bananas and I'm not talking the kind that monkeys like."

Monkeys.

I look across my room to where I'd pinned the picture May drew for me to the wall. It's her, Nolan, a monkey and me. As much as I wanted that to me my life just a few days ago, I can't have it. What I can have is time away with my best friend in Boston.

RISK   *Deborah Bladon*

Chapter 50

Nolan

"Can I help you?" That sounded about as civil as it's going to considering who I said it to.

"I'm looking for Ellie Madden." He scans the area behind me where a group of women has gathered around a new lipstick display. "She works here, right?"

"Who's asking?" It's an empty question. I know who he is. Tad Darling in all his fucked up, suntanned skin, blond haired, bastard glory is standing in front of me.

He gives me a once over, his eye catching on my wrist. "You rocking a Rolex, man?"

He's not. I take some perverse pleasure in that. "I am."

"Nice." He leans in close. Too close. I can feel his breath on my bare forearm. "You work here?"

"I own the place."

I don't look like I do at the moment. I was at home with May counting sheep. Literally, counting sheep in a picture book.

When Kristof called to tell me Tad had landed in New York and was headed straight for Matiz, I took off out the door. I didn't bother to change out of the jeans and concert T-shirt I'm wearing. I have no fucking idea how a T-shirt from the farewell concert tour of a boyband ended up hanging in my closet, but I put it on this morning.

297

This is what happens when I'm walking around in an Ellie Madden daze. I pledge my allegiance to five grown men who dance in sync to songs from the nineties.

"You're a fan of them too, hey?" He points to the T-shirt.

I'm burning this fucking thing as soon as I'm home.

"Why do you want to talk to Ellie?" I check the area behind him to see if Ellie is in sight.

"I'm her fiancé." He puts too much emphasis on that last syllable. So much so that he sounds like he's trying to fake a French accent.

Fucking douche.

"I'm her boyfriend," I begin as I tap my shoe on the floor, "I'd say we have a problem."

"Boyfriend?" he huffs out a laugh. "She didn't waste a minute, did she?"

"What do you want?" I cross my arms. I think I'm her boyfriend. I don't know what I saw going down between her and Wolf, but I know what I heard in her voice this morning when I finally listened to the six voicemail messages she's left me since Sunday. They're just friends she whispered into the phone on a sob. I want to believe her. I want to believe that now more than ever.

He mirrors my pose. "I want to speak to my fiancée."

"Your ex-fiancée," I correct him. "What do you want to speak to her about?"

"Things that are none of your business." He widens his stance. "I have something personal to

RISK   *Deborah Bladon*

discuss with Ellie. This has nothing to do with you, Crew."

"It's Nolan. Nolan Black," I correct him.

"Crew Benton owns this store," he quips with a grin. "I read that on the company website. You trying to pass yourself off as the owner, Noel?"

"Nolan," I draw out my name on my lips as I mentally note that I need to put someone other than Crew in charge of website design. "I am the owner of Matiz, and I'm Ellie's boyfriend. Two facts you'd do well to remember."

"Where is she?" His gaze darts around the store. "I'm only in town a few hours. I came to New York just to see Ellie."

"You're looking for Ellie?" Verna, one of the security guards, stops as she passes us. "Ellie took a few days off. She blew out of town for a girls' weekend. I wish I could have gone with."

I bite back the urge to ask where the hell Ellie took off to but I don't give Tad the satisfaction.

"Shit," he mumbles under his breath as Verna walks away. "This fucks up everything."

"Looks like you missed your chance." I blow out a breath with the realization that I might have missed mine too. "If we're done, the exit is the same as the entrance. It's right behind you."

"I don't get why she'd go to Boston," he mutters. "There's nothing left for her there."

"There's nothing left for you here." I point at the door. "Ellie's moved on. If you have a legal matter to discuss with her, I'll give you my attorney's name."

"It's not a legal issue." He shakes off my words with a jerk of his chin. "We settled months

299

ago. She gave it all away. Every penny I gave her went to charity. She'd give her last dollar to a beggar on the street."

"She'd do everything in her power to help anyone who needed it," I correct him. It doesn't shock me that Ellie helped other people instead of herself. "There's nothing left for you two to discuss so why are you here?"

"It's her sister's birthday today."

Sister? Ellie has a sister?

Tad examines my face. "I loved her. Whatever she told you about me, I loved her. I fucked it up. If I knew I had a chance to get her back, I'd take it. I'd give it everything."

I don't want to hear it. He broke her heart. I'm fucking breaking her heart right now. The last thing I want is to be like this clown.

"She's no good to the world on this day." His jaw tightens. "I'd have to hold her up to help her get through this day every single year we were together. Says a hell of a lot that she's not looking to you to give her that."

"Hold her up? Why?" I ask without thinking or planning or giving a fuck what he thinks.

I see the flash of satisfaction in his eyes when he realizes he holds a prize that I don't. My watch or my store or my goddamn misplaced sense of entitlement as someone important to Ellie doesn't matter right now. He knows something about the woman I love that I don't have a fucking clue about. "Ellie planned a trip to France for her sister's birthday five years ago. She worked two jobs while going to school to save for it."

RISK   *Deborah Bladon*

"They never went?" I shrug my shoulders. I doubt like hell Ellie would fall apart over a canceled trip. It explains her knowledge of French, though. She must have studied in anticipation of the trip. I can take her. I can take her and her sister and her nieces and May too. I can make this right. I can make us right again.

"Her sister died three months before the trip."

Died? Jesus Christ. Ellie's lost so much.

When I don't say anything, Tad goes on. "She's always blamed herself even though there was nothing she could have done."

"Why would she blame herself?" I can't honestly believe I'm asking Ellie's ex-fiancé anything about her, but he's willing to provide it, so I'm taking full advantage.

He glances at one of the sales associates as she tosses him an eager grin. "Ellie got shot the day her sister died. She saved that baby's life and she thinks it cost her sister her life."

Chapter 51

Ellie

I glance out the hotel window at the lights of downtown Boston. I haven't been here in years. I grew up here, made friends here and then when my mom died, my dad came from New York with his daughter to get me. She was my half-sister, and by the time she died, she was my sister, in every sense of the word.

"Annie's birthday is today," I whisper.

"I know." Adley hugs me from behind. "I ordered a small chocolate cake from room service. We're going to sing Happy Birthday in French for her."

I bow my head. "She'd like that but I can't do it."

"She would love it and you will do it." She rests her index finger against the glass. "Remember the first time the three of us came here together? You ran up every flight of stairs in that building over there to prove to yourself that you were fit enough to be a police officer."

I smile. "I am fit enough, but that's not all they consider."

She smooths her hand over my hair. "They have so many applicants that only a small percentage of people sneak through. You'll have an advantage after today. It sounds like you nailed your interview."

RISK   *Deborah Bladon*

I did. I'm confident that I'll get the job. I went into the office with all of my knowledge of the law and my experience to back me up. It's a temporary administrative position but it's something. I'll need to give up my job at Matiz if I'm offered this job, but I can deal with the cut in pay. I have some savings to fall back on and thankfully we live in a rent controlled building. I'll thank Crew for that when I tell him that I've accepted a new position with the NYPD.

"I know that you don't want to talk about the advice that Wolf gave you the other day, but did it help?"

I gaze out at the city and the moon beyond the skyline. "He's a grief counselor, so he understands loss better than anyone I've ever talked to. He told me that there's no time limit for mourning."

"That's true," she murmurs. "Everyone is different."

"I told him about Annie as soon as he explained what he does for a living. I asked him if he gets that a lot."

"I bet he does."

I turn to look at her. "He said that he loves helping people and he believes that talking about death can help celebrate life."

She moves so she's sitting next to me. "What else did Wolf say?"

"I told him about Paris." I feel the tears sting my eyes before I feel the lump in my throat. "He thinks it might be helpful for me to go one year on her birthday. I told him that I couldn't do that."

"Because you feel guilty?"

I drop my gaze to my lap as tears stream down my face. "Yes. It was Annie's dream to go. If I go now, I'll feel bad that she's not with me."

"Her heart was selfless, Bean." She reaches for my hand. "She'd want you to go. She'd want you to forgive yourself too. Annie would tell you that she didn't die because of you."

Adley was almost as close to Annie as I was. After our father had died, Adley's family took us both in. They nurtured us and included us in every Christmas, Fourth of July and Thanksgiving celebration.

They sat in the front pew when I walked Annie down the aisle on the day of her wedding. They came to the hospital when Annie had her twins and then again eighteen months later when she added another baby girl to her family.

They were also there, beside me, when we said goodbye to my sister. They held me at the funeral and helped to guide me through my life since.

I wipe the tears from my cheeks. "I wish I wouldn't have left her alone that morning, Ad. When I stopped by her place and she told me she had a headache, I agreed when she asked me to get her some ibuprofen from the pharmacy. If I had stayed with her instead, I would have known. She would still be alive."

"Ellie," she says my name soothingly. "The doctor told us that it was so fast. Even if you would have been right beside her, it was too late. You couldn't have changed anything. No one could have."

I push my hair from my face. "I don't believe that."

RISK   *Deborah Bladon*

"I'll tell you what I believe." Her eyes search mine. "I think fate put you in that store that day so you could save that baby. That was your destiny that morning."

"That means that Annie's destiny that day was to die?" I whimper. "How is that fair?"

"Life isn't fair." She touches my cheek. "One life was lost that day and one was spared. We don't get to decide who pulls what straw."

A light knock at the door draws both our eyes across the room.

"That's Annie's birthday cake." Adley taps my knee. "We're going to sing Happy Birthday in French to our big sister and then we're going to spend the weekend remembering her together."

"Okay." I nod. "I'll try for Annie."

"That's all she would have wanted, Bean."

***

"What's my favorite Las Vegas security guard doing in Manhattan on a sunny Sunday evening?"

I turn at the sound of his voice. That voice. It's a voice I'd recognize anywhere. "Jersey?"

"Ellie, it is you." He pulls me into a warm embrace. "I thought I was seeing things."

I feel the same way. I've been back in New York all of an hour and I've already seen a billboard with Shelby's face in Times Square and now a much kinder face in person. I take a step back to look at him. "Why are you here?"

305

"My daughter's getting married." He runs his fingers through his short gray hair. "Caroline. I told you about her, remember?"

I remember everything about Caroline, including the fact that she's Jersey's oldest daughter. "Congratulations. When's the wedding?"

"A week from today." He stomps his foot on the sidewalk. "Janine wanted to get here to help with the wedding planning. By help, I mean take over but she's the mother-of- the- bride so it's expected, right?"

"It's tradition for the mother-of-the-bride to run the show." I think that it is. That's what I've seen on television and in the movies.

"Why aren't you in Vegas? Are you taking a vacation?" His eyes light up.

"I live here now." I beam. "Things didn't work out for in Vegas so I moved back here."

He winks. "Janine is thinking the same thing. She wants us back here permanently before our great-grandchild arrives."

"Great-grandchild?" My lips twist into a smile. "Is Caroline going to be a mom?"

"You bet." He claps his hands together. "She's taking the fast track. A wedding and a baby all before the end of the year."

"I'm happy for all of you." I grab his forearm. "You're going to be an incredible great-grandpa."

"That I will. I'll do my best."

"I'm meeting someone." I glance down at my watch, realizing that I'm late for my informal meeting with the woman who runs a church mission here in Midtown. I'm going to volunteer there every Saturday morning. I have the time and doing good will help me

RISK   *Deborah Bladon*

focus on moving on from Nolan. I haven't heard anything from him in a week. "I better run."

He cranes his neck so he can see my watch too. "I'm meeting someone too. Two special someones."

"Caroline and her baby?" I rub my tummy as I giggle.

He laughs. "A friend and his baby. Technically, she's not a baby. May is five now. I'm taking her to see that new musical for kids. It's her first Broadway show and I get to be her escort."

"I know a five-year-old May," I say quietly. "May Black?"

I glance up the street to where Nolan and May are approaching, their hands held tightly together, her hair bouncing as she skips along beside him. She's wearing a red lined cape over her pink dress and a top hat. The magic wand in her hand is circling the air. I feel an urge to excuse myself and walk away before they get here, but the need to stay is stronger. "Yes. May Black."

"So you know her dad? Rigs?"

My eyes slide over Nolan as he nears.

I've only ever heard the name from Annie's lips and read his name in her journals after her death.

I saw him from a distance once as he sat on a park bench with my sister.

He had a sandwich for her in one hand and a toy for our dog in his other. He kept watch over my sister when we had nowhere to go. He gave her a safe place to be herself when she felt she didn't belong. He didn't care that she was so shy that she could barely speak or that she feared most people.

307

He befriended her. He cared for her and when her life was threatened, he protected her.

I should have known. I should have felt it.

He's Rigs. Nolan Black is Rigs.

Chapter 52

Nolan

It's the best fucking mirage I've ever seen. Technically, it's the only one I've ever seen. It's also the only one I ever want to see. Ellie Madden is standing next to Jersey on the corner of Fifty Second and Broadway in the same spot I met Kip.

They were talking like they were old friends until Ellie looked my way and saw my face. She has to see everything I'm feeling in my expression. She must know that I regret every single thing that's happened since I walked into that candy store.

I went to see Liam. I called him after I got his number from his brother, and he invited me to his office. The office where he sits with people who've lost those that they love. He counsels them and helps them deal with their sorrow.

That's why she was there at the candy store with him. She was trying to cope. She wanted this year to be different so that she wouldn't feel the breath-stealing pain that she feels every year on her sister's birthday.

Liam didn't tell me shit about any of this. He couldn't. He explained about confidentiality and friendship.

I had to piece it together myself based on what Tad told me and that sadness that's always there in Ellie's eyes. I spent the weekend uncovering every detail I could about the day that Ellie's sister died. I read the newspaper clippings about the shooting and then I called in a favor from the anchor at one of the local news stations and he found the archived footage of the news report from that day. I viewed it two hours ago. I watched it six times. I still can't believe my eyes.

"Look who I found," Jersey calls to May and I as we approach. "I found a beautiful girl that I met in Las Vegas standing on this corner waiting to cross on the light."

"You should never cross unless it's safe," May says as she breaks free of my grasp to run toward Jersey and Ellie.

She loves that old man as if he was her great-grandfather. I pray that doesn't change when his family expands. I doubt that their bond will break. He loves May as much as my grandfather would have.

May breezes right past him and jumps at Ellie, the top hat she's wearing flies off in the light wind. She wraps her arms around Ellie's legs, nestling her face against her stomach. "I missed you, Ellie. I thought you'd come back for more pancakes."

'I'm sorry that I haven't, May." She bites her bottom lip. "I'm sorry."

Any apologies need to leave my mouth, not hers. I'm the one who has to grovel and beg this beautiful woman to give me another chance. "It's good to see you, Ellie."

"You too, Nolan," she responds quietly.

Jersey clears his throat as he scoops up May's hat. "It's a small world, isn't it, Rigs?"

Startled, I feel panic washing through me. I look at Ellie. I wait for any recognition, anything.

RISK *Deborah Bladon*

"I've never been here before." May turns in a complete circle, her eyes cast above, soaking in the buildings, the sounds, and all the people milling about around us. "Daddy, why don't we come here? Look at everything."

Ellie kneels down. She takes May's little hands in her own. "May B, today I learned something very special about this spot."

"May B?" May giggles. "Oh, Ellie. I like that. Call me May B again."

"May B," Ellie begins again, her voice giving way to emotion. "Many years ago, before you were born, my sister, Kip, met a very special boy on this corner."

No. Fuck no. Ellie's sister is Kip? She was Kip?

I start to cry. I don't fucking know how not to.

"Daddy?" May reaches for my hand. "Why are you crying?"

"This spot is magical." Ellie taps her toes on the pavement, drawing May's attention back to her. "Your daddy can feel it. I can too."

May closes her eyes tight, her brow furrowing. "I think I feel it too."

"It's in here." Ellie taps the middle of her own chest. "If you stand very still you can feel the magic, can't you?"

"I feel it." May smiles as her fingers trail over Ellie's cheek. "You're crying too, Ellie. You feel the same thing that my daddy does?"

Ellie shifts her focus to me. Her eyes lock with mine. "I feel everything your daddy does. Everything he feels for me, I feel right back."

I crouch too, wrapping my arms around May and grabbing hold of Ellie's forearms. "There's more to the story, May. Daddy just learned more about the story this afternoon."

She turns abruptly to face me, her small hands darting to my shoulders. "Tell me. I love this story. I love magic."

"Kip's sister is the bravest person in the world." I try to keep my voice calm, even though everything inside of me is spinning. "She saved a life. She saved the life of a little princess."

"Like a real princess, Daddy?"

Ellie looks into my eyes. I take a deep breath, but it does little good. My pulse is racing, my mind is on full-throttle and my world is complete. This is what love is. All of this. The three of us. Me and Ellie and May.

"What was the name of the princess, Daddy?" May turns back to look at Ellie before she cups my cheeks in her palms.

I tilt my head slightly so I can see my beautiful Ellie. My warrior. My hero and the love of my life.

"Princess May. She saved Princess May on the day she was born."

Ellie sobs. She leans forward but I hold her steady. May turns and throws her arms around Ellie's neck. "Don't cry, Ellie. She saved the princess. The magical girl saved a princess in the story. I think the princess is me."

I nod as I cling to them both. I rest my forehead against Ellie's, whispering to her, "She is the princess. You saved May, Ellie. The baby you saved is our May."

RISK   *Deborah Bladon*

Chapter 53

Ellie

He pushes his fingers into my hair, holding me still as he kisses me. He kisses me like his life depends on it. I pull back. I have to.

"How is this happening?" I cling to the front of his T-shirt. "You have to let me think for a second."

"You've been quiet since we said goodbye to Jersey and May at the theater." He tucks my hair behind my ear. "I know it's a lot to take in, Ellie. I want us to go the shoebox apartment so I can show you the blanket May was wrapped in and the note."

"I want that." I do. I've wanted that since he told me that May was the baby at the pharmacy. On the walk back to my place after we said goodbye to Jersey and May, Nolan explained about the newscast footage and how he'd watched as I was wheeled out of the pharmacy on a stretcher. He saw the woman with the baby. The baby who was wrapped in the same torn quilt that May was wrapped in when she was found in the lobby of his building. I remember every detail of that quilt. I remember my blood spattering onto it after I'd been shot.

"I have to get Annie's journals." I motion toward the hallway. "I keep them in my shoebox. It's under my bed."

He takes a step in the direction of my bedroom. I stop him with a pull on his shirt. I didn't know if Adley would be here when I told Nolan I wanted to come here. I'm glad that she's not. I need time with just him to absorb everything. It's too much. I can barely wrap my mind around the fact that May was that baby. I can't grab hold of the reality that he is Rigs.

"You treated me like shit," I blurt out. "I'm mad at you."

He kisses my forehead. "You have every right to be pissed as hell at me. I was an asshole. I'm sorry, Ellie. I lost it when I saw you with Wolf."

"He was helping me," I explain. "This week is a hard one for me and I saw him there and he asked how I was doing and I lost it. I cried because Annie and I used to share a package of candy whenever we found enough change in the park to buy it. I went there for May. I went to the store to get a necklace for May."

"I've never been in love before." His arms circle me. "I don't know how to do this. I need you to guide me, to help me. I need you to tell me when I'm fucking shit up because I cannot lose you. I won't. You are my breath now. If I lose you, I lose me."

"Never stop talking to me." I bump my fist against his chest. "Never do that. We can work out anything if we talk. If you go radio silent, I can't deal with it."

"It won't happen again." He trails his lips over my forehead. "I promise I will talk to you if I lose my shit over something I see or hear. I'll discuss it with you, Ellie. I won't shut you out."

"I love you so much," I whisper. "I was scared that I lost you forever."

315

RISK *Deborah Bladon*

"You love me?"

I look up and into his handsome face. "I love you more than anything. You know that, Nolan."

"I hoped that you loved me." He moves his hands to cradle my face. "You haven't said it yet, Ellie. You didn't tell me that you love me."

"I love you," I shout. "I love you, Nolan."

"I love you too."

"Promise me you'll never shut me out again. Promise me you won't let your huge ego destroy us." My mouth curves into a smile.

"I promise and it's not that big."

"It's huge." I hold my hands out in front of me so they're two feet apart. "It's this big."

"You have my ego confused with my dick." He cups his hands over mine and brings them to his chest. "Let's put the past to rest so we can focus on our future."

"I'd like that." I reach up to brush my lips over his. "I'd actually love that."

***

I hold his hand in silence as he reads my sister's journals.

We'd taken them out of my shoebox together along with a Polaroid picture of Annie and me that had been taken four days before our father died and our lives changed forever. In the photograph we're standing in Times Square, our arms linked together as we smile for the camera. The woman taking it knew us. She'd been working the area taking pictures of tourists for spare change for months. When she saw us that day, she asked if she could snap a picture. We agreed and after she was done, she handed it to Annie. She tucked it into the pocket of the worn varsity jacket she'd gotten from the shelter.

"You're sure you don't want some water or something, Ellie?" He turns to look at me.

We've been sitting on the couch in the shoebox apartment for more than an hour now. We came straight here after we got the journals. I wanted the privacy this space offers and he wanted to bring me here to show me the blanket that May had been wrapped in that day he became a dad.

"I'm fine." I glance down at the page he's reading. "You were like an older brother to her."

His eyes search mine. "Why did I never meet you? Where were you when I was with Kip?"

"One time I was hanging on the edge of the park and I saw you two talking." I pause to read a sentence written in my sister's handwriting. "Mostly I was with my dad. He would ask people for money and I was his prop."

I see the pity in his eyes but I don't want it. My dad lived a life that was filled with regret. He lost his first wife, Annie's mom, to a heart attack when she was too young for anyone to know that her heart wasn't strong.

He worked through that pain by having a bottle of whiskey by his side and different women in his bed. My mom was one of them. She didn't tell him about me until she knew her life was over. I was supposed to go live with my aunt in Brooklyn until my dad came to Boston. He arrived with a bouquet of flowers and Annie by his side.

317

The loss of my mom after their brief reunion sent him into a tailspin. He drank more and worked less and soon the small furnished apartment in Murray Hill that we lived in wasn't ours anymore. We slept in the car until he sold that and the city's shelters became our home.

He closes the journal with shaking hands. "We need to talk, Ellie, about something I did for Kip."

I squeeze his hand tighter. "You did lots of things for Annie. You gave her food and gloves. Your friend Jeff told her about Paris and it made her fall in love with it."

"That was Crew." A smile ghosts his lips. "Crew told Kip his name was Jeff."

I scan his face, tears swelling in my eyes. "That was Crew? He knew her too?"

"Not well." He swipes the pad of his thumb over my cheek to catch a tear. "They met only a couple of times. Crew talked about Paris. She was mesmerized by it."

"I can't believe that was Crew." I hold his gaze with mine. "I still can't believe you're Rigs."

"I'll read these." He runs his fingers over the open journal in his lap. "I will read and cherish every word that she wrote in here, but I need to talk about something now. I need to explain why I did what I did."

"What did you do?" My stomach knots. I've read my sister's journals more than a dozen times. I've held tight to her thoughts and her words because they've brought me comfort.

"Kip was attacked one night," he begins, his shoulders tensing. "Do you remember that night?"

"I remember everything about that night."

"I was there." He closes his eyes. "I was walking through the park. I heard her scream. I ran. I saw things. There was a man on her, Ellie. His hands were all over her. He was hitting her. Holding her down."

"Yes," I mutter, my voice barely audible. "I remember."

"I pulled him off." He reaches for my hand. "I pulled him off and he took off. He ran. I chased that sick fuck until I caught him."

Chapter 54

Nolan

Ellie's staring at me. I have no idea what Kip wrote in these journals about that night but I don't want to read her words before I tell Ellie what happened in my own words. I want her to understand why I did what I did. I want her to know that I was trying to protect her sister.

"He hurt Kip," she says softly. "She was in the hospital for weeks. It's a miracle she survived."

I've never known the extent of her injuries. All I saw was blood covering a face I couldn't recognize. Her nose was battered and broken, her jaw hanging loosely revealing missing teeth. Her clothes were on, though. Her shirt was ripped but her body still covered. She rolled over to shield her face as I pulled the bastard off of her.

"Did he… do you know if he…"

"No." She moves closer to me. "He didn't rape her. Annie fought hard. She fought him off."

By the time I caught him and dragged him to the ground, his jeans were closed but his belt hung open, the buckle clanging as he ran.

I heave a sigh of relief. I wanted to call the hospital back then to ask how she was, but I was too scared that they'd somehow trace the inquiry back to me and I'd be brought in by the police.

"Please know that I only did what I did for her, Ellie." I turn so I'm looking right into her eyes. "I don't regret it. I would do the same thing again."

"What did you do?"

I want her to put the pieces of this together herself. I scanned the newspaper the next day and the day after that when there was finally a small story about a jogger finding a man's body on a trail in Central Park. His name was never released. No one reported on his cause of death. I took it as a sign that I'd done the right thing and I took off. I went to Miami for a week with Crew after I burned my clothes and shoes in the fireplace of my parents' summer home on Long Island.

I held my breath for months after that hoping that no one would ever know that I'd taken a man's life.

I don't waver at all. I keep her gaze as I say the words aloud for the first time. "I killed that man, Ellie. I beat him until he was dead."

She moves back on the couch, her hand falling from mine. Her head shakes, a quick jerk before he eyes fall to her lap. "No."

"Yes." I don't want this hanging over me anymore. My anger fueled my movements that night but it wasn't just the sight of Kip laying there that spurred me on. It was the realization that the man I'd punched until he stopped fighting back and I couldn't lift my arms, had been watching Kip for weeks. He'd approached her more than one time. He'd walked past as I talked to her, gawking at her thin frame hidden beneath her jacket.

"Nolan." She drops her head into her hands, her palms pressing into her eyes sockets. "You didn't. You didn't kill him."

I expected this. I anticipated it when I realized that she knew I was Rigs. I knew that she'd have to deny it before she accepted it. Hiding it from her will only tarnish what we have. Sooner or later I'll have to confess. I can't hide a secret this size from the only woman I've ever loved.

"Ellie." I reach for her leg. "I know it's a lot to take in."

"No." She covers my hand with her own. Her gentle touch a sign. She doesn't hate me. She hasn't judged what I've done. "You didn't kill him. He didn't die that night. He died in a jail cell last year."

"What?" My vision blurs as the guilt lifts. I've never regretted what I'd done but there were moments where I wondered about his family. I had flashes of shame when I imagined him coming out of that night alive and turning his life around. I brushed off those fleeting thoughts quickly whenever I thought about Kip and the way she looked the last time I saw her.

I wanted to go back to help her. I ran in that direction, with my gloves covered in the bastard's blood as sirens wailed their imminent arrival. When I reached the edge of the alcove where she was, I saw two people. Both of them were on their knees, tending to her. I ran then. I tucked the gloves in my jacket, dropped my head and I ran home. I threw everything in a trash bag and waited until the next day when I went to Long Island and destroyed my link to that night.

RISK   *Deborah Bladon*

"Annie helped the police." She searches my face. "She used to notice everything about every person she was around. That helped them tremendously. He was arrested a few months later after he attacked another woman in Connecticut. Annie identified him and he was prosecuted."

"A man died in the park that night, Ellie. I read about it in the paper."

Her lips thin as she closes her eyes. "My dad died in the park that night. He drank himself to death because he'd finally given up."

***

My own fear has kept me captive for more than a decade. I was so scared of being prosecuted for killing that man that I hid behind an emotional wall of my own making. The only person I let in was May until Ellie fell into my lap.

I take the empty glass of water from her hands and place it on the coffee table. After she had explained that her dad died from acute alcohol poisoning, I held her while she cried. She and her sister had no one at that point. Her best friend's family stepped up to the plate. They took the two girls in and gave them a safe place to heal and thrive.

Annie took the time to get to know one of the EMTs who had been there to care for her that night. They fell in love. They married and had three beautiful daughters. A brain aneurysm took her life the day May was born.

Ellie was rushed into surgery while her sister's husband, Clinton, rushed into the ER with his wife on

RISK   *Deborah Bladon*

a stretcher. Their daughters had been over at a neighbor's home that day for a playdate and when Annie didn't go to pick up her children, the neighbor went there and used the key they had given her to check on her friend. Annie was unresponsive and when her husband arrived with his uniform on, he tried everything he could to save her life. There was nothing. She'd suffered a major stroke and died in her bed.

"Can I see it now?" Ellie takes my hand and kisses my fingertips. "I want to see it."

"Twenty seconds." I kiss her hand. "I'll be back in twenty seconds."

I sprint down the hallway and unlock the cabinet in the office. I push a bunch of loose photographs aside as I dig in the top drawer for a plastic bag. I find it. I yank it out before I take double strides to get back to where Ellie is.

I place the bag in her lap and she doesn't move. She stares at it. "Yes. This is it."

"You remember it?" I ask as I lower myself next to her. "Do you remember it, Ellie?"

Her hand carefully glides over the surface of the bag and the blanket and note that is trapped inside. I'd put it in the bag on the advice of my attorney. He wanted me to keep it preserved in the event that I'd be faced with a custody battle.

She cranes her neck to try and read the note. "I remember it. It was such an unusual blanket for a baby to be wrapped it. I kept thinking that it looked like the torn piece of a quilt. I asked her where it came from."

RISK   *Deborah Bladon*

"The woman holding May?" I refuse to call that woman May's mother. That's not who she is. It took Kristof less than thirty minutes to learn her name after I told him that she was a witness to Ellie's shooting.

Jennifer Richardson abandoned her premature daughter in the lobby of my building sixteen hours after she gave birth to her. The note she left with May listed her time of birth. She wrote that she was doing it because she realized that her life didn't have room for a child. She wanted May to be safe and to live with someone who could give her what she needed. She ended the note with a vague promise that if things didn't work out for her, she'd be back for our daughter.

May was her backup plan which meant I'd never let her near my daughter.

"Where did she say it came from?" I ask because I'm curious. I want to know Jennifer's mindset between the time my daughter took her first breath and the moment she left her alone in a cardboard box.

"She didn't say much of anything." Ellie half-shrugs. "She didn't look well. She was so gaunt and I asked if I could help. I offered to buy her food and take her to a doctor."

That's not what she needed. Jennifer needed courage. She needed the courage to face her estranged husband to tell him that she had fucked a stranger she met in a bar and ended up pregnant. She obviously didn't do that. She's living with him in Texas now on a sprawling ranch, happy and child free. The shares of their tech company are riding high at the moment.

Their year-long separation was documented in the tabloids as he spent his time chasing after women half his age and she disappeared from the public eye.

Kristof will keep a distant eye on Jennifer in the event she ever decides to seek out May. I'll keep the blanket, the note and the information Kristof gathered to give to my daughter if I ever feel it's necessary.

I'm indebted to her that she didn't make another choice when she discovered she was pregnant. She made a choice to have our daughter and to give her to me and for that, I am eternally grateful.

"Do you think it was fate?" Ellie slides the bag back onto my lap. "Me and May, you and Annie? Was it all fate?"

I place the bag on the coffee table before I turn and face her. "I think fate is part of our story. I think risk is a bigger part. I took a risk for Annie. You took a fucking huge risk for May and we took a risk on each other."

"I'd risk anything for May." She scoots closer, her hands landing on my leg. "And I'd risk anything for you, Nolan."

"We're doing this until we die." I pull her into my lap. "You and I are in this until we're as old and gray as Jersey."

"I'm in." She kisses me softly. "You are my destiny. I can't even try and deny that."

"You're mine. I'll cherish you forever and celebrate every day I get to love you."

"I'll do the same. You, me and May."

RISK *Deborah Bladon*

Epilogue

One Year Later

Nolan

"I'm not a doctor." Ellie hands the piece of paper back to me. "What does any of this mean?"

I look down at the complex terminology splattered across the page. "It means that I can be up to full speed in no time flat. All we need to do is book an appointment and a new baby brother or sister for May B will be on the way."

Her brow furrows as she rips the paper from my hands. "We already did the home study for the adoption. Why are you having an appointment on your own? Also, May would tell you no speeding in that new car you bought."

"I bought that car so we could take Sunday drives out of this city. I bought it for all of us."

"You bought it so you could race around and pump up your ego." She waves her hands in the air as she puffs up her cheeks. "I'm on to you, Nolan Black."

"You're not a detective yet, Ellie Black," I point out. "I realize you will be one day because you are rocking the shit out of that administrative job you have at police headquarters."

"I am doing a great job." She tugs on the bottom of her T-shirt. Actually, it's my T-shirt. It's that boyband farewell tour shirt that my wife has now claimed as hers.

"I'm going to have the surgery to reverse the vasectomy." I catch the paper as it flutters out of her hand toward the floor. "I want us to have a baby, Ellie. I want to see you pregnant. I want it all."

"We're adopting a baby, Nolan." Her bottom lip quivers. "He's three, but you know what I mean. Jonas is going to be our son in just a few months."

"I'm already lining up season's tickets for the Yankees for my boy and me." I tap the brim of the Yankees cap on my head. "I'm talking about another child, Ellie. One that we create. It'll be a little bit of you and a little bit of me."

Her mouth falls open. I'm tempted to take advantage of that since both May and our foster son, Jonas, are with my parents at the shoebox apartment right now. They're cleaning the place out so they can move in. They promised to stay in New York full time to get to know our new son. Our blonde haired, blue eyed little boy loves them just as much as May does.

"We have such a beautiful family right now." She holds her hands next to her chest. "Do we have room for a baby, Nolan?"

"You fired all the nannies but Tilde, Ellie. We have all the room in the world."

She did that. The day after we got married six months ago, Ellie cleaned house. She kept Tilde on board so she could take care of May after she was done at her half days of school and to look after Jonas. Ellie and I are around the rest of the time so we can help our son adjust to being a part of our family and to listen to May tell us how much she wants a donkey.

In just a few weeks our daughter will start first grade and both Ellie and I will be there to watch her walk up the front steps of the school to start a new chapter of her life. Ellie is Mommy to May now. May asked the morning of our wedding if it was okay to call her that. The answer got caught behind Ellie's tears. I shed more than my share that day too.

"It will be a lot for us to handle." She smiles that smile that tells me that she wants what I'm offering. I see that look on her face all the time when I'm perched between her legs with my face or my cock. My hands make her happy too.

"We have each other, my parents, Sarah and her husband, Clinton and your nieces, Tilde, Eda and Dino if they can tear themselves away from each other to jump in and help. Jersey and his wife will babysit if we're in a pinch."

"Adley will want to help us too." She purses her lips. "Crew can too."

"He set her up with his brother for tonight." I yank the cap off my head. "You think she'll hit it off with Kade?"

"No," she says matter-of-factly. "Adley is going to marry Crew one day. Mark my words."

"I don't see it but I trust you." I pull her close. "Do you trust me?"

"With everything."

"I'm going to fuck you right here." I lift her onto the kitchen counter as she squeals. "We'll start practicing right now for baby making."

"You don't need any practice," she purrs as she tugs my T-shirt over my head. "You've got it all figured out."

"Do I?" I rip open the front of her blouse. Buttons go flying. They bounce off the counter and onto the floor.

"You ruined my shirt, Nolan." She fake pouts. "Do you remember when you ruined my panties that first night we were together?"

"I remember," I begin before I unclasp her bra and give her right nipple a quick lick. "I remember that it felt like my first time that night."

"How? It was far from your first time." Her hands drop to my jeans. "It was like your ten-thousandth time."

"Ellie." I cradle her delicate face in my hands. I rest my forehead against hers, smelling her sweet skin, staring into her blue eyes. "That night was the first time I felt anything inside. My heart broke open that night. You let the light in."

She leans forward to kiss me. "You're what dreams are made of."

I kiss her back, harder. "You're what beautiful lives are made of and I'm grateful every second of every day that this is my life."

THANK YOU

Thank you for purchasing my book. I can't even begin to put to words what it means to me. If you enjoyed it, please remember to write a review for it. Let me know your thoughts! I want to keep my readers happy.

For more information on new series and standalones, please visit my website, www.deborahbladon.com. There are book trailers and other goodies to check out.

If you want to chat with me personally, please LIKE my page on Facebook. I love connecting with all of my readers because without you, none of this would be possible.

www.facebook.com/authordeborahbladon

Thank you, for everything.

Preview of TENSE

A Two Part Novel Series Featuring Nicholas Wolf

"Do you like it? Some people have said it's too long. It's actually quite thick when you're holding it in your hands, isn't it?" The tone is low and throaty, emanating somewhere from my right.

Such is the conversation on subway trains in New York City. You'd think I'd be oblivious to it all by now. Most of those who have lived here for decades have an innate ability to silence the staccato sounds of voices, traffic, and the underlying hum that is constantly hanging in the air in Manhattan.

For those of us who are considered fresh transplants, the timbres of the city are still part of its irrefutable charm. I never thought I'd get accustomed to the constant buzz of the traffic when I closed my eyes to sleep each night but now it's the lull that helps me drift off. I've only been here two years but I know that I'd long for the frenzied energy of this place if I ever decided to move back home to Florida.

"I'd like your honest opinion." I feel the slight pressure of a strong shoulder rub against mine. "Chapter seven is my personal favorite. Have you gotten that far yet?"

I glance down at the thick book resting on my lap. I know, without a doubt now, that he's talking to me. I've already had two, one-sided, conversations today about the book. One was with a woman waiting in line at the dry cleaners. The other was just fifteen minutes ago with the man who runs the bodega by my office. In both cases, I just smiled, nodded and listened to them rattle on about the awe inspiring detective novel I'm lugging around Manhattan with me.

"I haven't," I say quietly without looking at him.

No eye contact will make it easier for me to ignore him if he persists. I'm not a rude person but I do know how to protect myself with a perimeter of ignorance. Men give up easily if you pretend they don't exist. Most men do, that is. This one doesn't seem to be taking the hint.

"Have far are you?" A large hand brushes against my skirt. "You at least got past the first chapter, right?"

Physical touching is a no-no. I scoot more to my left, trying to gain even a few more inches in distance from him. This train is bursting at capacity with commuters. Part of that is the time of day and the other is the route.

It's early evening and I'm headed for Times Square, one of the few places in the city I'd be happy never seeing again. It's too much for me. There are too many people, too much noise, the smells overwhelming and the energy frenetic.

"I'm not trying to accost you." He laughs. It's a sexy growl and a few women actually turn to see the source. Judging by the way they linger when they look at him, he's not hard on the eyes.

"I'm just trying to get to a book signing," I confess, hoping he'll leave me alone if I tell him, politely, that I'm not looking to hook up. "I need to get this signed for my boss. It's a gift from his wife."

"You're hoping to meet the author? Nicholas Wolf? I heard the line for the signing was around the block already. People have been waiting all afternoon to meet him."

"Shit." I finally turn to look at his face. "You're not serious, are you?"

He's as good looking as I imagined him to be based on his voice. Seriously hot. Like seriously, I will give this man my number if he asks me for it, hot.

Black hair, blue eyes, and just the right amount of stubble on his face are the appetizer. His perfect teeth, rugged jaw and his lips, oh those lips, are the main course. He's wearing a wool coat and jeans so who knows what dessert is, but it would be delicious. I know it would be so delicious.

"I'm serious," he says. "If you get in line now, the store is going to close before you'll get that book signed for your boss."

I roll my eyes. "I don't get the appeal. I have no idea why Gabriel likes it so much. He told me to read it so I read the first chapter and…" I point my thumb towards the floor.

"Thumbs down?" He cocks a dark winged brow. "You didn't like it?"

"It's too wordy. I was too bored to finish it."

He stares at the book before he speaks again. "I take it Gabriel is your boss? You're getting it signed for him?"

I nod sharply.

"Give it to me. I'd like to show you something."

It's not my book and since we're moving at breakneck speed inside a subway car, it's not as though he can grab it and run. I slide it from my lap to his.

"What's your name?" he asks as his hand dives into a leather bag sitting on the floor at his feet.

I watch his every movement. "Sophia. My name is Sophia. What's your name?"

He pulls a silver pen from out of the bag and before I can protest, he opens the cover of the book and starts writing.

Well, shit. I bet it's his number. I'm not going to stop him. I'll just buy another book for Mr. Foster and keep this one for me.

He closes the cover of the book, slides the pen back into his bag and turns to look at me.

"My name is Nicholas. Nicholas Wolf."

Coming Soon

Preview of WORTH

A Two-Part Novel Duet Featuring Julian Bishop

I notice him immediately. It's impossible not to. Julian Bishop is the man of the hour, after all. This celebration, complete with expensive champagne and stiff-backed wait staff, has drawn the crème de la crème of Manhattan's social elite. It's the place to be tonight, and with a lot of crafty manipulation and a fair bit of luck, I'm standing in the midst of it, wearing a killer little black dress and diamond earrings I borrowed from a broker who has sold more than her fair share of apartments with Park Avenue addresses.

"I got you another glass of champagne, Maya."

I turn toward my date for the evening, taking the tall crystal flute from his hand. I enjoy a small sip while I look at his hands. They're adequate, not too large, and not too small. Those hands, along with the brief kiss he gave me when he picked me up tonight promise a night of passion that would be forgettable at best. He's nothing to write home about or to write about at all, for that matter.

"Thanks, Charlie," I purr. "Where's your drink?"

He nudges the sexy-as-all-hell, black-rimmed glasses up his nose with his index finger. He has a nerd with a side of male model look. That's what made me stop at his desk two weeks ago to ask if I could borrow his stapler.

I don't staple. If I did, I'm sure I'd find one in my desk, hidden underneath the three dresses and two pairs of shoes I have tucked in the drawer. I never know when a change of wardrobe is called for. A girl has to be ready for anything when she's trying to claw her way up the hierarchy of the Manhattan real estate market.

"I had one. That's my limit." He squints as he looks at the bar. "Is she here yet? I heard someone say she's going to make an entrance."

I heard someone say she's a dirty, dirty slut.

That someone was me. I said it to myself. She's far from dirty or slutty. She's a lawyer, Harvard educated, with looks to rival her brains. Jealousy is a filthy accessory and I don't wear it well at all.

"I don't think she's arrived." I turn back to where Julian's standing. He looks identical to the way he did when I first laid eyes on him. That was a year ago. I was helping a friend and he was offering her a job. Our paths crossed, the energy flowed and then he left. I never saw the man again.

I would have settled for one tumble in the sheets of his bed. A brief encounter would have satisfied my craving but it wasn't meant to be. He continued on his happily-ever-path and I swam the dating waters of Manhattan occasionally snagging a Charlie in my net.

"I'm going to mingle," I say it like I mean it. "I'll meet you back here in thirty."

Charlie looks down at his watch. It's not impressive. That's not Charlie's style.

"Thirty minutes, Maya." He touches the lenses of his glasses with two of his fingers before he points them right at me. "I'm going to have my eye on you."

Good for you, Cowboy.

I take my champagne, my spirit of adventure and my too tight black heels and I walk across the room. I took my time getting dressed tonight just for that one split second that we all live for. It's that moment when the man you imagine running naked through a field of daisies with or fucking in a back alley, turns and looks at you.

I've been planning this for two months.

Plotting every word I'll say when his eyes meet mine. I'm counting on him remembering me because I've been told I'm not easy to forget.

"Maya Baker." The voice behind me is unmistakably his. Warm with a hint of control, deep with a promise of pleasure.

I start to pivot at the sound of it. It's a beacon, a pull that is too strong to resist.

"Don't turn around." A hand, steady and determined, rests on my hip. The fingertips assert enough pressure to control my movement. "I don't recall seeing your name on the guest list."

Something's caught Julian's cock's attention. I can feel it pressing against me in the middle of this crowded room while we wait for his business partner, rumored lover and person I'd most like to lock in a closet for eternity to arrive. "I was a last minute addition."

"A welcome addition," he adds. "Are you enjoying yourself?"

I feel the undercurrent of desire. It was there last year when we met. It's stronger now.

"I am now." I push my fingers into his on my hip.

His chest lifts and falls. "I'm needed on the stage. You won't run away before we have a chance to talk, will you?"

I turn my head to look up at him. Black hair, ocean blue eyes and a face that would make any woman lock her office door to imagine a moment alone with him.

I've done it. Many women in Manhattan have.

"You're as handsome as ever, Julian."

He rounds me, his hand still holding mine. "You're more enchanting than the day we met, Maya. I've followed your career. I have a position I think you'd be interested in."

Coming Soon

ABOUT THE AUTHOR

Deborah Bladon has never read a romance hero she didn't like. Her love for romance novels began when she was old enough to board the bus, library card in hand to check out the newest Harlequin paperbacks. She's a Canadian by heart, and by passport, but you can often spot her in New York City sipping a latte and looking for inspiration for her next story. Manhattan is definitely her second home.

She cherishes her family and believes that each day is a gift for writing, for reading, and for loving.

24356652R00197

Printed in Poland
by Amazon Fulfillment
Poland Sp. z o.o., Wrocław